Denendeh
(Land of the People)

Denendeh
(Land of the People)

Elizabeth Trotter

authorHOUSE®

AuthorHouse™
1663 Liberty Drive
Bloomington, IN 47403
www.authorhouse.com
Phone: 1-800-839-8640

First published by AuthorHouse   11/09/2011

ISBN: 978-1-4670-0123-6 (sc)
ISBN: 978-1-4670-0124-3 (ebk)

Printed in the United States of America

Dedicated to the Native Peoples of the Northern Territories
who struggled valiantly to achieve autonomy.

Many thanks to the following people—
Authorhouse for their never ending help and patience during
the computer change over

Moi Jones for her encouragement and clinical
recommendations
Nigel Carson, Irwin McFarland and Francesca Jane McFarland
for their constant support

The resolute and versatile students of Thebacha College who
never failed to enchant me with their many anecdotes which
gave me the inspiration to put it all down on paper.

Last but not least the constant advice with my research into
mushing, political, and legal matters from my native friends, and
others who sadly have long since cast aside their earthly bonds.

But what of life whose bitter angry sea
Flows at our heels, and gloom of sunless night
Covers the days which never more return?
Ambition, love and all the thoughts that burn
We lose too soon, and only find delight
In withered husks of some dead memory.

Desespoir
-Oscar Wilde

CHAPTER 1

Eric, aroused from sleep by a soft nibbling on his ear, rolled over lazily. He automatically stretched out a well muscled arm towards the pillow on the right side of the queen sized water bed, which he now shared occasionally with Sanja, his sole source of comfort since Tamalyn's tragic demise. The silky black Afghan licked Eric's face, then bounded on to the carpet with an "I want to go out" expression in her soulful dark eyes. "Okay Sanja, only if you promise not to get into a scrap with Tufty," said Eric to his pet in a voice reserved for a recalcitrant child. Tufty, a spunky, energetic, Jack Russell., who delighted in terrorising the neighbourhood canines, belonged to Charles and Louise Stratton. They lived in the adjoining house separated by a three metre privet hedge which had several holes made by Tufty for his escapades. Eric quickly threw on a terry robe. In the wake of the Afghan, he trotted barefooted to the porch door, where the brightening rays of the morning sun glinted like Halloween sparklers on the lily pond, in the middle of the rose-fragrant, dew-laden garden. It is going to be another hot day, thought Eric, as he picked up the morning paper. Giving it a cursory glance, he observed that the headlines spelled out economic gloom and doom. Grimacing, he shook his disarrayed blonde hair and deposited the paper on the worktop as he plugged in the coffee pot. He had just enough time for a quick coffee and cigarette before he continued packing.

While Eric waited for the coffee to perk, he reflected on the day when he and Tamalyn had first moved into the house with its shadowy elms, multicoloured rose bushes, and what Tamalyn considered as a very special feature, the lily pond. When Eric had presented Tamalyn with six little silver fish in a water-filled plastic bag, she had been as thrilled as a child with a new toy and rushed delightedly to deposit her charges in their new home. They had flitted happily among the water lilies for a week before Winston, a large grey Persian cat, discovered the treasure trove and devoured the lot with relish. Ever since then, Tamalyn's love for cats had waned and Sanja had shared her mistress's feelings by challenging aggressively any feline that dared put a furry paw on her territory.

Eric's thoughts then drifted to the quaint little staircase leading to the attic, which Tamalyn had referred to as the stairway to the stars, because they always looked so large and luminous through the skylight window. On numerous occasions Tamalyn had snuggled against him as they stood in the sparsely furnished attic which they named as their conservatory, gazing through the telescope at the Plough and other twinkling heavenly bodies. The consummation of their marriage had been repeatedly re-enacted under the stars and brilliant moon on many occasions by deserting the master bedroom for the more romantic location.

He missed Tamalyn. A sudden surge of desolate abandonment overcame Eric as he thought of her winsome smile and the warm kiss she had given him before she departed for the hospital where she had worked as a physiotherapist; only to reach it in an ambulance and be pronounced dead on arrival. A speeding motorist had zipped through a red light and left one more grief stricken widower to cope with the void in his life. Without Tamalyn life for Eric had become ephemeral. His depression was forcing him to leave the house over whose door step he had carried his happy laughing bride fourteen months previously. He loved the house and its location. Its warmth reached out to him. It seemed as if Tamalyn's presence pervaded every room, especially the attic, where the bright beams of the sun and moon swept voraciously into the dark corners as if to devour any traces of sadness that might be lurking there. Eric wondered about the elderly man and his wife who had agreed to rent the house. He had overcome his inner conflict and decided not to sell. He felt assured that he would one day return and be able to bask more comfortably in the happy memories which were secured like precious jewels in every nook and cranny.

Eric hoped that the tall austere man and his taciturn wife who were taking over the occupancy would not rob the house of its friendly atmosphere

The scratching of Sanja at the porch door and the strong smell of coffee, shattered Eric's reverie. As he opened the door, he observed Charles Stratton his amenable neighbour displaying his usual enthusiasm as he made his way across the yard. He greeted Eric with the remark that the aroma of fresh coffee wafting through his open window had been tempting and he was anticipating an extra cup being made available from the pot. Eric still holding the open door and laughing remarked

"Charles you have been using the same phrase since I moved in and became your next door neighbour."

They settled themselves at the kitchen table, each with a lighted cigarette, a cup of black coffee and chewed over the news bulletin's rhetorical reference to the economic slump.

"That was a wise move at the last minute, renting instead of selling your house Eric.

"Look at the headline on page two. BONANZA FOR FIRST TIME BUYERS. HOUSE PRICES ON THE SLIDE."

Eric acknowledged this statement with a shake of his head.

Charles Stratton was an eminent Queen's Counsel who had a vivacious red headed wife with a zest for partying. She was constantly badgering Eric to participate in her social soirees. Every weekend there were constant comings and goings and he always heaved a sigh of relief at noon on Sundays, when the raucous voices, tinkling glasses and uncontrolled laughter which drifted through open windows and the barbeque patio dissipated, permitting him to once again enjoy the sounds of nature which he loved.

While Charles rambled on about his judicial affairs, Eric's mind drifted to the fate of Sanja. He would miss the adorable animal who had been his constant companion since Tamalyn's untimely departure. It would not be a feasible proposition to transport the dog to Canada's Arctic where she would be confined in cramped accommodation and subjected to sub zero temperatures. Furthermore, because of the nature of his research which would require extensive travel, it would be unfair to leave the animal dependant on strangers for long periods of time. Tamalyn's sister, Becky, had come to the rescue and agreed to care for Sanja during his absence.

Eric's eyes clouded with sadness as they rested fondly on the Afghan's shining black body. This gave rise to Charles's assumption that Eric needed to be rescued from his obvious state of loneliness. He suggested that Eric and he should take a trip to Las Vegas before Eric departed for the stark, northern wilderness environment, sparsely populated with not more than sixty-three thousand three hundred and thirty one people which Charles considered pristine, hostile and cold. In his opinion, it was definitely bound to have a more depressing effect on Eric's already weakened psyche. Eric shook his head negatively and told Charles that he was not yet ready for frivolous relationships or social gatherings that required endless effort in order to be accommodating. He had already decided to leave a month earlier to help him become acclimatized before he became immersed in his Polar bear research. Eric was glad that he had studied Zoology and majored in Haematology. His experience, as Director of one of Canada's most prestigious Zoos, had afforded him the opportunity of accepting a two year contract with the Northwest Territories Government. He was convinced that a complete change of environment was the salve that would heal his intractable sorrow.

CHAPTER 2

Meira groaned loudly as beads of perspiration rolled down her forehead, the salt temporarily blinding her. It prevented her from focussing on the Medicine Man who leaned over and applied a cake of cool herbal ointment to her dampened brow. He then swept an eagle feather down her body, and it lingered above the heaving mound of extended stomach, which tried desperately to expel the burden that caused such agonizing pain. The Medicine Man proceeded to move the feather in a wide circle over her lower abdomen, and at the same time he chanted loudly in his Aboriginal language, as if to drown Meira's torturous cries.

Meira had been in labour for an agonizing four hours and was beginning to reach a point of sheer exhaustion. Even though the woman in attendance was trying desperately to get her to continue pushing, Meira hadn't the strength. She knew it was waning and just wanted to close her eyes and drift into the comforting light which seemed to beckon her. In one of her more lucid moments she knew that she must deliver the baby. It would be Trolin's first child and he waited anxiously, perched on a tree stump, his breath rising like white plumes in the frigid air. His thoughts centred on his young wife as her piercing cries made his head throb.

Why, he murmured dispiritedly, when Meira had not been well during her pregnancy, had he insisted on the child being born in the traditional way without the aid of white man's medicine? If Meira had attended the Nursing Station during her pregnancy, he was certain that her groans and cries would not now be resounding throughout the cabin. They escaped into the frosted landscape, mingling with the lone cry of a wolf somewhere under the brilliant moon gliding majestically across the silver plated sky.

Meira also heard the howl of the wolf, and allowed herself to drift back in time to a part of her life that she mentally fought to forget. She was ten years old. It was dark and the howling of a wolf made her shiver and draw the thin blanket closer around her frail body. From the opening, in the room where she lay with her two sisters and baby brother, she saw Uncle Tosh, her mother's new partner, who had arrived a year ago, throw another piece of wood into the stove. The sparks momentarily lit up the place where her Mama lay, close to the stove, surrounded by empty beer bottles. Meira cringed whenever her Mama and Uncle Tosh came home with crates of beer. It meant that there would be no milk for Riel, nor breakfast for Meira, Rosa and Lori. Neither would she be able to go to school because there would be no one to care for two-month old Riel or three-year old Lori. Sometimes her Mama and Uncle Tosh would drink the unfinished beer when they awoke, then they would argue and fight.

She witnessed her Mama receiving many beatings, the blood spotted wall an attestation to the rampant alcoholic savagery that governed their young lives. The shouting and battering by Uncle Tosh of their Mama would terrify the children causing them to scream. This made Uncle Tosh very angry and if Meira failed to quieten them they would be violently shaken and slapped with his large calloused hands. Each one of them bore the welts and bruises of his uncontrolled anger and cruelty. Meira had learned, at an early age, to stay quiet in order to avoid being physically abused and she had taken it upon her young shoulders to try and protect her siblings. She understood that Riel, being an infant, was unable to comprehend the violence. Meira loved him and she endeavoured to protect the baby by stuffing her candy coated fingers into his mouth and covering him with the blanket. This always quietened him. Rosa, when the opportunity presented itself, took candy from the Bay store and Meira kept a small cache which was an essential part of their daily sustenance, as well as being a pacifier.

When Meira and Lori attended school without a lunch packet, because there was nothing in the cabin except beer, some of their classmates would share their sandwiches with them. Their teachers discreetly handled the situation of their empty stomachs and also provided extra milk cartons for their little brother. The only time Meira felt safe was when Uncle Tosh went out on his trap line. Her mother's indulgence in alcohol decreased. She even found time to plait Meira's hair, prepare proper meals and give more attention to her children, especially Riel.

It had been a good winter and the furs were of excellent quality resulting in Uncle Tosh obtaining a satisfactory price from the Bay store. He and her Mama went out to celebrate. On the evening of the third day, when they had not returned, Meira knew she would have to find wood for the stove. Both Lori and Riel were sniffling and Rosa, who had a racking cough, was complaining bitterly about feeling cold. She threw the last piece of wood into the stove and left Rosa in charge of the two younger children. The iced particles of snow crunched under her feet as she made her way, beneath a woven cosmic curtain of multi coloured Northern Lights, towards John Duncan's cabin. Meira knew there would be lots of wood and she would be able to take more than two pieces because she had brought the sled. It was a long way and she could hear the wolves howling in the distance but she was unafraid because her first thought was the welfare of her little brother and two sisters. Before she reached the wood pile the sled dogs began barking and it made her nervous, but she quickly filled the small sled and turned towards home. As she neared the cabin she smelt smoke, then she saw flames, fanned by the strong wind, leaping high into the air. Meira released her frozen hands from the sled and ran towards the cabin which was a blazing inferno.

Her loud yells of Rosa! Lori! Riel! soared above the tops of the wavering trees, only to be lost in the sound of the icy wind and crackling flames as she sank to her knees. She covered her face with her tiny hands and sobbed loudly; a small lonely figure under a vast expanse of northern sky, weeping for her lost children.

With a violent scream and contortion, Meira pushed her son from her womb, into the hands of the waiting elder. Her agonizing scream made Trolin jump from his uncomfortable seat and hurry towards the cabin. He was met at the door by the medicine man who put his hand on Trolin's shoulder and told him that the Great Spirit had seen fit to allow his son to be born alive. To give thanks, and before he held the child, Trolin must build a sweat-lodge, purify himself and pray that the generation to follow would walk in a sacred manner acknowledging the unity and harmony of the Creation. After imparting this information to Trolin the Medicine Man returned to the cabin.

As the steam circulated throughout the sweat-lodge Trolin's life unfolded before him.

When he was two year's old, his Grandfather, a respected elder and Band Chief, began to influence his young life. He taught him his language and told him many traditional stories. Every time he took Trolin out on the land, he emphasized that he must love the earth and all things of the earth, and form a kinship with all earth's creatures, the sky and water. He taught Trolin how to hunt, trap and give back to the land what had been taken. Trolin's Dad, although he had been imbued with the same beliefs had departed from his cultural values and philosophy.

He was now languishing in a prison far removed from his traditional roots. Trolin recalled the incident which had put him there. His Dad's life had become embedded in alcohol which led him into a triangle of jealous violence. Trolin's Mother, weakened by tuberculosis, had spent many months in hospital. When she returned to her family, she was unable to cope with the chores of day-to-day living and took to her bed. This put tremendous stress on her husband and young family, comprising three boys and two girls.

Trolin noticed that his Dad had begun to drink heavily and very rarely came home when the Bar closed. He had become involved with a local Aboriginal woman named Martha, who had a dubious reputation for bedding down with anyone, who would provide her with liquor, and whatever other nonessential items she fancied. It was a wind swept, bright starry night, when Trolin's Dad arrived at the cabin in a cantankerous mood. Trolin was surprised to see him because the Bar had not closed but it was obvious that he had consumed an excessive amount of alcohol. He assumed that his Dad had run out of money and decided to stay at home for the remainder of the evening. His Dad sat at the table and brooded for a long time with his hands propped under his chin, a permanent scowl on his face. Suddenly he jumped up and snatched the rifle from the bracket on the wall. He went to the bedroom and returned with some bullets which he loaded. Trolin and his brothers were frightened because they had never experienced this divergent behaviour. Without speaking, he left with the rifle under his arm and Trolin heard the engine of the truck roar into life and take off with a squeal of brakes.

Some inner sense persuaded Trolin to follow his Dad and he quickly donned his boots and parka, jumped on the skidoo and went subconsciously in the direction of Martha's hut. When he reached there, he was horrified to find his Dad propped against the wall, eyes glazed, and the rifle on the floor beside him. On a blood stained mattress lay the naked bodies of Martha and a white man. Trolin blamed himself for not reaching the hut in time to prevent his Dad from committing the terrible crime. This scene had been firmly etched in his mind and he suffered many nightmares during and after the trial which resulted in a ten-year sentence being imposed.

Shortly after the catastrophe, Trolin's Mother died. The family was broken apart and the children were sent to foster homes. Trolin was placed with a very devout Catholic family, who insisted on his attending church and preparing himself for admittance into the fold of Catholicism. This religion seemed to be isolated from the profound religious and spiritual qualities of the aboriginal traditions which his Grandfather had taught him. While he realised that the Great Spirit was present in the Catholic church, nevertheless, earth consciousness and the ability to communicate with the spiritual world around him was not evident in the teachings he began to receive from the Priest.

Twice weekly, Trolin attended the home of the Priest, where he was initiated into the formal doctrines which to him were ambiguous. Trolin developed a great respect for the Priest, who was very patient, and at the end of the lesson would reward him with coffee, cookies and a pat on the head, so he endeavoured, to the best of his ability, to meet the expectations required. As the lessons proceeded the Priest appeared to Trolin to become over friendly. He would sit closer to Trolin and sometimes put his hand on his knee when he wished to stress an important point. At first Trolin dismissed it as an unimpeachable act of reinforcement but the Priest's hand became more forceful straying higher above his knee.

The uncomfortable position, in which Trolin found himself, intensified one evening when the Priest fondled him in a private area that Trolin had been taught by his Grandfather as being the vessel in which the seed of life was contained. The Priest, acutely aware of the discomfort he was inflicting on his young student, reassured him that what he was doing was only a natural way of expressing his fondness for him and lifting Trolin's hand he placed it on his crotch. The Priest's aberration became more aggressive each time Trolin attended until he was forced to submit to acts of sodomy.

He was devastated and was told by the Priest that he should not mention, to anyone, the acts which had occurred between them. He reiterated it was God's way of expressing love between two people and should not be revealed outside of the room in which they were enclosed.

Trolin was not appeased. His behaviour changed. He became very introverted and dreaded the visits to the Priest's home. The recurring nightmares of the tragedy in the hut were now replaced by the horrible acts the Priest was imposing upon him. He prayed, as best as a ten-year old could, to the Great Spirit to relieve him of the indignity he was suffering. His prayers were answered but not in the manner he expected. Trolin contracted tuberculosis and after losing a lung was hospitalized for many months. When he was discharged from the hospital the social worker placed him with another family, one that held the same beliefs as himself. He tried to bury his wretched past by submerging himself in his own religious formalities and the healing process began.

In his twenty-first year Trolin fell deeply in love with Meira whom he had known since schooldays. His marriage was a happy one because he and his wife professed an intense and abiding faith in the Great Spirit.

In the steaming red glow of the sweat-lodge, Trolin prayed for wisdom to raise his child, and others who might follow, as well as his grandchildren in the ways of the Great Spirit. He also asked for long life for himself and his wife so that their descendants could walk unimpeded in their traditional beliefs.

CHAPTER 3

Valerie glanced at the wall clock and thought that the minute hand seemed to move with enhanced alacrity. She emitted a long sigh, as she realized it was going to be a tight schedule, because there were still two patients requiring attention. As a favour to a friend she had been entrusted with the keys of a house which had been assigned to Dr. Eric McClure. She would need to accelerate her pace, if she hoped to be on time to meet the scheduled flight, provided the drifting fog banks permitted it to land. It had been snowing earlier but through the ice fogged window she could not discern whether there had been a respite.

Valerie weighed Elisepee's baby and noted that he had gained a little weight. As she drew the vaccine into the syringe there was a loud commotion in the porch and the door burst open to admit Aviatok dragging her eight year old grandson by his parka hood. Pogiak's left hand was wrapped in a blood-stained towel and frozen tears lay like frosted beads on his wind-burned cheeks. Pogiak had been demonstrating, with drastic results, to his white friend, the art of scraping and cutting the skin of a seal using an ulu. His left forefinger had been partly severed and would require suturing. This would take time which Valerie did not have. She hurriedly made a phone call to her friend, Daniella, and requested that she should meet the plane and bring Dr. McClure to the Nursing Station so that the Wildlife officer's instructions could be relayed to him.

Pokiak's injury would have to take precedence over the other patients' requirements and Valerie hastened to attend to her

12

young stoic patient. He never moved a muscle as she cleaned and sutured the badly severed finger and gave him his tetanus shot. His courage bore the mark of the true Inuit spirit in the face of adversity, the reprimand from his Grandmother and his lack of expertise in front of his friend, being the cause of the tears, which had now melted. As Valerie was about to record, on the chart, the medication dispensed to her last patient, Daniella holding a box and Dr. McClure clutching two large suitcases entered. A violent gust of icy wind preceded them which sent the furnace roaring. Eric removed his glove and held out a cold finger tipped hand to Valerie exclaiming that he didn't expect to encounter such freezing weather so soon. Valerie replied that it was normal for the time of year and she hoped he had a good flight. Daniella, who was smiling mischievously in the background interrupted with the remark that she would have to leave as three hungry children were waiting to be fed.

Valerie offered Eric coffee and as he removed his coat she was impressed with his height, breadth and appearance. The thought crossed her mind that he was a handsome man.

"Do I detect an English accent?" enquired Eric as he accepted the proffered cookie the only remaining one on the plate.

"Sorry, this is the last one. I overlooked cookies when I placed my order a few days ago so I will make another phone call when my last patient leaves. Isolation has many disadvantages and yes you are correct regarding my accent."

"Which part of England?"

"Lancashire, Lytham, St. Annes."

"I am not familiar with that area. I spent some time, in my youth, travelling the length and breadth of the British Isles. My favourite place was the Cornish coast."

"Did you have time to visit the Blackpool illuminations? Blackpool is close to where I resided with my parents in England."

"I have heard of the illuminations but unfortunately I missed them. How long have you lived here?"

"Four years, but prior to coming north I worked at the Royal Victoria Hospital in Montreal for eighteen months. My field is

Community Health, and this position became available just as I was about to make a move to the Australian outback."

"Does the isolation and frigid temperature not affect you?"

"No, I never have much time to think about isolation. I am always kept busy. There was another Nurse working with me but she left a few weeks ago and I am expecting a replacement soon. Now what about you Dr.McClure, where did you come from?"

"You may call me Eric. I came directly from Vancouver and I have a contract for two years to make a significant study on the world's largest Carnivores, the Polar bears. I will be gathering some important data which might help maintain the bears at an acceptable level. They are a considerable resource for the Inuit hunter and their decline is a concern. I will be working in close co-operation with the Canadian Wildlife Service and some of the hunters."

"That appears to be an interesting occupation Eric. You have certainly come to the right part of the world to study Polar bears." Valerie offered a coffee refill which he accepted, as she relayed the Wildlife's officer's message.

"You will be sharing your home for a few days with a biology student who is due to leave at the week-end. He is presently at the Science Institute in Igloolik, so if a stranger appears in your living room don't be alarmed.

"Valerie, I was advised to bring some groceries including wine and vegetables. I also brought a few cartons of milk which I need for my cereals."

They both went into fits of laughter when Valerie added "I hope you also brought some powered milk as well. Polar bears you will find but we do not have any cows".

A woman with a bit of humour, thought Eric, is refreshing.

"If you give me a few moments Eric I will accompany you" said Valerie as she handed him the keys.

Eric continued to drink his coffee as he watched Valerie tidy her desk and lock various cabinets. He liked what he saw; a vivacious auburn-haired woman, with a beautiful dimpled smile and huge green almond shaped eyes, who seemed to take good care of her slender figure. A tremendous attraction towards her enveloped him, only to be usurped by the recollection of his remark uttered a few days previously to Charles Stratton that he did not want to get involved in a relationship.

When they arrived at the house, Eric inspected the fridge to find a lone carton of pineapple juice and a mouldy slice of pizza. There were a few cans of soup and a can of beans in the kitchen cupboard.

As Eric put away his groceries Valerie remarked that he should join her for a meal as she felt sure travelling and sitting around airports all day would discourage him from commencing food preparation.

. "Are you sure it won't be too much trouble?"

"No Eric, no trouble at all. It is just as easy to cook for two people as it is for one. Besides I will enjoy the company. My house is the one next to the Nursing Station and if you make your way there at seven o'clock I promise to serve you a gourmet meal. I hope you like fish."

"I have no dislikes when it comes to food," replied Eric with a smile as he glanced at his watch. "I will see you in exactly sixty minutes."

Valerie had just enough lettuce, green onions and tomatoes to make a salad. It would probably be the last one she would eat until someone brought her more vegetables from the South. This was what she missed most of all, vegetables and fruit.

Eric arrived as Valerie was putting the finishing touches to the baked Arctic Char. She was pleasantly surprised when he produced a bottle of Chablis.

"This should complement the fish, Valerie. The food smells very appetising."

"It should be ready soon. If you wouldn't mind opening the wine, we will have a glass before dinner. You will find the bottle opener and cutlery in that drawer." as she pointed an oven gloved finger towards the cabinet.

"Where do I find the glasses Valerie?"

"Just open the cupboard above the cutlery drawer."

As Eric busied himself with the wine, and laying the cutlery beside the already placed table mats Valerie concerned herself with the contents of the oven.

Eric returned to the kitchen with filled wine glasses and handed one to Valerie.

"Happy days Valerie" said Eric with a smile as they touched glasses.

As Valerie responded she was aware of Eric's intense gaze and a faint flush coloured her cheeks. To hide her embarrassment she placed the glass on the counter top and opened the oven. Eric noticed the tinge and was overwhelmed by a feeling that this would be the first of many invitations.

During dinner, Valerie told Eric that she had completed her Nurse's training at Crumsal Hospital in Manchester and then branched into Public Health after doing Midwifery.

"Community Health here is very different to what I was doing in Preston, England. Here, I am expected to be X-ray technician, Lab technician and Doctor as well as a Veterinary Surgeon on occasions. Only last week, after taking some X-rays, I had to splint a dog's broken leg."

"What happens if a patient is seriously ill?"

"The Medevac team come in and take the patient out to hospital."

"So you are expected to diagnose each patient's illness."

"I am, but a Doctor and Dentist also visit the community. This is where I get my supply of fresh vegetables, fruit and anything else I care to order. I usually phone in my order to the store, pay by credit card and whoever is visiting will pick up the order and bring it to me. That is the reason you are able to enjoy the salad and fresh pineapple."

"I wondered how you managed to provide salad and fruit, Valerie, when you are living in such isolation. I suppose, like a Doctor, you are on call night and day."

"Quite right, Eric, but I took the position on the condition that I would be given separate housing as I did not want to live in the Nursing Station. The previous Nurse told me that she had people calling at the Station at all hours of the night. As long as the Nurse is in the Nursing Station people will keep calling, irrespective of the time. Because I live in a separate house I am not bothered too much after eight o'clock in the evening."

"Well, all I can say, Valerie, is that you require a lot of stamina to live under such stressful conditions."

"Not all that stressful. I take it in my stride and believe it or not I actually enjoy the job."

Valerie removed the empty plates from the table and went into the kitchen to pour coffee. Eric followed and thanked her profusely for providing such a delicious meal. He said he would reciprocate when he stocked his larder but she need not expect him to compete with her culinary skills. At this remark they both laughed.

Eric took the little silver tray from Valerie and preceded her into the living room where he placed it on the coffee table. When they were comfortably settled, Valerie decided to do a little more prying into Eric's life."

Are you married, Eric?"

"I was, but unfortunately my wife was killed in a vehicle accident fourteen months ago. There was complete silence before Valerie replied.

"I am so sorry, Eric, I didn't realize that you were still suffering the consequences, otherwise I wouldn't have asked."

"It's OK, Valerie. Sometimes it's good to talk about things that hurt emotionally."

Eric then proceeded to tell Valerie about his deceased wife, Tamalyn, their hopes and dreams and his reason for coming north. Valerie listened, without interrupting and before he attired himself to face the rigours of his new northern environment she knew the life story of Dr. Eric McClure.

When Valerie got into bed she lay awake for a long time. Her thoughts focussed on Eric and she came to the conclusion that she liked him. He had made an indelible impression on her and she hoped a close friendship would develop and endure.

Eric also lay in his bed and thought about the events of the evening. Even though he tried to dislodge the vision of Valerie sitting across the table, her auburn hair glinting in the candlelight, he found it difficult to do so. Eric turned on his side and tightly closed his eyes as a feeling of guilt engulfed him. It was too soon to tarnish Tamalyn's memory.

CHAPTER 4

Eric's late breakfasting was disrupted by a rattling of the door knob and a pounding on the door. When he unlocked it he looked down upon a small man with a cheerful face and smiling eyes. As Tomak Quitsuliak pushed past him uttering the words," No one in residence locks their door here," Eric stood dumbfounded. Tomak introduced himself by announcing that he had been assigned to work closely with Eric and he had arrived to take him out on the land. He threw himself on the settee and watched as Eric put on his boots.

"Those shoes are not suitable. You will need sealskin kamiks," stated Tomak, as he pointed to Eric's footwear.

"This is all I have," replied Eric, forcefully.

"We'll soon fix that. You come with me."

"Eric donned his down-filled parka and followed Tomak outside where a snowmobile was parked.

"Get behind me."

Eric squeezed behind Tomak's bulky figure and almost fell off several times as the machine twisted and veered around the corners of a few houses, before it was manoeuvred to a halt outside a co-operative store. Tomak preceded Eric into the building, where Eric observed several women sewing various garments, kamiks and mittens. He inspected some of the items and was quite impressed with the quality of the work. Tomak, who was conversing in his language with a very comely woman displaying a wide smile, pointed to Eric's footwear. She followed Tomak's gaze and shook her head in the affirmative. After rummaging through a large cardboard box, she produced a sturdy pair of sealskin kamiks and indicated that he should put them on his feet. They were a perfect fit and felt comfortable. He could understand why Tomak considered his boots unsuitable.

"This is my wife Melak." said Tomak. She smiled, then pointed to a sealskin parka and spoke to her husband, who relayed to Eric that he should be wearing a more suitable garment instead of the one on his back.

Melak held Eric's parka between her thumb and forefinger. Again she conversed with her husband while she shook her head negatively.

"Not warm enough for the land this coat." relayed Tomak as Melak handed him the sealskin parka.

"You wear this one. My wife says it is your size."

Eric put on the parka and again it was a perfect fit. "How much are these items?"

"Government will pay." replied Tomak. "You take and Melak will fix it with Mr. Sands."

"But I don't think I can do that."

"You can do it." Leave your things here and Jonas will take them to your house later."

Tomak pushed Eric, arrayed in his new clothes, towards the door and several of the women smiled and nodded approval as he passed them. After another short bumpy ride, they arrived at a government office where. Eric dialogued with some of the officials and was assigned a snowmobile. Soon he was moving along behind Tomak across a white wind-churned land devoid of a tree line that swept endlessly towards a misty ice-fogged horizon. His skin tingled and felt as if it were being pricked by a thousand sharp needles, as the mighty force of the wind hurled frozen particles of snow at him. The sensation caused him to pull the parka hood closer around his face. They travelled for quite a while and although it was bitterly cold Eric found it invigorating. The land was awesome and a perfect natural environment for such magnificent animals as Polar bears. Eric had many thoughts in his head and felt that the decision to move north had been the right one.

Tomak invited Eric to his home where he again met Melak, their two daughters and four sons. Tomak and Melak were descendants of the first nomadic people who had roamed the frozen north for centuries, surviving on what food the land offered in winter, existing on what the tundra provided in the short summer when it came to life like a painted canvas with multi coloured flowers, berries and fauna. Eric learned how Tomak, when he was a small boy, helped his father. He was taught at an early age to stand motionless beside ice holes and harpoon seals. The blubber was required for rendering seal oil for the Quillik, the seal lamp which provided light. The seal meat was an essential part of the daily diet. The skilful manoeuvring of the umiak, a light type of sealskin canoe used for harpooning whales was another important skill that a good hunter required.

While the harpooning of whales could be dangerous, the killing of a Polar bear was evidently a mammoth task with which to contend, testing to the utmost, the strength, stamina and skill of the hunter. These survival skills had enabled Tomak to support his family and they were now being passed on to his four sons.

His daughters were being taught women's work which included being proficient with the ulu in scraping the skins of animals and stretching them. The women chewed the hide to soften it and this affected their teeth. They were also required to make various garments from animal skins because, as Eric had already found out, man made fibres were inept and did not have the power to keep out the piercing, relentless cold winds that swept the barren land. Unless a person was suitably clad death from hypothermia would be imminent in a short period of time. Eric was fascinated as he received replies to his many questions.

Melak offered Eric some food. He was hesitant about accepting it because the smell nauseated him, but rather than offend his host he ate it and managed to swallow every bite without regurgitating it in an unsavoury manner. Tomak, as he consumed his food with gusto, informed Eric that muktuk, delicate little squares of whale blubber that fermented all summer in rancid seal oil was a delicacy. When the meal was over Eric returned to his house. He entered in his diary that he had been initiated into true northern culture by participating in a feast of northern delicacies.

During the night violent cramps in his stomach awakened Eric. He was forced several times to make a quick dash to the bathroom where he was explosively sick. On each occasion he remained there for quite some time before dragging himself back to bed. Eric lay on top of the bed feeling as if the room were spinning around him. When he made a final attempt to reach the bathroom he collapsed on the floor.

Malcolm Magee, an undergraduate at Queen's University in Ontario, who had spent the summer working on a scientific project concerned with the brilliant floral kaleidoscope on the tundra, had been offered a ride from Igloolik in a private plane. This enabled him to arrive earlier than anticipated.

As he entered the house, he observed the parka and kamiks behind the door and knew that the new tenant had arrived. Whistling merrily, he ventured into the kitchen where he poured himself a glass of juice before he proceeded, glass in hand, along the hall towards his bedroom. He inclined his head towards the open door on the right and saw the crumpled figure of Eric on the floor.

"Is everything all right here?" asked Malcolm in a concerned tone. Not receiving a reply he entered the room and knelt beside the supine form of a man who appeared to be seriously ill. Quickly, Malcolm went to summon the nurse, who arrived within minutes and immediately assessed that the situation was serious.

Eric had an extremely high temperature and was delirious; therefore he was too ill to be moved to the Nursing Station. After removing the soiled clothing and cleaning the patient, with Malcolm's assistance, she managed to get him into bed. Valerie then hurried to the Nursing Station to fetch the equipment required to start intravenous fluids and antibiotics. She suspected botulism and hoped that in a few hours Eric's raging temperature would have stabilized, so that she could obtain a history of what he had eaten twenty four hours earlier, in order to make a proper diagnosis.

Malcolm, whose project was completed and who intended leaving the same afternoon, offered to postpone his departure because of Eric not being in a fit condition to be moved to the Nursing Station. He received some instructions from Valerie and settled into the new position of Nursing Assistant with aplomb. It was late evening before Eric showed any sign of recovery.

"Eric, I never expected to have you under my care as a patient so soon," Valerie said with a smile as she wiped his face with a cool cloth.

"You were in another world, one of dementia, but I am glad to see that you have returned without any serious consequences."

Valerie was then able to ascertain that he had eaten muktuk, indeed a delicacy of fermenting whale blubber which appeals greatly to the palate of the Inuit. Eric smiled faintly as Valerie reprimanded him for consuming so much muktuk.

"I was only being a polite guest, Valerie," replied Eric "but I take your point, it is not always sensible to indulge in foods to which one is unaccustomed without first gently acclimatizing the system. You can rest assured that I will be more careful in future as this has proven to be a cataclysmic experience."

Valerie made her patient comfortable for the remainder of the night and left him in the care of Malcolm. Eric was on his feet within a few days but he still felt a bit wobbly, so on Valerie's advice he spent the remainder of the week recuperating.

When Tomak came to visit Eric he was not at all surprised that the muktuk had made him ill. He remarked jovially that on Eric's next visit he would be served raw fish but the very thought of ingesting such a morsel made Eric blanche. Valerie laughed when Eric relayed Tomak's raw fish remark and related that she had just finished removing, with forceps, a circular fish bone from the throat of an Inuit child.

"So as to get sufficient protein the children are allowed to chew on fish bones. "The little one I attended was turning blue in the face and choking. It was quite scary."

"I don't envy your job, Valerie," said Eric and he poured her a glass of wine. As he proceeded to pour water for himself, Valerie extracted a video from her bag.

"I thought you might be interested in watching this story, Eric. I don't know what your spiritual beliefs are but I am a firm believer in reincarnation."

"Reincarnation?" repeated Eric quizzically, raising an eyebrow.

"Perhaps it sounds rather passé, in comparison with the many theological doctrines that are in vogue today, but there are so many lessons to learn in life. One life is just too short to make up for our numerous shortcomings. People's paths are continually crisscrossing, as they proceed through their various karmic lives. Actually, I feel strongly that we have met in a previous life. We are kindred spirits."

Eric thought for a moment before replying. "I know I feel very comfortable in your company, Valerie, but whether that feeling could be construed as being an aspect of reincarnation, I am not sure. I would need some more enlightenment on the subject before I could arrive at a concrete conclusion."

"How do you feel about the film, Eric? Are you interested in looking at it? You might gain something from the content even though you have no knowledge of the subject.

"Go ahead, Valerie, I have no objection," answered Eric as he pointed towards the video machine. Valerie inserted <u>Somewhere in Time</u> into the machine as she and Eric, with filled water glass and wine bottle beside her, settled themselves comfortably for some pleasant viewing. When the film ended, Eric remarked that he had enjoyed the story.

"From the way in which it was presented, it could possibly sway one into believing that the passage of time in one life was but a step towards a long journey comprising many lives." He added that it was food for thought and he was prepared to read some literature on the subject which Valerie offered to bring to him on her next visit.

After Valerie had gone, Eric theorized on the complex subject of reincarnation and the thought that he and Tamalyn could be together again in a future life became comforting. He also analyzed his feelings towards Valerie, which led him to believe that despite the fact there was a strong magnetism it was a matter of chemistry. He rationalized that he was too practical, in the scientific sense, to permit himself to be goaded into accepting unproven facts. However, he could afford occasionally to luxuriate in these whimsical thoughts.

CHAPTER 5

Eric covered the packed sleds with a tarpaulin while Tomak harnessed the dogs. Eric was quite excited at the idea of spending a weekend with Tomak on the land. It was a good beginning to his research. With humour in his voice, he stated to Tomak, as he completed his task, that he hoped there wasn't an excessive amount of muktuk because the health nurse would not be easily accessed. Tomak, with a glint in his eye, replied that there were other delights in store for him.

As the dog team fanned out across the vast expanse of glittering, ice-covered land Eric followed behind on his snowmobile and sled. He had learned from Tomak that the dogs were essential because they would act as a warning if a bear happened to be in the vicinity, especially when he and Tomak were asleep in the tent. Polar Bears, the largest of the bear family, some of them reaching a standing height of eleven feet, are solitary animals, quiet and difficult to see because they blend in so well with the snow-covered environment. Their sense of smell is so acute that they can smell dead whale or seal meat fifteen kilometres away.

Eric, being a zealous dog lover, was appalled at the way in which the husky dogs were treated. They were not considered as pets and were expected to survive in gruelling, inhospitable temperatures and Arctic storms existing on a diet of a few pieces of frozen seal meat. He wondered how they had the strength to pull Tomak, who was quite a sturdy individual.

The beauty of the land fascinated Eric, as the faint mellow glow of the sun which would soon be obscured, transformed it into a magical kingdom of glacial mounds and peaks with sparkling turrets, caused by the effects of the ever changing light. He found the journey, to where they stopped to pitch the tent for the night, stimulating.

While Tomak staked out the dogs and fed them, Eric grappled with the tent in a wind that threatened to demolish it before it was properly secured. His next job was to hack some ice, to be melted in a pan on the primus stove, which would be needed for hot drinks. Because Eric was not yet attuned to the new environment he spent a considerable amount of time on these tasks. Eventually Tomak and he were enjoying a well earned rest and hot beverages with some of Melak's now frozen bannock. Eric declined to accept the dried meat which Tomak offered him and instead was quite content to munch on a chocolate bar.

After supper, when Eric went outside he noticed that the dogs, already covered by snow, were curled up with their heads under their bushy tails, their backs to the howling wind. He described the scene to Tomak and expressed concern that he didn't think it possible that the dogs would be able to detect a marauding bear in this position. Tomak assured him that his team of dogs was well experienced in Polar Bear country and he need not have any fear Even though they gave the impression of abandoning themselves to sleep, they were always alert.

Eric felt a sense of relief as he zipped himself into his sleeping bag. As he stared at the sibilant lamp he thought about Tomak's distant ancestors who had crossed the Bering Land Bridge ten thousand years ago. Several distinctive cultures had been developed which depended on a way of life adapted to Arctic conditions. One of these, the second eastward migration from Alaska, named Thule people of which Tomak was a direct descendant, moved into the Canadian Arctic about a thousand years previously. Eric marvelled at the tenaciousness of a culture that could exist in such harsh, extreme and primitive conditions. He leaned towards Tomak.

"Tomak I am extremely interested in your culture and would like to learn more about it. Did you, as a child, and your family live in a snow house?"

"Winter was spent in an igloo and in summer we lived in a skin tent."

"I presume the tent was made from the skin of Caribou."

"Quite right, the Caribou is a very important animal to the Inuit people. It provides food, clothing, tools and other material. Seal, whale and walrus are as equally important. To hunt the whales and stalk other sea mammals we used the skin of the seals to make the Umiak. The whalers were the people who introduced us to wooden boats and firearms in exchange for fresh meat."

"Before the use of firearms how did the Inuit kill Polar bears?

"They were killed with a spear made from wood and bone and the hunter had to get quite close to the bear to be sure of his aim. Polar Bears are powerful, dangerous animals and because this primitive weapon was used they were not over-hunted. It was an honour for a hunter to bring down a Polar Bear with this method. Some of those Inukshuks which we passed could be an indication of a Polar Bear kill. Once firearms were introduced bear numbers began to decline. However, in 1949 there was a Game Ordinance introduced requiring every hunter and trapper to be licensed, and the season for hunting was limited, but the bears appear to be on the decline again.

"I had in mind to ask you about the purpose of those large stones in the shape of a human form, which could be described as true symbols of the north, referred to as Inukshuks".

"An Inukshuk can have many meanings. They have been a vital part of our landscape for thousands of years. The particular area might be a good camp site, an ideal fishing area, a warning of a dangerous river, a food cache or a signpost from one area to another. They never topple and their durability against the relentless gales that sweep the land impart the knowledge that we are not alone. Our ancestors and others have left a mark of recognition. To us, the shapeless stones are old friends."

"So it is really an important feature that characterises habitation of this vast icy land, Tomak."

"We also used kilamitaks, Eric, small stones wrapped in skin and tied with thongs, with a loop to fit the middle finger, to target birds. It would be swung around the head with great momentum before being aimed at the bird. The bird became immobilized because the thongs would wrap around the legs."

"The Inuit are very innovative people, Tomak."

"In my father's time we never used a watch or clock. The sun was our timepiece and calendar and the stars our compass. Nature gears the hunter's time. Are the whales going to say Tomak needs to hunt us today so we should put in an appearance? The migration of the Caribou takes place at a particular time of the year and if the hunter is not around at that time then the family will not have any meat. In winter, fur bearing animals are in their prime so trap lines have to be worked according to Inuit time. We were people who never worked according to a nine to five schedule, nor did we work for other people or organizations, but we worked hard even though we were, and still are referred to as being lazy, because we don't conform to white man's time. We were a proud independent race of people with close-knit family ties until the government intervened. The only outside contacts we had were fur traders and missionaries. Now our lifestyle has changed. When the government officials took over, they introduced us to a welfare state by building houses and bringing us together in a community setting, insisting that our children be educated, otherwise we would not receive the child allowance. So as not to be separated from our children, we stayed in these communities and became more and more dependent on the government for services similar to those in southern Canada. A lot of illnesses such as smallpox, influenza and measles depleted the Inuit population because we had no immunity. The government, of course, thought they were introducing us to a better way of life but my generation still yearns for the old ways and life on the land."

"Tomak, will your sons really settle for that way of life now that they have become used to southern consumer goods and other items. I know your youngest son has travelled to the city of Vancouver in western Canada and spent ten days there as part of a student exchange. During the conversation I had with him, he told me that he found the trip exciting and worthwhile and he hopes one day to travel farther. His ambition is to become a pilot."

"I know I cannot control my children's lives but I can still teach them their language and traditional life skills which can be put to good use. You heard my first son saying that he hopes to be a tourist guide. Another thing that bothered me for a long time was the loss of our language. Without that we have no identity. I am glad that the government, on the advice of our political groups, is insisting that it be taught in the elementary schools. "Bilingualism is also an asset, Tomak, but if your son does become a pilot and works for an international airline he will need to be fluent in English, and if he obtains employment with Air Canada he will also require to be fluent in French. If he becomes a pilot in an airline owned and operated by the Inuit, which will operate only in the north, then his language will be very useful. The many business organizations, that are now being formed by the Inuit, are going to need staff with good English skills if they hope to conduct business with southern and overseas consortiums."

"If our language dies we are a lost people. The young cannot communicate with their elders anymore and our heritage is in danger of passing into oblivion."

"It is good, Tomak, that the Inuit are now taking control of their own political and economic development. In that regard they can be assured of a better future for themselves and their descendants. Strange to say Tomak, but many southern Canadians have no knowledge of the Northwest Territories or its inhabitants. If I were to ask a passer-by on the street could he or she tell me anything about the Northwest Territories, nine out of ten times, I would be met by a blank stare."

There was no reply, and as Eric directed his head towards Tomak he observed that he had nodded off. Eric snuggled deeper into his sleeping bag and allowed his roving thoughts of the Inuit to subside, but before he finally succumbed to sleep, the vision of a dimpled smile and auburn hair glinting in soft candlelight filled his mind. He smiled and closed his eyes.

On the second day, after a more hazardous journey, they were once again enclosed in the shuddering tent as the wind beat against it with ferocious energy. The conversation developed into an evening of myth telling and the indomitable powers of the Shaman, but Tomak's true story was captivating.

"Agiak was a young girl who had been promised, on the day of her birth, to be given as the wife of the infant son in another family, when they became of marriageable age. When the young man grew up he left his community and got into bad company in the town. Agiak went to visit him, in the company of a member of her family, and became pregnant. Meantime the young man decided to marry another woman and forget Agiak. Agiak's father went to see him. He told him that if he did not keep his promise and marry his daughter he would get the Shaman to deal with the situation. The young man laughed and told Agiak's father that he had no intention of keeping the promise, which had been made between the parents of both families. He stated he was not frightened of the Shaman because he did not believe that the man could evoke any powers, good or bad. When Agiak's father returned to his community he sought the help of the Shaman. The young man obtained a position with an oil company in which a member of my family was also employed. Both men were working in a building adjacent to another a few metres away. The supervisor sent the young man to fetch a tool from the outside building. When he failed to return within ten minutes, my relative went to look for him and found a boot lying on the ice, and in the distance he saw the young man being trailed along by a Polar Bear. The incredulous part of the story is that it was not an area ever frequented by Polar Bears."

"How can that be explained, Tomak?"

"Quite simply, the Shaman sent the bear to seek out the young man and punish him. One should never underestimate the power of the Shaman. Before the missionaries and health officials appeared, people sought the help of the Shaman medically and spiritually."

"Do the Inuit still believe in the Shaman?"

"The elders and some of my generation who have not been swayed by the Churches' teachings do, but the young people appear to have different values because of other outside influences. I enjoyed the old days much better. We always had a celebration in February for the sun's return. Myself and other children ran to the igloos, blew out the lamps, and from the ceremonial flame new wicks would be lit. It was a time for dancing and story telling, everyone looking forward to a new harvest blessed by the sun."

"Many of the Inuit's myths are revealed in their carvings and prints. As a matter of fact, your second son's carvings have made quite an impression and I intend purchasing some of his work when I return. "I am rather proud of my son's achievement as a Carver. He is slowly making a name for himself."

The men's voices were beginning to tire because of the extra strain imposed on their vocal chords by trying to compete against the howling of the wind. They lay, prisoners of their own thoughts, each tightly wrapped in his meditative cocoon, Eric's mind once again enveloped in dinner for two, auburn hair, candlelight and reincarnation. What he was experiencing in the lonely, extensive, primitive and unpredictable wilderness created the realization, that life surely extended beyond the bounds of planet earth into a realm of sanctity. The mystical grandeur of the land, with its sparkling glaciers and ice sculptures; its floral jewels, abundance of marine mammals, fish and other magnificent animals, had the power to inhibit the projectile that embedded life in the fast lane, and draw upon the more subtle spiritual desires hidden in the depths of man's psyche. Despite the raging storm outside, Eric experienced an inner peace, a feeling that had eluded him for a long time.

As they made their way back to the settlement, Eric felt a warm glow of excitement at the thought of getting together with Valerie. She had been constantly in his thoughts and he hoped that the mutual respect, which they had for each other, would grow into a more permanent and lasting relationship. He felt as if a healing process, regarding his deceased wife, had taken place and plans for a brighter future were already formulating in his mind. He had no doubt that Valerie had the capability to bring some joie de vivre into his crippled life.

Time went quickly, as Eric involved himself whole heartedly in the land of the polar bears, and his knowledge and understanding increased considerably, giving him the feeling of having attained a satisfying achievement in all areas of this fascinating occupation.

Eric's first year had been a very busy one but he had enjoyed every moment as he worked with the team counting, examining and affixing collars to polar bears. His relationship with Valerie had also become a little closer, but his travelling had kept them apart for most of the time

Eric and Tomak travelled to the Hudson Bay area, home to the largest concentration of Polar Bears in the world. When they landed at Churchill, a busy seaport inhabited by over a thousand people, they were driven to the meeting place where Eric absorbed some more valuable information. The main topic on the agenda was the proposed establishment of a National Park for the protection of the Polar Bear denning area just east of the community.

He was shown a tundra buggy, a large reinforced steel vehicle set atop mammoth wheels which gave it immense height. An eleven foot bear, on hind legs, would only be able to press its black snout against the window pane and this appeals to the tourists. There is a small platform which can be used for photographing but only under close supervision. When they reached the town dump there were several bears scavenging amongst the garbage. Two cubs were sparring as they tested each other's strength.

Polar Bears are marooned during summer until the ice forms in mid November. While some of them lie around conserving energy, because they haven't eaten, a few find their way to the dump in search of food. Wildlife officers are constantly on patrol because bears and people are a dangerous combination. Bear traps have to be set and the fresh seal meat will attract the offenders to the cages. The entrapped bears are taken to Polar Bear Prison where they are tranquilised, examined, and tagged. They are then transported by helicopter a hundred miles or more north of Churchill. This exercise is referred to as 'arrest and deportation.' The next stop at the edge of the coast gave Eric a view of a larger number of reclining bears, impatient bears padding backwards and forwards, and hungry bears digging in the snow hoping to find a morsel of food. On the perimeter of this congregation, several Arctic foxes roamed, well out of reach of the predators, anxiously hoping for a kill so that they could satisfy their hunger on the Polar Bear's leftovers.

The High Arctic is the Ice Kingdom of this large, splendid, mysterious animal whose cunning intelligence, enormous strength, and ferocity enables it to endure the eternal fight for survival. Eric observed several huge males. The male bear can weigh between seven hundred and fifteen hundred pounds. Not having eaten anything during the summer months, the male will attack and kill anything that moves. A bear can pretend to be asleep and in two leaps be covering the unsuspecting prey. Bears may look ungainly but they can move fast. They have powerful sight. Their tactic is the element of surprise and a sudden attack is the key to surprise.

In this perilous time, at the edge of the coast, a female has to pay particular attention to her cubs, otherwise they could become fodder for a hungry male. Although the female of the species is only half the weight of the male, she will attack if it comes too close to her cubs. She will fight viciously, even to the death, to protect her family. The mortality rate for cubs is twenty to forty percent. However, if a female is starving, she too will also eat her cubs in order to survive and breed again.

The Inuit hunter will not use the liver of the Polar Bear because the high concentration of Vitamin A makes it poisonous.

A drama unfolded as a bear cub strayed from its mother while she was playing with its twin. The stray cub was rolling playfully on its back in the snow when a large male swiftly moved in and attacked it. The mother quickly came to its rescue but it appeared to be badly injured. The little cub lay on its side as blood poured from its wounds. The distressed mother commenced to lick the severe gashes and the tundra buggy had to move in to shepherd the attacker a long distance away from the scene. It was a tricky situation because the smell of fresh blood could have caused a horrific melee. It was a while before the injured cub was able to rise. It slowly and painfully hobbled after its mother and the other cub, as she led them away from the huge carnivores that waited expectantly to put their huge paws on the sea ice.

Nature gave the Polar Bear paws like snowshoes to enable it to spread its massive weight, and the soft hairs covering the paws keep the bear from slipping when running on the ice. Eric felt sad as he watched the little injured cub making a valiant effort to survive. The Ice Kingdom was a cold, harsh environment where inhumane practices dominated the survival of its wildlife.

During dinner, Tomak intimated that Churchill was also a haven for Ornithologists in spring and summer because of the colossal number of birds, some of them rare that visit the area every year. Birds on their migratory flights take advantage of the rich feeding provided by the low sedge marshes, while others use the suitable vegetation for nesting and rearing of chicks. The Polar Bears also attract an enormous number of tourists which benefits the town economically.

One of the Wildlife officers then told Eric a story about his friend who resided in Churchill. He was awakened by the sound of cupboard doors banging in his kitchen and descended the stairs to find a Polar Bear rummaging around, flicking tins and packages on to the floor. He quickly vacated the premises, in bare feet and shorts and sought help. The bear had to be tranquilised and removed with great difficulty. His friend was out-of-pocket for the enormous amount of damage caused by the marauding animal. The story brought forth gales of laughter as well as a warning that the residents of Churchill have to be alert while Polar Bears are congregating in the area waiting for the ice to form.

"Ours is a rich wilderness land, Eric," said Tomak with a huge smile, "all 3,426,320 square kilometres of it within the Northwest Territories boundary line." He then added with a resounding laugh, "not forgetting, of course, the unique people who inhabit it."

Eric nodded in agreement and replied, "It is a land of extraordinary rugged contrasts, both in wildlife and population; a colourful mosaic of ethnic groups trying to overcome their differences, to enable them to band together as a force, and become landlords in their own land."

Eric made a decision to take Valerie to Churchill, when the opportunity presented itself, so that she could enjoy what he had just experienced.

CHAPTER 6

Meira tenderly placed her son in the swinging hammock. As she gazed at him she could see a slight resemblance to her long dead brother, Riel, in his strong features. She sighed forcefully. How much longer would the thoughts of that dreadful night keep haunting and tormenting her? Although the nightmares were becoming less frequent, she still suffered from pangs of guilt, blaming herself for having left her sisters and brother alone in the cabin. Her mother, of course, had put the blame on Meira's young shoulders and abandoned her to the care of a relative. Meira's quality of life improved in her new home, and she managed to finish her grade ten education, before finding a job as an office assistant in the Bay store.

Meira returned to her beading, a craft she had learned from her adoptive parent. She was quite skilled in the art and much of her work on slippers and mukluks was displayed in the co-operative which catered to tourists. She was making a pair of mukluks for Trolin who would soon be returning from a caribou hunting expedition.

Trolin and she had been in the same class in school before he became ill. She remembered the first day he had been brought by the social worker to the home in which she resided. He was shy, didn't talk much and spent a lot of time alone in his room. It was only when the Chief began taking an interest in him by taking him duck shooting and hunting did he respond and become more communicative and friendly. Later, Meira learned the cause of his introverted behavioural problems. Since that time she refused to have anything to do with the various religious denominations that attempted to inveigle her into their clutches.

Trolin and Meira had many things in common. Their lives had been traumatized by near similar incidents, alcohol being the root of the trouble which led to disaster. Therefore, they did not frequent bars or permit alcohol in their home. For Trolin, this caused many unhappy incidents between himself and his brothers, who drank heavily, abused their women and children, and expected Trolin to provide them with enough meat to see them through the winter.

Meira lifted the piece of paper on which she had written a poem for Trolin. She liked to write and was forever surprising him with little rhymes and poems. She was sure he would like this one entitled <u>Moon glow</u>. She read it aloud

> *Silence shrouds the depths of night*
> *As across the wide expanse of sky*
> *Like a majestic queen adorned with light*
> *Rides the silver moon, aloof and high*
> *Would she dare cast a flickering beam*
> *Over pale white birch and towering pine*
> *To where a lonely hunter tall and lean*
> *Rests on a bed of spruce and forest vine*
> *Oh! Queen of light my tear dimmed eye*
> *Longs to fondly gaze from such a height*
> *Upon the stalwart form that alone does lie*
> *With furtive creatures that roam the night*
> *My arms, like your ribbons of silver thread*
> *Would reach out in a loving warm embrace*
> *To enfold closely the raven black head*
> *And gently touch the slumbering face*
> *My restless heart will not cease to yearn*
> *Nor will the void that is dark with pain*
> *Be comforted, like the moon's caress*
> *Till my love returns safely to me again*

Meira smiled, as she folded the piece of paper and slipped it inside the mukluk she had just finished beading. She still had some beading to do on his caribou jacket but that would be taken care of long before he left on his journey to Europe. As president of the Trappers Association, Trolin, in the company of some members of other native trapping organizations across the north, was going to take a stand against the ban on furs. The native contingent would try to persuade government officials, and other animal rights groups, that the livelihood of the native was in great jeopardy unless the ban was lifted. The case they hoped to present was based on a way of life that had existed for more than a thousand years, where traditional skills were used to procure food, material for clothing and tents as well as crafts. Even though sweeping changes were very evident as land claim negotiations proceeded, there were still some Dene people who lived close to and relied on the land for food and making a living. The group would stress that the leg hold trap had been banned and that a more humane trap was already being used.

Trolin was quite excited about the forthcoming journey. He had never been farther from his Hamlet than Edmonton, Toronto, Calgary and Vancouver. He had already borrowed a camera from one of the Royal Canadian Mounted Police members in anticipation of the European trip. Even though Trolin tried to control his excitement by appearing nonchalant, as the time of his departure drew nearer, Meira was aware of his concern that the mukluks and jacket were incomplete. She knew he would be pleased to see the finished mukluks and she placed them neatly, side by side, on the small table in the bedroom. Meira decided to have some smoked fish before joining Nuniye. As she emerged from the smoke house she heard a faint rustle among the trees adjacent to the house. She looked around, but failed to detect anything other than a wood grouse, that flapped its wings wildly as it flew out from among a scattering of rust coloured leaves. Meira missed having the dogs around. Their fierce barks and growls usually deterred unwanted animals.

It was still late afternoon when Meira joined Nuniye who was having his usual daytime nap. She had been working on beading and decided to rest her tired eyes.

Meira was awakened by a terrific thumping noise against the back porch. Quickly slipping out of bed and grabbing the rifle she crept towards the window beside the porch and observed a Black Bear, on its hind legs, attempting to enter. She pondered on the best possible action to take. To shoot through the door of the porch would be foolhardy, because if she did not manage to kill it outright a wounded bear would be more dangerous. Before she could fully contemplate any other source of action, the bear managed to claw the door off its hinges and force its enormous bulk through the opening. On impulse, Meira raised her rifle and fired. The bear, with a yelp and a growl, lumbered over the demolished door and disappeared into the bush. Meira's next step was to phone the Wildlife officer and he and a companion were on the scene within minutes. They were able to track the wounded animal by following blood droplets. They had not travelled more than a few hundred metres before they found a dead bear. Meira was saddened that she had been forced to take the bear's life, but wild animals are a perilous force with which to become entangled, and she had to think of her own life and that of her child. The skin and meat she would be able to use and she felt sure that Trolin would be proud of her brave effort to protect his son. Meira went back to bed but nervous exhaustion kept her from sleeping properly so she commenced to bead Trolin's jacket.

Meira's heavily pregnant sister-in-law arrived as she was about to bathe Nuniye. She could smell alcohol from Rachelle and knew that she had not curbed her appetite for the drug, despite her promise made only a few days previously.

Meira commenced to lambaste her vocally, pointing out that she had already brought a Fetal Alcohol child into the world, who required special care and attention, and to give birth to another child in the same condition would be inhumane. Rachelle ignored Meira's remarks and proceeded to pour tea, which had just been made before she arrived, into a mug.

Meira shook her head dejectedly. There were so many brain damaged children in the north and it grieved her every time she looked at Rachelle's daughter, Maya, or a similarly afflicted child. Maya was severely incapacitated both physically and mentally and would remain in that state for the remainder of her life. Meira laid the blame for all the self abuse, evident in every community, on the strangers who first came to the land,

and the government which had taken control of their destiny and reduced them to an impoverished people forced to rely on welfare and other hand-outs.

The Chipewyan, Slavey Dene, Sahtu Dene, Gwich'in and Dogrib Dene, now referred to as the Dene Nation, were self reliant resourceful people and accomplished hunters, who had lived by a code of ethics which helped them survive unimpeded, until the explorers, voyageurs, trappers and traders came on the scene. Then everything changed. A new way of life was introduced when some of the native women married these strangers who invaded the land. The children of the marriages were then exposed to two separate cultures, that of their native ancestors and those of their white forefathers and became known as the Metis.

Meira remembered a conversation she once had with a College professor who told her about the British introducing opium to the Chinese. She compared that situation with the present one, the introduction of alcohol, that had so many people dependent on it, but she considered the effects much worse because of the numerous suicides, untimely deaths and mentally scarred children.

Although she realised that time does not stand still, nevertheless, she was concerned at the rapidly vanishing way of life to which she had been introduced by her adoptive Slavey parents. The moon nearest to Easter, the day the sun dances, referred to as the moon of the geese, when small birds appear; a sign that the geese have passed on their way north because the smaller birds ride on the bigger ones on the migration route. Many times Meira's adoptive father had pointed them out to her as they flew out of a flock of geese towards the shore to feed. Spring, the time of year, more gentle, when creeks and rivers discard their icy mantle and the men in the family prepare for the spring hunt.

Summer fishing camp, Meira's favourite time of year, when the whole family work in unison, gathering and storing enough food to sustain them during the winter. Now, only the families that had not broken the link with their past were living off the land, the other unfortunates linked to a lifestyle totally alien to their forefathers' customs and guardianship of the land.

Trolin's two brothers' lives had been directed by Social Services and they had been placed under the jurisdiction of separate families after the death of their Mother. Neither of them had native foster parents, which resulted in lifestyles that were not inspirational, and immersed them in a culture that excluded hunting and trapping. Their lives were aimless and boredom set in. This caused them to turn to alcohol which shattered what little bit of heritage to which they felt they belonged.

Trolin had tried many times to help his brothers overcome their problems, but his attempts were never very successful. He had hoped that the deaths of two men, as a result of drinking gas line antifreeze, who had been friends of his brothers, would have a sobering effect on them.

This was another very serious problem in the North, the alcohol abuse also included consumption of other substances with alcoholic content which led to blindness and death. All Trolin could do was pray that they would eventually realize the error of their ways and conform to a more caring way of life. It saddened Trolin to watch their disintegration and that of their wives who also imbibed, all of them slowly poisoning their bodies and whose fogged minds could not foresee a brighter future for themselves or their children. As Meira renounced her rambling thoughts, Rachelle noisily poured another mug of tea.

"When will Trolin be back Meira? We need some meat."

"I hope soon, Rachelle, because there is a Scientist coming to consult with him on the bear population."

"I heard about your encounter with the bear. I am glad I did not have to cope with that experience and especially in my condition."

"I never really experienced any fright until after I had used the rifle," said Meira as she replenished her empty mug. I am going to skin the bear shortly and I will send you some meat later in the afternoon."

"Has Trolin heard anything further about the Land Claims?

"No, Trolin is quite concerned because the Gwich'in, Sahtu and Dogrib have formally withdrawn from the Dene Nation. They want to take control of their own affairs. It seems impossible to resolve the different interpretations of the treaty between the Government and the Dene. According to the government we gave up our Aboriginal title for treaty rights but the Dene insist that they signed a peace treaty which included sharing with Europeans. It is difficult to deal with the Government. Many of our people are still resisting the changes that are being imposed on them, but we are custodians of the land on which we have hunted and trapped since time immemorial. There is great confusion at the moment and Trolin maintains that united we stand, divided we fall."

"Maybe the Government wants to create confusion among the people. That would give them more power over us. Too much has been forced on us too soon

. It is impossible to expect us to change from our nomadic lifestyle to a southern one overnight. I don't understand any of it, Meira. I only hope Trolin will be able to convince the assembly to stay together. The cracks will denote weakness."

"Since Trolin became actively involved with the Dene Nation organization I see very little of him. He is always travelling but I don't mind as long as something can be accomplished in our favour and the Dene Nation, as a whole, is satisfied."

As Rachelle prepared to leave, Meira once again reminded her of the disastrous results that would prevail if she continued to imbibe in alcohol. In response, Rachelle disappeared with a wave and a smile.

Meira turned her attention to Nuniye, who was babbling happily on the table, where she had set him so that she could attend to his personal needs. Of one thing she was sure and that was his upbringing. He would be taught to share. Sharing was a law by which the Dene had lived because of the harsh climate and conditions of the land. Being a nomadic people, they travelled in small groups to where food sources would be found and everyone shared in the catch. He would also be taught tolerance, another law that had been strongly evident. Recently it appeared that tolerance was in short supply because of the estrangement of various groups from the parent organization that was formed to protect the rights of the Dene. She felt certain that by the time Nuniye shed his childhood years, the Dene would be in complete control of their own destiny and harmony with creation and each other would once again be an important part of their lives.

CHAPTER 7

Eric tapped each foot against the door jamb to dislodge the snow, before removing his footwear and placing it on the mat in the hallway. He carried his luggage to the kitchen, where he unpacked and deposited his soiled clothing in the laundry bag. Before proceeding to the bathroom to store his toiletries, he opened the fridge to grab a beer and was surprised to notice a bowl of stew and some bannock, with a note attached which read "Heard you were returning today; nothing like a bowl of caribou stew to appease the appetite of a weary traveller—Valerie." With a grin Eric lifted the telephone and on the second ring a cheery voice answered.

"Valerie, what a pleasant surprise to find a home cooked meal awaiting me. Any chance of you sharing it with me?"

"I would be delighted, Eric. Just give me thirty minutes to finish a report then you can regale me with your trip's anecdotes."

Eric hurriedly disposed of the remaining luggage, popped the stew into the oven, had a quick shower, and was about to lay the plates and cutlery on the table when Valerie arrived, bearing a precious bottle of red wine. As she removed her parka, assisted by Eric, he surprised himself by giving her a quick hug exclaiming how pleased he was to see her. Valerie responded by placing a slight peck on his cheek. The warmth generated by their respective actions set the scene which led to an evening of tempestuous passion, that left them both struggling for equilibrium, and a strong desire to nature the bud of love that had flowered so quickly.

Daniella, observing that Valerie was busy, settled herself into a comfortable chair with a magazine. Several times her attention was drawn to Valerie's smiling face and debonair attitude, which she considered as being quite unusual, having regard to the fact that the waiting room was crowded and the passage to and from the clinical room hectic. When she entered Valerie's office, she remarked on the complete transformation of her friend and requested the prescription which might put some zest into her own life. Valerie laughed and replied that nothing had changed and she was just having a good day. Daniella retorted that Valerie looked like someone who had just fallen in love, because the eyes were really the mirror of the soul, and her eyes revealed more than just having a good day.

"Level with me, Valerie. Is it that scientist who arrived from Vancouver who is making your eyes sparkle, although he hasn't been around very much?

Valerie hesitated a moment or two before answering. She replied that Danielle's assumption was correct and that she was well and truly smitten, adding quickly that the feelings were reciprocated. Daniella threw her arms around her long-time friend saying that she shared in her happiness and hoped that she would soon be acting as matron-of-honour.

"Not so fast, Daniella, Eric lost his wife in a tragic accident after fourteen months of marriage, and he moved North in an attempt to heal the wound. I am sure he is not prepared to jump quickly into another marriage until a reasonable length of mourning has elapsed. Maybe it will just turn out to be an affair on the rebound but I would settle for that because he is a hell of a nice guy."

"Oh, sorry Valerie, I didn't realise that Eric had sustained such a loss but it is good to see you sparkle and if he has that effect on you, who knows, anything can happen. Jack and I are having a little get-together on Saturday evening and you and Eric, if he is available, are very welcome."

"Is the occasion something special Daniella?"

"Actually it's a private send-off for one of Jack's employees."

"You mean it's for Sara. I knew she was going but didn't know exactly when. That should be a relief, Daniella."

"Maybe it will be my turn to sparkle now. I know she has a tremendous crush on Jack, although he keeps emphatically denying it, but this last month with the usual 'I'll be late for dinner, honey, Sara and I and have things to finish,' happening two or three times in the week certainly laid my spirits low. To tell you the truth I will be glad to see the end of her."

"Then why are you giving her a send-off at your home? Surely the office party would have been sufficient."

"To please Jack. He suggested it and if she is going what have I got to lose?"

"That's very thoughtful, Daniella, but I doubt if I would be able to comply with such a request from my husband if I were in your shoes." Daniella shrugged her shoulders "That's life, Valerie; you have to accept the bad as well as the good."

Valerie then produced Daniella's test results and confirmed that she was indeed pregnant.

"I knew it Valerie and believe it or not this will be my last child. Four is an even number. I already have two boys and one girl so I hope this will be another girl."

"My heartiest congratulations, Daniella, there is no reason why you should not have another healthy child regardless of sex. How will Jack receive the news?"

"I think he will be happy and excited because he has often said that we should have another daughter who would be a playmate for Deana . . .

"Good, I am sure he will be delighted," said Valerie as she examined Daniella's lower eyelid. Here are some iron tablets, just follow the directions on the box. The doctor will be here on Thursday so I will make an appointment for ten o'clock. See you then Daniella."

"Thanks Valerie, keep smiling and don't be doing anything that I wouldn't do."

With those last words and a big grin from ear to ear Daniella exited the nursing station.

Daniella was the last patient to leave the clinic so Valerie poured a coffee into the caffeine stained mug, kicked off her shoes and seated herself at her desk to update the pile of files scattered in disarray in front of her. With her pen poised over

Daniella's chart her mind reflected on her friend. From the first introduction to Daniella, a few days after Valerie's arrival, a firm friendship formed which had strengthened as the geese flew back and forth, heralding the arrival of several springs and long dark winters, broken by the ever present kaleidoscope of the Northern Lights

Valerie had brought Daniella's third child into the world, and was immediately appointed Godmother by delighted parents, who were happy to be the recipients of a daughter, while already parenting two delightful sons. She remembered Jack's effusive thanks for a job, well done, when she had placed the tiny bundle in his arms and watched him stroke, with great tenderness, his daughter's downy head. Jack had flirted outrageously with her when they had first met and he displayed many other characteristics of the Arian male. While admiring Daniella's patience with Jack's occasional unrestrained behaviour, she was of the opinion that underneath that seemingly devil-may-care attitude, Daniella was hurt and resentful of Jack's flirtatious approaches to all women who crossed his path. Valerie felt sorry for her friend, because several rumours had been circulating, that Sara's duties as personal assistant were far exceeding those described in the job description.

The fact that Sara already had a husband made matters worse. Valerie was privy to information that Sara's husband had applied for the transfer to Yellowknife because life in the community, due to his wife's philandering, was becoming unbearable.

Valerie did not envy Daniella's forthcoming situation when she would be placed in the position of hosting a farewell dinner for her husband's paramour.

She was still in the same pose with poised pen when Eric pushed his head around the door and announced that he had been watching her for a full minute while she appeared to be lost in her thoughts.

"Would a dollar buy them? Valerie?"

"I will give them to you free of charge, Eric. We have both been invited to a farewell dinner on Saturday evening and I hope you are free to accept the invitation."

"I will be delighted to escort you, Valerie. I have no aversion to making it known that we can now be considered as an Item, It is a good way of becoming acquainted with other people in the community."

Valerie then proceeded to tell Eric the story behind the proposed dinner. His response was, that having met Daniella when he first alighted from the plane, he was so impressed by her dazzling smile and conviviality, that he would never have suspected under such an effervescent exterior, lurked the dregs of unhappiness.

"The same could be said of you Eric. One would never suspect that you are cloaking hidden depths of sadness. I was truly unaware that such catastrophic circumstances had affected your life until you bared your soul."

"Touche Valerie. Millions of people are carrying burdens, some more sorrowful than others, yet they can maintain a placid or convivial appearance without denoting inner turmoil. Perhaps you personally have some deep seated grief of which I am yet unaware."

"No, thank goodness. Nothing really destructive or horrible has as yet, touch wood, encroached on my life with the exception of my patient's complaints and illnesses. I have lived with birth, pain and death but this can be expected in the profession I have chosen. To change the subject Eric how about a cup of coffee?"

Thanks, Valerie but I haven't time. I just called to say that I have to go out of the community again for a few days but I will be back in time for Saturday's rendezvous."

"Take care Eric, I look forward to seeing you Saturday."

Eric placed a kiss on top of Valerie's head and his parting statement in a laughing voice before he exited was "I hope to find some other goodies in my fridge when I return, Valerie."

"You'll be lucky" murmured Valerie under her breath as she returned to the unfinished work on her desk.

This statement was provoked by Eric announcing that he had to leave for the remainder of the week and Valerie hoped her disappointment hadn't been too obvious. She had been anticipating another evening of dinner, wine, candlelight, soft music and whatever else the ambience might have contributed, but on second thoughts decided that she must not go off the rails completely.

She chided herself that it would not be fitting to throw herself wantonly at a man who had enthralled her with his first kiss. Maybe last evening's coming together, in such a joyful and passionate embrace, could possibly be attributed to a sense of isolation and lack of romantic involvement with the opposite sex for quite some time. Nevertheless, it appeared to have had the desired effect on Valerie to want to pursue it to its ultimate conclusion. However, being held in high esteem in the community, as Public Health Nurse, she must not blot her copybook by being over zealous and immersing herself in a love affair that might peter out, like a puff of smoke from an extinguished candle flame. Still, she had found it difficult to control the excitement she felt, when Eric had entered her office and planted a kiss on top of her head before leaving. She had been involved in two previous relationships but neither of them had produced the same dynamic effect.

Valerie decided to have a light supper before sorting through the closet to find something suitable to wear on Saturday. Normally, on an occasion such as the anticipated event, she would not choose anything too dressy, but since she was going to be escorted by Eric she intended to be a bit more adventurous.

Having settled the dress question, she concentrated on her hair and decided that a trim was in order. Daniella, being an experienced hairdresser and a former hairdressing salon owner, was the only person capable of giving her a stylish hairdo. She dialled Daniella's number and when she answered Valerie detected a note of despair in her voice.

"Are you feeling OK, Daniella?"

"Of course, Valerie. Just feeling a bit tired."

"How did Jack react to the good news?"

There was a slight hesitancy before Daniella replied. "Well, he was not exactly overjoyed or over the moon as I had hoped. He has been working really hard lately and probably the thought of a crying baby in the wee small hours of the morning wasn't, at that particular time of announcement, conducive to a burst of enthusiasm. He won't be home again until after nine tonight."

Valerie, not wanting to comment on Jack's deplorable reaction, decided to make her request.

"Well, Daniella, maybe I shouldn't be making this request but if you can spare about fifteen minutes to trim my hair before Saturday I would appreciate it."

"Certainly Valerie. I will be happy to trim and shape your hair. Now that you have romance in your life you must always look chic. By the way, is Eric going to be accompanying you on Saturday?"

"Yes he is Daniella. We are both looking forward to having a delightful evening."

"Super, Valerie. How would after supper tomorrow evening suit?"

"Suits me fine, Daniella. See you then."

As Valerie replaced the receiver she felt sad that her friend's expectations regarding Jack had not been realised. Maybe there was some truth in Daniella's assumption that Jack was overworked and he would, when the reality of the situation eventually hit him, express his true feelings more positively.

Next evening, Daniella confided in Valerie that the relationship between her and Jack seemed to be disintegrating and she was becoming more certain that he was truly in love with Sara. The thought of Sara leaving, according to Daniella's distraught voice, appeared to be upsetting Jack so much that he was actually calling out her name in his sleep. Valerie tried to console her distressed friend by pointing out that overwork causes stress. Jack was probably dreaming that he was still in his office and calling on Sara in relation to some important task to be carried out

"Maybe, Valerie, but I still have my doubts. Anyway, what do you think of the hairdo?"

Valerie gazed at her reflection in the mirror held by Daniella and nodded approval.

"You have done a super job, Daniella. I am looking at a new me. I don't know what I would do without you because I am hopeless when it comes to hairstyling."

"I expect you will be requiring my services more often, Valerie, now that Eric is an essential part of the scene."

"I most certainly will" was Valerie's laughing reply.

"How about another coffee, Daniella. I am not going to offer a glass of wine in your state of health."

"I am taking your advice Valerie and cutting wine out completely. Even my coffee consumption, and you know how partial I am to coffee, will be drastically reduced, so I am refusing a refill but thanks for the offer. The children were doing their homework when I left so I must get back and monitor their progress."

"Thanks Daniella for doing such a superb job on my hair. You are an angel."

"I wish my husband thought so," answered Daniella with a deep sigh as she passed through the open door.

Valerie had just closed and locked the door behind Daniella when the telephone rang. I hope this isn't another one of those nights when nasty wounds, caused by over indulgence in alcohol, require to be stitched entered her mind.

As soon as she answered the line went dead, but on a re-ring she was pleasantly surprised to hear Eric on the other end of the line.

"What happened the first time I called, Valerie? I could hear you speaking.

"I couldn't hear anything Eric, the line was completely dead. It happens often in this environment.

"Can you hear me now?"

"Yes. Your voice is perfectly audible Eric. Where are you?"

"I am at the Institute in Iglook. Lots of interesting material here. Thought I would just take a few minutes to say Hi and tell you that I miss you. I would rather be with you this evening, sipping wine and listening to a voluble speech on reincarnation. You might manage to convert me to your way of thinking."

"Really Eric. Have you read any of the material I gave you?"

A cursory glance through it is all I have been able to achieve, so far, but I promise you I will devote an evening to the subject when I return."

When is that Eric?"

"Saturday, just before noon Valerie."

"I'll be waiting at the airport."

"I hope you miss me Valerie. I have been thinking about you all day."

"I do miss you Eric but I haven't had much time to think. My time has been utilised by getting the charts updated before the Doctor arrived. Now that's over for another month I can let my hair down. Incidentally, I had my hair cut this evening."

"Not your beautiful hair, Valerie."

"Yes Eric, but nothing drastic, just shoulder length."

"I can't imagine how you look with shorter hair"

"You'll see Eric. It's very trendy."

"OK Valerie, it can't be soon enough. See you Saturday."

Valerie replaced the receiver and gleefully threw herself onto the settee where she reminisced on the conversation she just had with Eric. She felt elated and treated herself to another glass of wine as she conjured all sorts of pictures in her mind of life with Eric on a permanent basis.

Eric's flight was delayed for four hours, but the sight of Valerie's smiling face and sparkling eyes banished the tedium of the long wait he experienced at the airport, prior to departure. Before he eased himself on to the back of the snowmobile, he enfolded Valerie in his arms and gave her a warm kiss on her frozen lips which she eagerly returned.

"So happy to see you Valerie. Let me see the new hairstyle."

Valerie pulled down the hood of her parka and Eric gave a whistle of appreciation.

"Enchanting Valerie. I love it."

I knew you would consider it trendy Eric."

"I certainly do. It's delightful and suits your heart-shaped face. I never imagined it would be so attractive.

Valerie drove Eric to his residence and on entering the living room he observed the place setting and inhaled an appetising smell emanating from the kitchen.

"I knew you would have a culinary surprise waiting for me. Valerie," said Eric with a loud laugh.

"You are being pampered Eric but I consider your friendship worth the effort."

"Eric kissed Valerie on the cheek. "Thanks my love. I appreciate your concern for my welfare."

After partaking of a delightful late lunch, Eric announced that he was going to be immersed in paper work until party time. Valerie replied by indicating that she had to attend the clinic to remove some sutures from a child's leg.

There was a small gathering, already imbibing in various alcoholic beverages and in party mood, when Valerie and Eric arrived at the residence of Jack and Daniella. Valerie noticed that Sara was ensconced in a wing backed chair while Des, her husband, perched on the arm. They appeared to be in deep conversation. Jack emerged from the kitchen with a tray of drinks and exchanged greetings with Valerie and Eric. Very soon the room was crowded and Valerie and Eric moved around chatting comfortably with the other guests.

Around midnight guests were startled to hear Jack and Des, both of whom had consumed an excessive quantity of alcohol, embroiled in a fierce argument in the kitchen. Daniella hurriedly forced her way towards the fracas, followed by Sara and very soon the ferocious dispute escalated into a more vitriolic and dangerous situation, where violence was imminent. The threatening poses of both men necessitated restraint by an RCMP officer, who was an invited guest, and Eric who happened to be positioned just outside the kitchen when the argument erupted. As Eric grabbed Jack's arm, Des's fist lunged towards Jack who ducked the blow. Eric received full force of the attack which threw him against the edge of an open cupboard door, causing a deep laceration to the side of his head, and a badly bruised eye sustained when he first encountered Des's hard fist. At this stage, several other male party guests had to intervene and eventually some semblance of peace was restored. Both Daniella and Valerie were in a state of shock, as indeed were most of the female guests. It was several minutes before the kitchen was cleared to enable Valerie to assess the extent and seriousness of Eric's injuries. It was evident that the head wound would require suturing, and a cold compress was immediately applied to the bruised eye which was already darkening; and one to the head wound to control the bleeding

When they emerged from the kitchen, all the guests had departed and Daniella sat alone on the settee, weeping softly into a large tissue. Valerie put her arms around Daniella, and tried to comfort her with reassuring words to the effect that Eric's injuries were not serious, and once the hangovers had dissipated, both Jack and Des would be contrite.

"Just a storm in a teacup, Daniella. Tomorrow everything will be forgotten." While uttering these words, Valerie knew that Daniella was deeply ashamed that her husband's indiscretion would now be publicised far and wide and everything wouldn't be forgotten. It had been obvious from the tone and context of the altercation, that Des had been accusing Jack of having an affair with Sara. Jack's response of "So what?" had prompted the attack.

"I will have to transport Eric to the clinic Daniella to insert a couple of stitches to the head wound," said Valerie as she proceeded towards the closet to retrieve her parka. Daniella immediately regained her composure and apologised for being thoughtless in not maintaining her role as hostess, as she sprang into action and went to assist Valerie and Eric who were donning their outdoor attire.

Before departing Valerie whispered "Keep your chin up Daniella everything will be OK. You'll be surprised. Jack will be on his knees in a few hours begging your forgiveness."

Daniella murmured as they both kissed her "I'll phone you later to find out how you are Eric. I feel so ashamed."

Eric and Valerie were of the same thought as they stood outside under a canopy of aurora streamers which bathed the glistening landscape in an eerie glow.

"Why can't man exercise more control over the dark side of his nature and elevate his thoughts to a higher level of consciousness. It is better to play among the stars than grovel in the dirt and succumb to self inflicted mortifying indignities." stated Eric sadly.

As Valerie sutured Eric's head, they discussed the untenable situation in which Jack had placed himself and arrived at the conclusion that once Des and Sara left the community, the situation in the household would return to normal.

"This is the second time you have come to my rescue, Valerie. I have a heck of a headache but I am sure a couple of pain killers will relieve it."

"I will give you a strong tablet Eric which will make you sleep more soundly. You will have quite a shiner for a few days but your dark glasses will hide the disfigurement"

"All week I have been dreaming of this night filled with love and romance and now look at me. One eye completely closed, part of my head shaved, and a stitched ugly wound."

"There will be many more nights Eric so don't worry about it. I will take you back to your residence and once I administer the medicine you must go to bed immediately."

Valerie, before she left Eric's bedroom, made sure that he was comfortable. As she stooped to kiss him goodnight he produced a neatly wrapped little parcel.

"Not to be opened until you reach home Valerie. I had envisioned a different scene for presentation but things haven't worked out as planned."

Valerie took the parcel, thanked him with another kiss and switched off the light. Curiosity got the better of her and she opened the gift when she reached the snowmobile to discover a beautiful ulu necklace made of silver and ivory.

What a delightful gift from a delightful man, she thought, as she made her way across the sparkling icy terrain.

CHAPTER 8

Eric was waiting, in the small crowded airport for his luggage, when he was approached by a distinctively handsome native man, whose beaded braids reached across his broad shoulders and fell almost to his waist. The elaborately embroidered bandana and fringed caribou jacket added to the outstanding mode of dress. Immediately he knew he was being addressed by Trolin. After the usual customary greetings the conversation resorted to polar bears and the environment which Eric had just left a few days previously. Eric's luggage finally appeared and he followed Trolin out to the truck.

"It's good to be below the tree line again, Trolin. I have been used to being surrounded by trees all my life and I found it rather strange at first, without a bush or tree in sight, but the desolate Arctic wastes have their own particular beauty, which can be quite spectacular at times."

"This north is an enormous tract of beautiful land, Eric, occupied by diverse cultures. A thousand years ago our ancestors settled in the north above and below the Arctic circle. They were dependent upon whatever resources the land had to offer. Now is the time for the native people to take control of their own destiny, but many obstacles require to be moved before this can take place. It is a mind-boggling slow process."

"It will eventually happen, Trolin. There are definite signs in the East that a new mould is being cast."

"As you well know Eric, every land has its secrets. Take Egypt and China for instance. Their treasures lay hidden for centuries until the Archaeologists came on the scene and began digging. The same situation exists in our land. Rocks four billion years old have been discovered also gold and oil both valuable resources. I'm sure other treasures will come to light. The wildlife is another rich resource and it needs to be protected and managed. Who better to do this than the native hunter and trapper, who has been born and bred in this land, and has complete knowledge of the wildlife, their seasons and habits."

"I am in complete agreement with you, Trolin."

The conversation continued in this vein until they reached a log cabin hidden among the snow laden trees. On entering, Eric was struck by the natural beauty of the tall, lithe woman who greeted him. She was almost as tall as her husband with a mane of blue black hair that reached to her slim waist. The dark brown eyes and sparkling white teeth, in a perfectly shaped oval face, made a pronounced contrast against the pale tan skin.

Certainly a woman who would turn heads in a crowded street, thought Eric. She smiled and after he had been seated offered Eric a can of coke then busied herself at a table in the far corner of the room. Eric and Trolin continued the conversation, along the same lines as those discussed on the journey from the airport, until plates of stewed moose and bannock were placed on the table. Eric thought the food was delicious and complimented Trolin on having a wife with such good culinary skills. Meira blushed, and coyly hung her head, obviously embarrassed as Trolin extolled her virtues as a good wife and mother. She lifted Nuniye, who had been amusing himself with a wooden toy on the floor, and disappeared into another room. When Eric finished his rather large mug of coffee, he suggested leaving and checking into the motel as he had a special telephone call to make to Vancouver. Trolin nodded in agreement and as Meira was unavailable to be thanked for her hospitality Eric followed him out to the vehicle. A firm arrangement was made for the following morning to take Eric out on a quick tour of the area before the meetings commenced.

Eric went through the contents of his briefcase and set aside his notes and list of questions. He stepped into the shower and was forced to terminate sooner than anticipated because the water changed quickly from being very hot to extremely cold. Wrapped in a towel he felt the urge to speak to Valerie and dialled her number.

"Hi Valerie. How are you?

"Fine thanks Eric pleased to hear you have arrived at your destination safely. What is the weather like there?"

"Not as cold as where you are. It feels good to be among trees again. How are things with you, Valerie. Still busy?"

"You know my schedule Eric always on call twenty four hours a day. No serious situations at the moment just pregnancies to monitor."

"How is Daniella?"

"Still under the weather mentally, not physically because Jack hasn't returned from Yellowknife yet. He phoned to complain that the meetings were taking longer than anticipated. Daniella's imagination is, of course, running wild imagining Jack in the arms of Sara. My attempts at consoling her are futile, falling on deaf ears, but in her condition all this stress is not good for the blood pressure."

"I thought the reconciliation after that dreadful going away affair would have been the turning point."

"I'm afraid not Eric. Daniella is the type of person who forgives but does not easily forget. Her vivid imagination is driving her crazy and I hope Jack doesn't have to attend any more meetings in Yellowknife until after the birth. I don't believe he is associating with Sara, because I have heard through the grapevine that Des and Sara have once again become a loving couple, who rarely socialise on the same scale, as demonstrated when they lived here."

"A loving couple like us Valerie? I miss you and your appetising meals but I participated in a delightful feast of stewed moose this evening."

"At a restaurant Eric?"

"No. I was a guest at Trolin's table and his wife Meira prepared a wonderful wild meat dish. What a beautiful woman she is. Definitely a person who would turn many heads in a crowd."

"Are you trying to make me jealous Eric?"

"No my love, just making a statement. I can't help admiring a beautiful woman and I mean beautiful with a capital B. You are beautiful Valerie, in a different sort of way, so the statement is innocuous."

"When do you think you will be returning Eric?"

"Probably towards the end of the week. Is there anything special you would like me to bring home besides the fresh fruit, veg and wine?"

"No thanks Eric. The items on the list I gave you will be sufficient."

"I will be contacting you again Valerie before I leave, and if anything else occurs to you in the meantime I will be happy to add it to the list. Have a good week Valerie. I love you."

"Take care Eric, love you too."

When Valerie replaced the receiver she felt a twinge of jealousy. Since the fateful night, when Eric had been injured at Daniella's house, the friendship between them had become more intense. The fantasies she had painted in her mind, regarding a settled life with him, appeared to be on the brink of materialising. She had fallen head over heels in love with Eric and to hear him complement another woman's beauty made her feel uneasy. This made her think that maybe she was reading too much into the relationship. As she fingered the ulu chain around her neck, which she wore constantly, she dismissed the twinge as a natural reaction to a careless frivolous remark and prepared to retire for the night.

Spiralling frosty vapours exited from their mouths, as Eric and Trolin made their way next morning to the conference room where the agenda would focus on archaeological and ecological matters. Everyone was in agreement that it would be foolhardy to commence divesting the land of its rich mineral wealth, without taking into account, the fragile environment of the tundra where rocks, four billion years old, had been discovered.

Again it was stressed that raping of the land must be avoided and the habitat of the bears and other creatures be protected against the onslaught of people, snowmobiles, machinery and heavy equipment, until there was a firm agreement among the Inuit, native groups, government, mining, oil and gas companies.

It was agreed by a show of hands that many dialogues are needed before the economy of this land is in native hands. The conference ended after questions and answers had been dealt with and the following day was to be devoted to ecological matters.

When Trolin and Eric arrived at the cabin it was obvious that Meira had again gone to great lengths to promote native hospitality, by preparing a caribou stew smothered in dumplings. It so appealed to Eric's palate that he had no hesitation in accepting a second helping.

Eric found Nuniye to be such an engaging child that he commenced to amuse him, while Trolin conversed with his brother for a considerable period of time, outside in the truck. Meira sat silently watching Nuniye and Eric frolic. Occasionally she would smile and intervene when the child would exercise his juvenile authority in an obstreperous manner.

When Trolin re-entered the cabin his face expressed anger, and as Meira prepared coffee he conversed with her in the Slavey language. A family feud, thought Eric, as he continued to amuse Nuniye.

As Eric was about to depart, he expressed his pleasure at having partaken of such a tasty and satisfying meal and Meira, in her usual quiet manner, acknowledged his thanks with a smile. He spent the remainder of the evening making notes and writing a report on the day's activities.

Next day was spent in a series of meetings. Eric gleaned some information regarding eskers, those ridges of sand and rock that streak and wind like ribbons across the tundra. Although they only cover a small percentage of the barren lands they, nevertheless, form part of the ecological structure. The eskers, because of their sandy consistency and height are used as denning areas and corridors for many species of wildlife. Besides being important to wildlife, Eric learned that esker material can be used for building purposes, similar to quarries, where the rock is used in road making. The native members of the group were consistent in their views that the eskers should not be plundered or exploited by mining companies for their own use. Eric was also given access to further information on other bears occupying the land and the meetings occupied the whole day.

Eric had invited Trolin and Meira to join him for a meal at the restaurant. They had declined his invitation, so he ate in the company of two meeting members who imparted further knowledge to add to his growing data bank.

The penultimate day was usurped by a short meeting and a further consultation with Trolin, which again touched on the fragile political situation existing between the government and native groups.

"I understand you are going to London Trolin in the hope of dispelling the many misconceptions that Europeans have regarding native trappers."

"As a member of the Dene Cultural Institute I, along with over a hundred strong delegation of Dene and Inuit, will be a prominent part of the British Royal Museum display. I am really looking forward to the trip."

"What will the display entail Trolin?"

"It took quite a few months for the comittee to come up with ideas. The input was good and we settled on the idea of "The Living Arctic" to encompass all native artifacts, traditional clothing and tools. A model of an Inuit community encased in glass will form the entrance and the lighting will reflect the rapidly moving changes in the Arctic sun."

"It seems to be an ideal way of drawing attention to the plight of the trapper, Trolin, who relies on the fur harvest to make a living."

"A life-sized notch logged trapper's cabin containing a cut-barrel stove, small table and radio, together with a teepee erected above a spruce bough floor will also be on display, along with the more modern northern house where television, fridge and contemporary furniture form part of today's habitation. The most important item is the new humane trap."

"It sounds impressive enough to raise the negative understanding that Europeans have towards the fur trapper to a more positive one. The meetings to put together such an elaborate exhibition must have encroached on your Land Claims work."

"They did, Eric. There are many problems regarding land division and we have been at the bargaining table with the Inuit on numerous occasions. The agreement on boundary lines is the stopping block. As an example the Dogrib people want the boundary line to include part of the Contwoyto lake area because the rich gold mine there was on the Inuit side in the last agreement. Also the Chipewyan, who live south of the 60th parallel, but have hunted and trapped traditionally in the Northwest Territories have aboriginal rights to be considered. Likewise the Dene from the provinces to the east, who spend all year North of 60, want their land to be on the west side because their traditional values are more akin to the NWT Dene/Metis. To sign a bilateral agreement with the Inuit would assign these groups to a different territory. Then there is the Thelon Game Sanctuary with its wealthy abundance of wildlife, an area on which tourism would have a dramatic impact. The Tungavik Federation of Nunavit leaders don't even want to discuss this copious area and an arbitrator may have to be appointed by Ottawa to seek a fair solution regarding the boundary line. If we could dispense with this aspect of the agenda, and the Federal approach to aboriginal rights which the organizations consider restrictive, then we could proceed to work together under more amenable terms."

"The situation is very complex, Trolin, and the negotiators appear to have a long struggle ahead of them."

"If the division negotiations could be disposed of then other issues could be dealt with. The Dene/Metis have formed a northern alliance with the Tungavik Federation of Nunavut and the Council of Yukon Indians to work on areas of commonality."

"It is just a question of all parties involved in the negotiations for autonomy being satisfied before any significant progress can be achieved, Trolin."

Eric's commiseration on the untenability of the current situation was accepted by Trolin as bona fide, and the firm handclasp as they parted company forged a bond in a newly formed friendship.

When Eric returned to the hotel he phoned Valerie.

"Hi, Valerie. How are you my love?"

"Existing Eric. Can't wait to see you."

"Just one more day Valerie and I will be heading north again. I am going to Trolin's place for another delicious meal tomorrow evening".

"A meal Eric, or just to sit and gaze at his beautiful wife?"

"Now, now, Valerie, don't be sarcastic. It doesn't become you. You know I am only interested in you."

"It is just a natural reaction. I wouldn't really be human if I didn't experience a touch of jealousy now and again Eric."

"Nothing to worry about Valerie I will be with you soon and all those doubts regarding my romantic integrity will be dispelled."

Eric finished assembling all the invaluable data obtained during his investigative foray into the habitat of the bears and prepared for his visit to Trolin's residence. He had already arranged that he would make his own way and as he walked briskly across the crunching snow he felt elated at the thought of returning to Valerie. Before his contract finished he decided he would ask Valerie to marry him. He was confident that she would accept and his heart sang as he planned the scenario for the proposal.

The feast of ptarmigan proved to be another sumptuous meal and while indulging in coffee and homemade cookies Trolin's mistrust of the non native population became evident.

"When the white man first set foot on this country he plundered its treasures, all for greed. Wolves in sheep's clothing were sent to turn our forefathers away from their own religious beliefs. All that they held sacred was considered unholy. The children were removed from their parents and sent to schools where punishments were inflicted and stern disciplines enforced."

Eric recollected having a similar dialogue with Tomak and replied.

"But, surely education isn't such a bad discipline, Trolin. In other countries their peoples are suppressed by lack of education. In order for a country to advance and hold its own in the world of commerce the people must be educated."

"I agree, Eric, but not to the extent that their language and customs are completely eradicated. That's why, in collusion with other native groups, we fought hard for our language to be part of the school curriculum. Our children must learn to be proud of their heritage. As I understand it, in England, some families can trace their ancestors for hundreds of years. If the tables had been turned, I'm sure they wouldn't have relished the idea of another culture from across the sea blatantly attempting to extinguish their illustrious past, along with the most precious thing of all, their language."

"You are right Trolin in that respect, but there is no reason why natives cannot co-exist with the non native community and learn from each other."

"The saddest part is the rape of many of our children by the so called 'men of the cloth.' I was a victim of the debauchery inflicted by these vultures who fed on children's innocence. They hid behind a cloak of piety and spouted Christianity to gullible parents and it is still going on."

"I can tell you Trolin that situation is prevalent, not only in the north, but in many countries. Children are now being taught that such atrocious behaviour is unacceptable, so prison sentences are now being imposed on those who have been found guilty of such an abominable offence.

"It is just as well that the man who seduced me is dead otherwise I would gladly take great pleasure in sending him to prison.

From the bitterness intoned in Trolin's voice, it was obvious that he was still suffering the consequences of the mental and physical abuse inflicted upon him as a young innocent boy. Eric empathised with Trolin at the many injustices that had been administered to native people through the years. He agreed that the time was imminent for the people of the north to take complete control of their own destiny, lands and resources. Because of the ethnical and geographic differences, division would be necessary, but the end result would be a new north governed by its own people.

Meira had just finished pouring a third refill of coffee into Eric's cup when a loud scuffling noise in the porch sent Trolin running to the door. He hastily closed it behind him. A raucous quarrel ensued between Trolin and the visitor. Meira became visibly distressed as the voices became louder. She shook her head sadly and remarked that Trolin's brother always made trouble when he commenced drinking alcohol. Eric discerned that a lot of pushing and shoving was being demonstrated as dull thuds mingled with the raised voices. A loud explosion sent Meira screaming to the porch where she found Trolin lying outside the entrance bleeding profusely from a wound to the chest. Meira's continuous screams alerted Eric to immediate action. He went to her assistance and found her cradling her husband in her arms. By the time they had managed to transport Trolin to the Nursing Station, life had left him. The Royal Canadian Mounted Police officers became involved and Trolin's brother was placed under arrest.

Meira's friends and some of Trolin's relatives rallied around her. Eric attempted to proffer his condolences several times but Meira was in total shock and could not respond. Eric made his way back to his motel room where he spent the night turning and tossing in his bed, unable to sleep. He wished he could have spoken to Meira before he left the following morning, but he had no idea where she was, so he wrote a short letter and enclosed some money which he stated could be applied towards funeral expenses. Eric felt sad as he boarded the plane, that a young vibrant man, in the prime of life, with such strong ideals, and so much to offer to a land on the verge of a new beginning, should die under such horrific circumstances, leaving his young wife and son to fend for themselves.

Valerie immediately detected the change in Eric's mood when he arrived at the airport. Sardonically, she quipped that having to tear himself away from the beautiful talented woman was evident in his glum expression. She regretted having spoken so flippantly when she learned the truth of his sombre mood.

"Well, life certainly hasn't been dull since you arrived in the North, Eric."

"It certainly has not Valerie. It has been an ongoing roller coaster of ups and downs. It's becoming difficult to predict whether tomorrow will be just another normal day or one filled with traumatic events. On par with your daily experiences, love."

"Yes Eric there is a slight similarity but this weekend is going to be a very quiet one. No report writing, visiting, or wild parties. I am not sharing you with anyone."

"I am glad to hear that Valerie. I feel emotionally drained."

"Leave it to the nurse Eric, to apply her own particular brand of healing. We are going directly to my house where you will be treated like a Sultan."

Eric raised a quizzical eyebrow but made no comment or protest when Valerie veered of the road which led to his place of abode. On arrival, she took Eric's case and dumped most of the contents into the wash bag while Eric stretched out in an easy chair and sipped a beer. He couldn't help reflecting on the sorrowful scene he had witnessed of Meira's beautiful tear-stained face, cradling her badly injured husband in her arms and Nuniye clinging to her shoulder, his small face hidden among her hair, sobbing loudly. His reverie was interrupted by Valerie emerging from the kitchen with a tray on which lay some letters and two mugs of coffee.

"I collected your mail and brought it here Eric."

"Thanks, Valerie. You are my housekeeper, cook, secretary, nurse, but above all a kind, thoughtful, lovable woman for whom I care very much."

Valerie responded to this complement by ruffling Eric's hair as he proceeded to open his mail. There was complete silence as he scanned the contents of the various envelopes, while Valerie drank her coffee and contemplated her next move to try and assuage Eric's tension.

"Valerie, here is an invitation which we must accept. Charles and Louise are celebrating their twenty-fifth wedding anniversary."

We?"

Yes, my love. I am taking you out of here for a short vacation. It's time you had a change of scenery. We are going to be pampered in a five star hotel."

"But how can you take leave on a short contract, Eric?"

"I have been asked to attend a conference in Vancouver around that time so you should apply for leave Valerie."

"That's a super idea Eric. Something to look forward to."

Valerie felt enthralled with the idea that had just been presented. As she continued sipping coffee she mentally made a shopping list. Her wardrobe consisted mostly of garments suitable for the environment in which she resided, so a complete new range would be required to complement the elegant surroundings Eric had in mind. She smiled as she looked across at Eric who was frowning as he studied an account.

"Eric you are now going to have an aromatherapy massage, followed by a warm towel wrap to relieve the tensions of the past week. Then I am going to cook your favourite meal followed by a delicious dessert."

Eric immediately discarded the bill, jumped to his feet, and with a broad smile on his face took Valerie by the hand and led her to the bedroom.

It was an evening of subtle fragrances; soothing remedial treatment; unbridled passion; hot heavily scented towels; gourmet feasting; and tender meaningful lovemaking, which convinced Eric, as he lay enveloped in the lavender scented bed, that he was making the right decision to propose marriage before his contract ended. He had no wish to remain a widower for the remainder of his life and his strong feelings for Valerie were dominating the deep feelings of loss occasioned by Tamalyn's death. Eric also spent the following day soaking up all the attention lavished upon him, until satiation sent him into a deep sleep, secure in the knowledge that Valerie truly loved him.

Tomas and Eric attended a meeting the next day with a group of visiting students who were shown films of both men confined in a helicopter searching for bears. Eventually they were in a position to affix collars to two female bears to enable them to be monitored and gathering blood samples as well as collecting data on a large male bear Because the male of the species conical head shape, from snout to muscular neck is not conducive to retaining a collar, their activities were reduced to examining, weighing, measuring, tagging and drawing a blood sample. Timing is an important factor in this dangerous occupation. On the first sign of recovery by the anaesthetized animal, they quickly returned to the security of the helicopter, where they supervised its return to normality before continuing on their quest.

Before lunching with the students there was a question and answer session.

Tomas wound up the discussion by informing them that he and Eric's last trip would be Baffin Island and Banks Island in the western Arctic, after which all the valuable data amassed would be analysed.

Valerie's day began with rubella vaccinations before the Doctor arrived. It then became another mad hectic rush, assisting in examinations, dispensing medicines, and spending valuable time persuading one stubborn patient to divulge the name of his contacts, to prevent further spreading of a venereal disease he had contracted. She even had to go so far as to threaten him with RCMP intervention if he failed to comply with her request. The information obtained would also add to her work load. Several medevacs also had to be arranged and when the hour hand pointed to five o'clock Valerie felt exhausted. She certainly did not feel like entertaining but there were several frozen casseroles in the freezer. She had by this time become aware of the Doctor's likes and dislikes and there happened to be one dish available which would appeal to his palate. He had brought her the habitual fruit, vegetables and wine so dinner preparation would not be a difficult chore.

Valerie had everything ready when Doctor Raymond Park arrived, and he ate his meal with relish, complementing her on the appetising cuisine, as he finished his last crumb of apple pie. They reclined in more comfortable chairs away from the dining table to enjoy coffee and liquors

"You know I don't like talking "shop", after hours Valerie but I am concerned about Daniella's high blood pressure and blood disorder. She isn't a well woman and I may have to send her out to hospital for a spell."

"She didn't have these pronounced problems during her last pregnancy, Raymond."

"She is much older Valerie and her obesity does not help."

"I did put her on a diet before she became pregnant which she followed religiously. She also attended the exercise classes twice weekly and was in good shape before her marital problems materialised."

"That probably accounts for the obesity and her present condition. As you well know, Valerie, some people with ongoing unresolved problems turn to food for comfort. What is the present position in the marital relationship?"

"Well, the source of the problem is no longer in the community but it is difficult to convince Daniella that the relationship is ended, especially when her husband travels regularly to Yellowknife, where the third party now resides. When Jack accompanies Daniella to the antenatal classes he is very attentive towards her."

"Her weight will have to be controlled. I am going to leave a letter for her indicating this and emphasising a proper diet and exercise should be started immediately, otherwise she will be sent out to hospital.

I do not think she will be happy at the thought of leaving her family unattended, Raymond."

"That's the idea, Valerie. She will probably make the effort rather than run the risk of being medevaced. Sometimes you have to be cruel to be kind."

"I think she will follow your advice Raymond, but to ensure that she has support I will have a quiet word with Jack. When he is made aware of Daniella's unsatisfactory condition I'm sure he will move mountains to co-operate."

"Now, Valerie, let's change the subject. You know I am not going to give up easily. Come to Winnipeg for the week-end and I'll treat you like a princess. Discard your Cinderella image and let your hair down."

Valerie laughed merrily as she looked at the handsome Doctor who sat opposite her. She was sure that his roguish smile, twinkling brown eyes, and mop of unruly dark brown curly hair, would cause many increased pitter patters of the heart in the opposite sex. On his very first visit to the nursing station, he had displayed a keen interest in her. Even though she always maintained a professional attitude during his visits, it had not deterred him from pursuing his quest of trying to form a more significant relationship. If Eric hadn't arrived on the scene she might have been tempted to fall prey to his charms. His sense of humour and caring bedside manner put his patients at ease. On occasions when he was unable to attend and replaced by another Doctor, Valerie was inundated with telephone calls requesting that appointments be cancelled if Doctor Park was not going to be in attendance.

"I would love to accept your offer Raymond but I don't think Eric would be too pleased."

"So you are involved in a serious affair, Valerie?"

"Yes, Raymond, believe it or not, I am in love with a wonderful man."

"Ah! My loss Valerie. He is a lucky man but if there is a breakdown in the relationship, I'll be waiting in the wings."

Doctor Park announced that he had to leave immediately as he had been offered a ride on a chartered flight which had several available seats. He smiled, as he placed his empty glass on the side table and announced that he would not be available the following month as he was attending a conference. As Valerie helped him into his heavy parka he reiterated his concern for Daniella. He was assured that Jack's support would be enlisted to help Daniella achieve the goal, which Valerie would set for her, so that no further weight would be gained.

As soon as Doctor Park left, Valerie settled down to write a letter to her parents informing them that she had, at last, found true love. She gave them an impressive description of Eric, emphasising that his devastating handsomeness, combined with his joie de vivre made him irresistible, and stressed that she was ecstatically happy with this man who had stolen her heart. Valerie also stated that he would be accompanying her to England in the near future so that he could be introduced to the family. When Valerie had suggested this visit to Eric at the week-end, he expressed delight at being invited to meet the family members, which led Valerie to believe that Eric was more serious than she realised about the relationship.

Valerie sealed the envelope and prepared to relax with a glass of sparkling white wine when the telephone rang. Half clad, she answered it to hear a distraught parent requesting her to come quickly as her daughter had swallowed an enormous number of barbituates. Valerie ascertained that the girl was not unconscious and requested the parents to bring her to the clinic immediately. She dressed quickly and spent the next hour inducing vomiting and using a stomach pump while the distressed parents kept repeating "Why? Why? Why?

When Valerie finished attending to the pale faced girl she had to deal with the 'new to the north' parents and learned that their daughter had been suffering violent mood swings for several weeks. They thought it was teenage tantrums and didn't seek medical help. Valerie informed them that a referral to a Psychiatrist would need to be made, and they should contact her the following morning after she had spoken to Doctor Park, who would arrange the time and place of the appointment.

She explained to the parents that it is a well known fact that high incidences of suicide are found in the North during the season when there is a lack of light. This causes a *biochemical imbalance in the part of the brain that regulates main body functions. Some people are badly affected by the Seasonal Affective Disorder Syndrome. Many symptoms of the syndrome such as mood swings, a craving for carbohydrates, loss of libido, insomnia, mild to severe depression can all be attributed to lack of sunlight during the dark cold months of winter. The quotation seemed to pacify them and they escorted their daughter from Valerie's office feeling more enlightened as to the irrational and destructive behaviour of their only child.*

Valerie gazed at the unfinished glass of wine which had lost its sparkle. As she emptied the contents of the glass into the sink, she breathed a sigh of relief that the long arduous work day had finally ended.

CHAPTER 9

Meira opened the letter to discover that she had been accepted into the Teacher Education program in Fort Smith. After Trolin's tragic death, a cold numbness had engulfed her, mind and body, making her move around like a puppet on a string for a considerable period of time. It was only when she had gone out on the land, with some of Trolin's relatives in the springtime, that she was able to cast aside her mantle of sadness and come alive, like the land that was shedding its darkness and icy overcoat, opening its arms to a new beginning. She had a small son who would be reliant on her for a number of years and she began to realise, as the sole provider, she should enter a profession that would enable her to make a more comfortable life for herself and Nuniye. She had always been interested in teaching and Trolin had encouraged her, on several occasions, to make application to the college but she had declined. Her excuse had always been that she wasn't yet ready to become immersed in lengthy studies, whereas the real truth was that she had no wish to leave Trolin, regardless of the fact that he travelled extensively. She realised that he could not, on account of his many obligations to the various committees, accompany her to Fort Smith and she could not bear the prolonged separation. Trolin had always been of the opinion that the educational facilities in the North should have more aboriginal teachers, especially in the elementary schools, where native children could be immersed in a learning system staffed by familiar faces, who could address them in their own language. Now that he was no longer part of her life she would commemorate his memory by carrying out one of his dearest wishes and become a teacher.

Meira had many things to organize before she commenced a new phase in her life. She couldn't bear to be parted from Nuniye and although she knew the program would be demanding, she decided to take one of Trolin's nieces with her to act as babysitter, instead of leaving him in the care of her sister-in-law. She had been offered suitable accommodation and as she gathered together cooking utensils, bedding and clothing, she discovered Trolin's mukluks which had lovingly been prepared for his trip to Europe. She put her hand inside one mukluk and withdrew the poem she had written. Meira re-read it and the words caused her eyes to moisten, as the last line of the poem incisively reminded her that never again would she wait for Trolin to return from a hunting trip. As she handled the mukluk, a thought suddenly occurred to her. Dr. Eric McClure had been very helpful and kind after Trolin's attack and eventual demise. In appreciation of his kindness she would wrap the mukluks and send them to him as a gift. There were few white men, in whom Trolin would have placed implicit trust, but he had mentioned to Meira that Eric was a fair minded man who had empathy with the aboriginal population. He had stated emphatically, on more than one occasion, that he respected Eric's views and Eric would always be made welcome when he came to visit. On reflection of Trolin's remarks, Meira felt that he wouldn't mind Eric being the recipient of his mukluks and she commenced to pen a letter.

> Dear Dr. McClure:
> You were most kind to me when you discovered Trolin had been fatally injured. It was only with your help that I was able to get my husband to the Nursing station.
> Your gift of money towards the funeral expenses was also very much appreciated.
> In consideration of your thoughtfulness I am enclosing mukluks I originally made for Trolin but sadly he never lived to wear them. Although the acquaintance was short, nevertheless, Trolin had

a certain amount of respect for you and I am sure he would want you to have them. If Trolin had been alive I know he would have presented you with some little gift before you left Fort Smith.

Sincerely, Meira

As Meira prepared to wrap the mukluks, she was interrupted by Nuniye's cry of pain. She stooped to pick him up and gently rubbed the bruise which had appeared on his forehead where it had come into contact with the leg of the table. When his sobs had subsided Meira placed him beside her and completed the task of preparing the parcel for postage.

She had just lowered Nuniye to the floor when Rachelle came bounding through the door in a frenzy of excitement waving a letter in her hand.

"Meira, I have been accepted into the Academic Studies program in Fort Smith. I'm so excited about it and so is Magda, who will be glad to get away from all the trouble Dorin has caused."

She congratulated Rachelle and informed her that she too would be spending two years in Fort Smith. Meira was dubious as to Rachelle's sincerity about undertaking serious study. Rachelle had not resolved her drinking problem and she loved to party. Her love for excessive amounts of alcohol had caused the abortion of her last child a month previously.

"Magda will have his hands full babysitting Meira but I understand there is a day nursery there. I asked Magda to apply for the Heavy Equipment program and the kids could spend the day in the nursery but he doesn't want to do that. I hear you are taking Angie with you to look after Nuniye."

"Yes, Rachelle. It will help to relieve Agnes' burden by taking one of the children. She has enough to worry about at the moment with Dorin behind bars. It is good Magda is going to be the baby sitter otherwise you could be faced with a huge bill if you place three children in a nursery. Besides, Maya needs constant attention and she wouldn't be accepted into a nursery.

"I suppose not Meira. Anyway, we are looking forward to a change. I am sure you are too after all you've been through. I've admired you for a long time Meira. You are always helping others and you didn't deserve to lose out because of Dorin. I don't know how he could have so cold bloodedly murdered his own brother."

"He keeps saying he has no recollection of the argument and of harming Trolin. Had he been sober it would never have happened Rachelle. That's the reason I keep telling you that overindulgence in alcohol can have dire consequences, not just on one family but on many families. The pain and suffering can be unbearable causing one's senses to become fogbound. I know, Rachelle, I have experienced it and now poor Agnes has been left devastated because of Dorin's gratification of his desire for the drug."

Well, it's good that you are getting out of here Meira and leaving all the bad memories behind."

"There are more good memories Rachelle than bad but my main reason for going is to graduate as a teacher, an achievement I know Trolin would be proud of if he were alive."

"When I am finished in Academic Studies, I intend entering the Nursing program. That career has always appealed to me Meira. It would also mean spending some time in Yellowknife and I just love that city. I would probably be able to find a position in the hospital there once I am qualified."

"Do you realise Rachelle that you have many years study ahead of you. There will be no time for bar hopping. I am sure your goal could be achieved if you would only realise that you have a serious problem and do something about it."

"I know Meira. I have a problem but please don't keep lecturing me. I will do something about it one of these days. You'll see."

"Sounds good Rachelle. I look forward to seeing you graduate in your nurse's uniform. It will be a long haul but worth it. How about a coffee?"

"No coffee Meira. I just came to give you the good news. See you later."

Rachelle left the cabin in the same flurry of excitement with which she had entered and Meira turned her attention to Nuniye. She noticed he was beginning to exhibit a leaner look and was increasing in height rapidly. It was obvious that he was going to be as tall as his deceased father, but his features still bore a strong resemblance to Riel.

As Meira prepared a meal for herself and Nuniye, she dwelt on Rachelle's words that she should be looking forward to a change after the tragedy which had crushed her emotionally. Her life seemed to be beset by tragedy, especially losing the people she loved so dearly, but she had emerged from the depths of grief with a new strength and intended forging ahead towards her goal with a fierce determination to succeed.

Eric turned the package over in his hands several times before he proceeded to unwrap it. As he lifted out a mukluk a piece of paper fluttered to the floor. He picked it up and became fascinated as he read each line of the poem. The words so mesmerised him that he sat down and re-read it more slowly, absorbing each word and meaning which was obviously directed towards a very special person. He was slightly perplexed and couldn't fathom who would want to express such delicate feelings along with a gift of mukluks. He was about to withdraw the matching mukluk from the parcel when Valerie entered with a cheery greeting and planted a kiss on his cheek.

"What beautiful mukluks, Eric. Did you have them made to measure?"

"No, Valerie. I don't know where they came from and this was inside one of them. It fell out at my feet."

Eric handed the poem to Valerie and her eyes widened as she absorbed the contents. She was about to make a comment when Eric brandished the envelope he had just found hidden in the other mukluk. When he had finished reading Meira's letter it became clear to him that the poem was not intended for anyone, other than Trolin, and had obviously been erroneously enclosed in the parcel. Valerie agreed with him as she examined the beautifully made footwear with such fine embroidery and beadwork.

"What a lovely thought, Eric. They are so decorative and a very useful gift. Meira is a very talented woman. She also writes impressive poetry."

"The poetry wasn't for my eyes, Valerie, but it does disclose a great depth of feeling which she had for her husband. I will return it along with my thank-you note."

"I've just called in for a second, Eric, to borrow your coffee pot. Mine's defunct, fizzled out this morning, and the Doctor likes coffee with his liquors. Do you feel like joining us for dinner this evening?"

"No thanks, Valerie, I am going out on the snowmobile with Tomak and a few of his friends this afternoon, then we are all congregating at Tomak's place. It will probably be a late night so I'll stay here and see you tomorrow, my love."

Eric embraced Valerie and when she departed he sat down and re-read Meira's letter and the poem, then he pulled on the mukluks and felt pleased that they fitted so comfortably. He decided to reply to Meira's letter and after settling for a cup of tea in lieu of the much desired coffee, he commenced to write.

> Dear Meira:
> What a lovely surprise to receive such beautiful mukluks. They fit perfectly. The fact that they were made for Trolin makes them all the more special. Your thoughtfulness is very much appreciated and I will treasure this gift.
> I am returning a poem which was inadvertently left in one of the mukluks. I took the liberty of reading it and found the contents very touching. The sentiments expressed in your poem can only lead me to believe that you had a deep and abiding affection for your husband. You will have an ache in your heart which only time can heal, but the precious memories of your life with Trolin will be stored in the recesses of your mind forever.
>
> Sincerely, your friend, Eric

Eric read what he had written and satisfied himself that his thoughts and feelings on the acceptance of the gift and the poem were succinct. He then sealed and stamped the letter before he readied himself for the snowmobile trip.

As the three friends skimmed across the tundra, Tomak and Tarquiv in the lead, Eric again felt an essence of serenity within himself. He was thoroughly enjoying his sojourn in the Northwest Territories and every day presented a new challenge. In a few months the last year of his contract in the polar area would be finished. The more he thought about it he was surprised to feel a great reluctance to leave. He decided there and then to seek an extension and spend another year becoming more acquainted with the land, its wildlife and people. The land was like its people, a cornucopia of moods; sombre, exuberant, colourful, stoic. It never ceased to amaze him that yesterday's largesse could be tomorrow's penury as man and animal strove to maintain their proper place in its extensive, inimitable reservoir of cold savagery and spectacular ebullience.

Eric noticed the land was changing as the icy grip of winter began to loosen its formidable hold. Beneath frozen surfaces were enormous quantities of blue green water waiting to divulge its rich treasures.

Tomak and Tarquiv seemed to be competing against each other in a game of speed, Tarquiv in the lead. Eric decided to join in the sport and soon he was in line with both of them. When Tomak accelerated, Eric kept pace with him and Tarquiv fell behind. As they sped across the frozen bay the isolation gave him a great sense of freedom which appealed to his adventurous spirit. Again his mind reverted to the land. It had allure, like a beautiful woman who captivates and holds spellbound the unsuspecting swain. It also had the power to encourage man to draw on the profundity of his inner self and recognise his own spirituality. He could now understand why Valerie was loathe to leave and her words "it grows on you" began to make sense. His thoughts were disrupted as Tomak slowed down and looked behind. He came to an abrupt halt and Eric, who had preceded him, turned and came back to where he sat. There was no sign of Tarquiv and Tomak's agitation was evident as he stressed that they should retrace their path. After fifteen minutes hard driving Tomak suddenly stopped and warned Eric, by a frantic wave of his hand, to follow suit. A large crack in the ice led to a black jagged chasm which indicated that someone or something had assaulted the smooth glossy surface. There was no visible sign of the machine or its rider and they both sat immobilized, like black sculptures against a stark background, as they stared in horror at the spot, where their friend had presumably disappeared. There was absolutely nothing they could do. For either of them to venture across the cracked ice could spell disaster. Only the resemblance of an oversized breathing hole led them to believe that a tragedy had occurred.

"The sea lice will get him" said Tomak sadly.

"Sea lice?" replied Eric in a startled and questioning voice.

"Yes, there are enormous numbers of these voracious shrimplike creatures found in polar waters. They are likened to the piranha fish and they will hunt and devour their own kind. If a wounded man or animal happened to fall into the icy depths these amphopods would be able to follow the trail of blood, swarm over the body and leave nothing but bare bones. It's not the first time that skeletal remains have been found and the elders will tell you that the sea lice are creatures to be feared."

"I had no idea that such creatures existed here, Tomak."

"There is nothing we can do, Eric. We will have to go back and report this disaster."

Two unhappy riders, who had so joyously covered the trail with their missing friend a few hours earlier, quickly detoured and cautiously made their way back. Tomak had the unhappy task of breaking the news to Tarquiv's wife and family.

Eric spent a considerable time dwelling on the unfortunate calamity. He looked at his watch and deliberated whether or not he should phone Valerie. If Doctor Park was still at her residence he did not wish to disrupt the visit which was usually part social and part patient diagnosis/prognosis. He decided to take a chance and was glad to learn that Doctor Park was just on the verge of leaving.

As soon as he arrived, Valerie detected that his usual sang-frond attitude had been replaced by one of dejection. He threw himself disconsolately into the armchair and asked for a double whiskey. The fact that he had not greeted her with the usual kiss, or asked how her evening went, alerted Valerie to assume that a major incident had occurred. She handed Eric the drink and sat quietly opposite him waiting for the inordinate silence to break. Eric sat passively with the glass in his hand. He stared at the contents for a second then placed it on the side table before he divulged the source of his misery.

"Valerie, it is difficult to believe that I have been witness to so many deaths in my life. Tamalyn, Trolin, Tarquiv. Three T's. It seems so sinister, in fact it's downright scary and I'm not a superstitious man."

Valerie observed that Eric was in shock. She immediately evoked her nursing skills by providing some medication and removing the drink. She also tried to placate him, by attempting to reassure him it was just a coincidence that all the deceased persons' names began with the letter T, but he was not appeased.

"It's a bad omen, Valerie. Each death has been occasioned by catastrophic circumstances and not a natural passing."

"Everyday there are people all over the world whose lives are being shattered by exposure to grim and devastating tragedies. As an example Eric, last week fire in the Carlin household left only one badly burned survivor to face the loss of his wife and six children, as well as his house and possessions. The incidents in which you have been involved happened in such close succession, Eric. In your scientific and well organized mind there is no palpable explanation as to why you have to bear emotionally the consequences. It is all part of your karma Eric but we will not go into that now. What you need is a good night's rest and tomorrow you may be able to look at the situation in a different light."

LIke an obedient child, Eric allowed himself to be sent to bed after ingesting a sleeping draught, while Valerie became absorbed in perusing her medical records.

CHAPTER 10

It took Eric a few months to come to terms with the devastating disaster which he encountered on the icy tundra. Despite this, it had not compromised his decision to extend his contract, and headquarters in Yellowknife had acceded to his request. He decided not to inform Valerie of the good news, until they were together in Vancouver when he would also pose the question of how she felt about a legal long term commitment. If her answer was in the affirmative, then they would choose a ring and both of them would visit her family a few months later as an engaged couple. Not until a reasonable time had elapsed, as a token of respect to Tamalyn's memory, would Eric stand at a church altar and make marital vows. He thought most people would consider the idea passe but his ethical convictions outweighed the urge to tie the knot quickly.

Meantime, they decided to spend a week in Churchill which Valerie had been very keen to visit after listening to Eric's fascinating description of the place where the polar bears congregate while waiting for the ice to form.

Eric was excited as a schoolboy as he packed the appropriate clothing to wear in the beautiful city of Vancouver.

Likewise, Valerie was as eagerly excited as she browsed through the closet, choosing and discarding various garments which had been hanging there since she first arrived. Her purchasing list lay on the dresser and occasionally she would lift the pen, and add to the already growing number of items, which would make a sizeable dent in her savings. She decided to put a mackintosh in her bag, because the last holiday she spent in Vancouver had been marred by continuous rain for three days, and she had no intention of being caught off guard during this special vacation. As she zippered the bulging bag a loud knock announced the arrival of Daniella. Valerie had spoken to Jack a while ago about how vital his assistance was in helping Daniella to curb her excessive appetite. He had responded by resorting to being a more caring and attentive husband. The transition was amazing as if Daniella had taken on a new lease on life and Doctor Park, on his last visit, had been more than pleased with the test results. She had commenced to glow and was once again her cheerful self, outrageously funny at times, and always smiling. Even Eric had remarked that the change was amazing.

"Hi Valerie. It's only me" she exclaimed as she put her blonde head around the bedroom door.

"Come in, Daniella. I have just finished packing. Have a look at my list of purchases. I'm going to be drastically over weight with all these items. Is there anything special you would like to add Daniella?"

"No thanks Valerie. I think you have enough to cope with. Your holiday is going to be spent traipsing in and out of shops instead of relaxing and enjoying the gorgeous scenery. I can understand the need, of course, for the makeup, lingerie and designer clothes," she added with a burst of laughter.

"Eric's days are going to be spent attending the conference so I will spend my time shopping Daniella. You are quite right the need is there to make myself beautiful for the man with whom I have fallen deeply in love."

"I think Eric is the perfect man for you Valerie. You make a lovely couple. I am so pleased that you have found love and happiness at last. I take it there is an understanding between you which is going to lead to bigger things."

"Well, Daniella, it is said actions speak louder than words and Eric's actions lead me to believe that bigger things are on the horizon."

"I hope so, and soon Valerie, but wait until I regain my proper shape before the big day, otherwise I won't be able to get into a bridesmaid's dress."

Valerie giggled and replied that Daniella would be the first to know if wedding bells were about to ring.

"Let's get started on the hair Valerie. You haven't much time."

As Daniella worked on Valerie's coiffure she remarked that Jack had applied for a management position in Inuvik. If he was successful, and they moved there, it would be easier for the children to access and spend time with their grandparents in Whitehorse. She added that quite a number of children in the north are deprived of grandparents and other family members because of vast distances and excessive plane fares.

"Oh no, Daniella, am I going to lose my best friend?"

"Valerie, this is the north where friends are transient."

"Yes, I know Daniella. It does have its disadvantages."

"You'll be OK Valerie. You will have Eric as a permanent fixture in your life, and who knows, you too might be on the move since Eric is only a contract employee, but we will always keep in touch."

"I think I would like to remain in the North Daniella. I really love my job and the people. Geographically it's very beautiful, a raw beauty that can sometimes take your breath away. I cannot see myself in a large city like Vancouver which is also beautiful but rather crowded and the air impurities are overwhelming."

"Who knows what fate has in store for either of us Valerie. I only hope Lady Luck is benevolent."

The conversation between the two friends continued until Daniella held the mirror in front of Valerie to confront a sleek new hairdo which complemented the attractive interesting face.

"Wow! Daniella. You have surpassed my expectations. Well done."

Daniella gathered together her equipment and gave Valerie a warm hug as she wished her a happy holiday.

The journey had been long and tedious, and as soon as Eric and Valerie reached the hotel they both fell asleep once their heads touched the pillows. After a refreshing night's rest and a happy union of bodies and minds they chatted amicably over a tasty breakfast in the crowded dining room. Valerie was in sparkling form and as her lovely almond shaped green eyes gazed above her upheld cup at Eric, he reached across the table and grasped her hand.

"Valerie this isn't quite how I had planned this particular moment but you must be well aware of the deep feelings I have towards you. Will you do me the honour of becoming my wife?"

Without a moment's hesitation Valerie accepted.

"Yes, Eric. I am happy and proud to accept your proposal of marriage."

Eric pressed Valerie's fingers to his lips and informed her that he couldn't resist making the request at breakfast instead of during dinner. A more romantic setting, with dinner, flowers and champagne in the room was what he had in mind for the proposal, but the engagement would be celebrated in that setting once they had acquired the ring.

The following morning Valerie chose an emerald, her birthstone, surrounded by diamonds. As Eric slipped it on her finger, she was engulfed by such a deep feeling of ecstasy that her eyes brimmed with tears which trickled down her cheeks. Eric tenderly wiped them with his handkerchief, before he lovingly embraced her and they sealed their commitment to each other with a loving kiss.

When they returned to the hotel Eric had to leave her and she spent the afternoon shopping. Occasionally she would extend her hand and admire the ring which sparkled on her finger signifying a new important phase in her life. Valerie phoned her mother who was euphoric at the news and her father delighted that his favourite daughter was no longer alone, thousands of miles away from the family home. The wedding was discussed in great detail and when Valerie put the phone down she was elated at the thought of the forthcoming nuptials.

The evening was one Valerie would never forget. During dinner, amid the flowers and bubbling champagne, in the quietness of their room, they toasted themselves and made plans for their wedding and future together. Valerie was pleased that Eric had been offered another year's extension which would give them both time to consider long term employment, preferably in the North, which they both loved.

The following evening Eric took Valerie to the house where he had first commenced married life with Tamalyn. He informed the relieved tenants that he would not be returning to reside there on termination of the lease as anticipated. As he stood in the hallway with Valerie, a strange feeling overcame him, as if Tamalyn was giving her approval of his decision and choice, along with a warning. A coldness enveloped him and he shivered but the feeling passed as quickly as it came and he dismissed it as fanciful. Valerie noticed and asked him if he was cold.

His reply "Have you ever heard the old saying Valerie, someone just walked over my grave," made them both laugh.

Next evening, Valerie in one of her new designer outfits accompanied Eric to the home of Charles and Louise Stratton. When Charles learned that Eric and Valerie had just become engaged, he made it a stupendous celebration which lasted until breakfast the following morning. They were both exhausted when they arrived at the hotel and Eric laughingly exclaimed that he would need two matchsticks to keep his eyes open in the conference room. After a quick cold shower he felt much better but the excitement had been too much for Valerie and she was sound asleep before Eric left the room.

When Valerie opened her eyes she observed that it was 4:05p.m.and realised that she had missed a hair appointment. The realisation caused her some consternation as she wanted to look her best for the introduction to Eric's sister and family who had invited them to dinner later in the evening. She realised she would have to rely on her own expertise and spent the next two hours soaking in the bath and styling her hair. She was still in her bathrobe when Eric entered with a small bouquet of red rosebuds. As he presented them to her, he remarked that she smelt delicious, good enough to eat, and proceeded to remove the bathrobe as he nibbled at her ear and worked his way down the beautiful lean body that gave itself up, without retaliation, to Eric's loving ministrations. They both fell asleep and when they awoke were horrified to find that there was only half an hour in which to shower, dress and reach the rendezvous in time for dinner. Despite their late arrival they were received with open arms and Sanja, whom Becky had given to Eric's sister because of unregulated commitments, was overjoyed at seeing her missing master. She covered him with slavering kisses and never left his side all evening. It was a joyful reunion for Eric and his family and they accepted Valerie into their circle with extravagant praise for her extraordinary adventurous spirit. They enquired whether the marriage ceremony would be performed in Canada or England and Valerie replied England. Instead of expressing disappointment, they let it be known that they would be prepared to travel to England for the occasion as they intended visiting relatives there. As soon as a date had been agreed their relatives would be informed to expect them.

Valerie expressed her delight that some of Eric's closest relatives would be a party to their union as man and wife. The evening ended with a firm promise that his sister, her husband, and three teenage children would be waiting at the church the next time they met.

Discussion on the events of the evening and the forthcoming marriage lasted for more than an hour after they arrived at their hotel. As Valerie snuggled in Eric's arms she said a silent prayer thanking God that their paths had once again crossed.

Valerie spent the last day shopping and was forced to buy an extra case to hold all the extra items. When they had been in Birks buying Charles' anniversary present, Valerie had purchased a personal gift for Daniella, a pair of solid gold earrings.

The flights home were smooth and on arrival they went directly to Valerie's house.

"Will you be moving in here permanently, Eric?"

"Not at the moment, Valerie. I will remain as tenant of the government house meantime but I spend more time here than I do in my own place. When we return from our honeymoon Valerie and Eric McClure will be the tenants of this house.

"Valerie McClure," mused Valerie. "It sounds nice. I think it suits me Eric. Don't you?"

"Definitely, my love."

Valerie prepared the coffee pot and while she waited for it to perk, she phoned Daniella.

"Guess what, Daniella? The bells are about to ring."

"Valerie, you are joking. Are you serious?"

"I have never been more serious. Eric and I are engaged to be married. I have the ring to prove it."

"I am coming right over" said Daniella breathlessly.

Valerie replaced the receiver and got another mug out of the cupboard. Before long, Daniella was hugging and kissing them both alternately and mooning over the ring which she had taken from Valerie and placed on her own finger.

"Valerie it is so beautiful. I bet it cost quite a few dollars. Look at the size of the stone? It's enormous.

"It is an expensive ring Daniella, but Valerie is beyond worth." replied Eric as he proudly placed an arm around his fiancée.

"I am so happy for both of you. Have you named the date yet?"

"It will be a summer wedding Daniella, but I am going to be married in England because all my family resides there."

"Well, I can't say I am not disappointed because I am, but I understand, Valerie. If I could afford it I would be there but with three children and a new baby it would be impossible."

Valerie hugged her dearest friend and told her that she would have a special video made of the whole event, especially for her, and she accepted the suggestion with good grace.

"Have you any honeymoon plans?"

"Yes Daniella. We are going to be touring Europe for a month and Eric is renewing his contract when we return."

"Lucky you. I've always wanted to visit Europe. Maybe my dream will be realised some day."

Valerie then presented Daniella with the earrings. She was so pleased with the gift that she insisted on wearing them and preened in front of the mirror for a full minute as she admired them.

They talked incessantly for a long time before Daniella departed with a happy smile on her face.

CHAPTER 11

Over a light lunch, Eric and Valerie reminisced on the wonderful heady spring and summer they had enjoyed Now that winter had once more drawn her icy shroud cross the tundra, another cycle of relentless Arctic storms had begun. It did not detract from the radiant thoughts that were ever present of viewing from the air the spectacular migration of the caribou herds, camping, fishing, and sitting in the komatik listening to the cacophony which indicated the ongoing cycle of Nature's winged and feathered bounty. Amid softly falling white petals of snow flakes, gliding in a boat past Nature's sculptured icebergs, whose architectural geometrical forms conjured in the mind fairytale edifices. The never ending sunlit days full of fun and laughter when they lost track of time, not realising that it was 4:00 a.m. instead of 4:00 p.m. They both agreed that swimming with the whales in Churchill was an experience never to be forgotten. Every year the beluga whales return about the first week in July to Hudson Bay, where they wait in large pods to enter the Churchill river once the ice breaks up. The warmth and shallowness of the river is ideal for the calves to thrive and the adults to abrade their dead skin. They are inquisitive mammals and edge close enough so that the swimmer can get a close up view of one of the ocean's longest living and fascinating sea creatures.

"I have to go off again, Valerie, for a few days but I know you will be kept busy with wedding showers."

"I will, Eric, and I want to spend some time with Daniella before she goes out to hospital to give birth. She hasn't been her usual vibrant self for the past few days." She held a letter towards Eric. "Have you time to read this. It arrived today from Mum and Dad. They are both dying to meet you. Mum has made arrangements for you to stay with Auntie Margaret until the big day. You will adore Auntie M. She is a terrific cook and I guarantee you will have gained a few pounds before you meet me at the altar."

"Not now, love." said Eric with a laugh. "I'll read it when I get back from my trip."

Eric took Valerie in his arms and gave her a passionate kiss.

"Eric, if you weren't about to leave I'd say you have mischief in mind."

"I have, my love, but it will keep. Just think, only five more weeks and we are off to England to fulfil our destiny."

Eric ran his hands lovingly through Valerie's hair. He held her close, longer than usual, before he lifted his bag and disappeared through the door. Valerie removed the used lunch dishes from the table before she re-read the letter from her parents. They had reiterated how overjoyed they were that Valerie and Eric were having the marriage ceremony in England, and were waiting with bated breath to meet their new, soon to be, son-in-law. From the photograph which Valerie had sent, they expressed the view that he was a handsome man with a kindly face. Her two sisters had already bought their bridesmaids' dresses with matching accessories. Her Mum had purchased an ensemble, fitting for the mother of such an elegant bride, as her beloved daughter, and her father would wait until Eric's arrival, when the matter of his attire would be discussed with the bridegroom.

Valerie replaced the letter in its envelope, happy in the knowledge that she had such a warm loving family, and prepared to return to the clinic.

A few days later Daniella surprised everyone by giving birth to a baby girl weighing five pounds one ounce. She was perfectly healthy but was put into an incubator for a short while because of a slight breathing problem. Valerie noticed that Daniella had turned very pale.

"How are you feeling Daniella?" Let me take your blood pressure again. She was worried to find it very low. On examining

Daniella again, she found her patient haemorrhaging quite badly and after putting her on a drip and transfusion she immediately phoned Dr. Park. His response was not very encouraging.

"You must get Daniella medevaced immediately Valerie before it becomes a matter of life or death. As you well know she is going to need the surgical performance of a hysterectomy. You can't wait for the medevac team to arrive. The situation could become critical. Are there any planes there at the moment?"

"There is a charter plane which brought some government officials a few hours ago but hasn't left yet because the weather is a bit iffy."

"Contact the pilot immediately and explain the situation. Ask him to phone the Airline and see if he can get permission to take the patient out and stress it is really an emergency, a matter of life or death."

On these fraught words Valerie replaced the receiver and buried her face in her hands. "Dear God," she prayed," help me get Daniella to hospital in time to save her life." She couldn't wait for the medevac team to arrive. Valerie would have to rely on her skill, which appeared to be rather inadequate, in relation to the chronic nature of the situation; and the skill of the pilot, to get them quickly to hospital.

Valerie returned to the clinic waiting room where Jack was weeping unashamedly, being comforted by Daniella's mother Kate, who was trying to show some restraint. Valerie gazed into her tearful eyes and relayed the information that it was imperative that Daniella be medevaced without any further delay. She then hurriedly prepared Daniella for departure, leaving her assistant in charge of the infant, who had made an early entry into a world, where her mother lay at death's door and her father, so distraught, he was barely able to comprehend that he had a new baby daughter.

Permission was instantly given by the Airline once the pilot explained the circumstances and the interior of the plane was quickly altered to suit a patient on a stretcher, nurse and equipment, especially bricks to keep Daniella's legs raised. It was a rocky flight as well as being a very unpleasant journey and Valerie worked feverishly in a desperate attempt to stabilise the rapidly deteriorating condition of her dearest friend. She valiantly fought to hold back the tears that she felt would choke her as she realised Daniella might not live to reach the hospital.

Suddenly, she was jolted from her oppressive thought pattern by a distinctive change in the sound of the plane's engines, a shuddering, and the pilot's frantic voice," Mayday Mayday we are going down. Prepare for an emergency landing."

Valerie was so transfixed by the sudden pitch of the plane, which appeared to be out of control, in a downward spiral, that she failed to respond. There was a tremendous explosion as the plane hit the icy terrain and disintegrated, scattering debris across the frosted landscape.

Valerie lay on her back, in a semi conscious state, her right leg cruelly twisted in a grotesque position. The shock of being exposed to the extreme cold seemed to clear her dulled senses. She tried to move her left arm but knew instantly that it was broken. Every time she tried to move it caused unbelievable pain to her injured leg, and her back felt as if a thousand hot irons were being applied to her spine. The effort caused her to remain perfectly still for several seconds. Valerie turned her head and saw the stretcher a short distance away. She knew she had to make an effort to reach Daniella who appeared to be still strapped in the stretcher.

She made several agonising attempts to crawl towards the stretcher, and when she finally reached it, she discovered that Daniella was dead. The stretcher was attached by the safety belt to part of the plane that had detached itself from the main body and since Valerie had been beside her she realised that she must have been thrown out with her. There wasn't a scratch on her and her limbs appeared to be normal. She smoothed back the frosted hair from Daniella's face and noticed the gold earrings she had brought her from Vancouver. Her eyes were open wide and she had a hint of a smile on her face, as if, at any moment, she would burst into her witty spiel of conversation or a gale of laughter. Valerie tried to close Daniella's eyes but they were frozen. She realised that her own chances of survival were pretty slim unless she attempted to keep herself warm. Daniella no longer needed her assistance and she struggled to pull a blanket from the stretcher but everything was frozen. After what seemed an eternity, Valerie realised that it was impossible to cover her exposed body, although by now she seemed to be impervious to the cold and pain that had previously been excruciating. She slowly turned her head in the opposite direction and detected the nose of the plane from where she lay but no sign of the pilot.

As Valerie lay on the icy cold bed beneath her she momentarily closed her eyes but was suddenly startled by the sudden appearance of the moon. It hung like a huge lighted silver bauble from a Christmas tree, as it cast its effulgent glow across the grim, desolate scene. Her mind churned out image after image from her first day at school, when she relinquished her mother's hand and bravely entered a new dimension; to the present time which encompassed a life full of love, joy and contentment, about to culminate into a lifetime commitment with Eric. Slowly, she lifted her hand towards her neck to finger the ivory and silver ulu necklace, but it wasn't there. Frantically, she grappled around on the ice with her undamaged arm searching for the necklace but her frozen fingers failed to locate it. Before she could reflect on its loss a vivid picture crossed her mind. The final touches were being made to her wedding dress. She had only one more fitting before she would proudly walk, clasping her father's arm, down the long aisle towards the love of her life, who would be waiting at the altar. She could see his smiling face so clearly as her father put her hand into Eric's outstretched one, but Kahlil Gibran's words surfaced from the depths of her mind, 'If in the twilight of memory we should meet once more, we shall speak again together and you shall sing to me a deeper song.' As Valerie's eyelids drooped she emitted a long, deep sigh.

As soon as Eric entered the house, he immediately phoned Valerie's residence and failed to get a reply. He then phoned the clinic and was informed that Valerie had gone on a medevac with Daniella. He ascertained from Deidre that Daniella was seriously ill and Jack and his mother-in-law had gone home, in a very distressed state with the new baby.

Quickly he donned his parka and made his way to Jack's residence. While Kate busied herself in the kitchen, Jack poured his heart out to Eric emphasising how badly he had treated Daniella by having an affair with Sara, when in fact he truly loved his wife. He stressed that if Daniella's life would be spared he would never again stray from being a faithful husband. It was only at this point that Eric realised just how acute Daniella's condition was.

Kate emerged from the kitchen with a baby's bottle in one hand and a towel in the other. She tenderly lifted her little granddaughter from the cot and placed her on her knee for feeding. In the midst of all the fuss and excitement, Eric had forgotten to congratulate Jack on the birth of his daughter. He proceeded to do so by shaking Jack's hand and expressing pleasure at the new arrival. He then took a peep at the silky haired infant who suckled contentedly on her bottle.

"Have you decided on a name for this beautiful child yet?"

"She will be named after her mother, Daniella. Jack and I hope she has inherited the same love and warmth that her mother so freely dispenses to everyone."

Jack, once again, allowed the tears to flow freely down his cheeks and Eric could see that he was fully repentant as well as being truly traumatized.

During the following two hours, Jack talked incessantly about Daniella and their life together. When he had poured Eric a "drink for the road" he glanced at his watch. Looking worriedly towards Kate, he stated how surprised he was that Valerie hadn't telephoned as promised.

"I'm going to phone the hospital now, Mum."

"Do you think you should, Jack."

"Yes, I can't stand this waiting around."

Jack eventually got through to the hospital and there was a look of shock and consternation on his face as he turned around to address Kate and Eric.

"They haven't arrived there yet."

"Oh! No!," shouted Kate in a loud voice as she jumped from the chair and grabbed the phone from Jack's shaking hand.

Statements to the effect that there has to be a mistake and the patient must have already been admitted, maybe she has been wrongly registered under another name, were hurled frantically along the humming telephone wire adding drama that was escalating at a rapid pace.

Jack, becoming more agitated reclaimed the telephone from his, by now hysterical, mother-in-law and left a message with the hospital clerk that Valerie should contact him immediately on arrival. He then proceeded to dial the Airline.

"George, Jack here. I have just phoned the hospital and Daniella has not yet arrived there. Surely they should have reached their destination over an hour ago?"

"Jack" there was a moment's silence, "I was just about to contact you. Apparently there was a Mayday picked up two hours ago by a passing jet so we have a rough idea where the downed plane is. It's near enough Churchill for a full scale ground search to be launched. I'll keep in touch."

Jack let the phone fall from his hand and collapsed in a heap on the settee, his head buried in his hands.

"Jack. Hi, Jack. Jack are you still there?" could be heard from the dangling phone. Eric picked it up and when George realised that he was no longer speaking to Jack he repeated the same sad story. Eric turned as pale as Jack and his hand also trembled as he listened without interrupting. He was completely stunned and replaced the receiver without a proper acknowledgment of the news which he hadn't, as yet, fully digested. Kate was by this time in an uncontrollable state of anxiety and this jolted Eric into a state of raw reality. He took complete charge of the situation by administering two good stiff whiskies, one to the demented lady who was sobbing loudly, and the other to Jack who kept repeating "It's too late. It's too late." By this time the three children, who had been in bed asleep, when the commotion started, were now awake and standing sleepily at the entrance to the living room. Eric shepherded them back to their respective rooms, at the same time trying to reassure them that their Grandma and Dad were very upset because their mother had been medevaced. He told them not to worry as things would probably be sorted out by morning.

Eric then returned to the living room. He poured himself a double whiskey and commenced to speak to the two deeply troubled occupants, in an attempt to reassure them and himself that all was not lost; by the same time the next evening, Jack and he would be with Daniella and Valerie, rejoicing in the fact that they had been safely rescued.

"But it's too late for Daniella. She was bleeding to death when she left here, and even if the plane did land safely in an isolated area, Daniella would not survive." interjected Jack.

"We can only pray, Jack, that a miracle will occur and our loved ones are found quickly."

Jack laid his tousled head back on to the back of the settee and closed his red rimmed eyes, while Kate constantly wiped her falling tears and occasionally sniffled as she sipped her drink.

Eric sat quietly reflecting on his relationship with Valerie and his forthcoming marriage. Surely, God wouldn't be such a cruel God as to snatch away, for a second time, a life of love and happiness which he was experiencing with Valerie. His first marriage had been idyllic and he had no doubt in his mind that marriage with Valerie would be as equally idyllic. He had been so devastated by Tamalyn's untimely demise and to have to face another trauma of such horrific dimensions would be hard to bear. Maybe God, in his Infinite mercy would see that he had suffered enough and dispense pity by restoring Valerie to him with just a few cuts and bruises; better still uninjured and just a little shocked at having found herself and her patient marooned somewhere on a desolate icy stretch of land, far from civilisation. It's strange, he thought, that only in time of great need does man turn to God for help. For three hundred and sixty-five days of the year his thoughts are focussed on other aspects of life and its many facets, while God remains on the periphery, like an invisible guardian in the subconscious mind, waiting to be called upon if needed.

Eric felt he had been blessed when he met Valerie. She was the serum that had helped heal the painful wound but to be sorely afflicted by a fresh wound would really affect his psyche. The more he thought about it, the more distressed he became and no matter how hard he tried he couldn't put things into their proper perspective. He had a deep gut feeling that the situation was more serious than Jack, Kate and he realised. He poured himself another drink and waited. It was a long night.

When the call came, that the wreckage had been found and there were no survivors, Eric wept copiously. He returned to his house and spent the afternoon making phone calls to his and Valerie's family. He felt as if he were enclosed in a bubble which would burst at any moment and release him from the captivity of death. Next evening, George called to offer his condolences.

"This was found on the ice beside Valerie's body, Eric. I thought you should have it."

Eric tried to prise as much information as he could about the experience of the pilot, the age of the plane, servicing etc., but knew inwardly that nothing could be determined regarding the fateful accident, until a complete investigation had been carried out. George kept stressing that the weather had played an enormous part in the accident, and only on account of the life and death situation, which was ironic, did he allow his pilot to attempt the journey. Irrespective of the results of the investigation, nothing would bring back the precious people who had perished.

As soon as George left, Eric opened the envelope and removed the contents. He held in the palm of his hand the broken ulu chain and then it struck him forcibly, that no more would it grace the neck of the woman he had loved so dearly. Eric wept bitterly.

CHAPTER 12

Meira was halfway through her first term and mid term tests had been more than satisfactory. When she first arrived at the college and attended orientation, she was pleased to learn that the Principal was aboriginal and a former graduate of the program. She had an extraordinary rapport with the students besides being a perfect role model. In Meira's mind this gave the program more impetus and she thought if the principal can do it so can I. With this in mind, she worked and studied diligently, the resulting report inflating her already enthusiastic image of her ability to achieve the high standards set by the program.

She, Nuniye and Angie had settled well into the trailer provided by the college and the facilities offered were spacious enough to procure the privacy required for study. Rachelle, Magda and their children had been allocated a three-bedroom house which delighted Rachelle, because the enclosed back yard was a suitable playground, where the children could let off steam without constant supervision. The fact that Rachelle was distanced from Meira was a consoling factor. Past experiences had resulted in Meira's household being disturbed at all hours by the fractious behaviour of both Rachelle and Magda while under the influence of alcohol.

Meira liked the neat attractive town on the banks of the Slave River with its large cathedral and quaint little picture postcard Anglican church. It also had two well stocked combined food and clothing stores, as well as a drug store and various variety, craft, hardware and book stores which Angie enjoyed browsing through with Nuniye in tow. The town also bordered on the Wood Buffalo National Park, a wilderness area covering 17,300 square miles, larger than Switzerland, where buffalo, moose, bears, wolves and other wild animals roamed. The area also had three sets of rapids which attracted tourists from many parts of the world. There were numerous cross country ski trails, snow shoeing and dog sledding activities which made Meira feel at home. She had no qualms about relocating for a two-year period to this southern part of the Northwest Territories and so far Angie had not displayed any signs of homesickness. This made it easier for Meira to apply herself to class lectures without having to worry about Nuniye's welfare. The only disturbing factor, which bothered her greatly, was the three bars where alcohol was dispensed liberally. Her aversion to it had already led her into a fierce argument with several students because they had attempted to persuade Angie into joining them for a night of partying. This was the only worry that nagged her constantly.

Angie as a young child had been exposed to a life similar to her own. Although Angie had given, on more than one occasion, an indication that she repelled the lifestyle her parents had imposed upon her she would sometimes express the desire to go with Doreen, another babysitter she had befriended, to the bar but swore that she only drank coke.

Meira had never smelt beer or spirits on Angie's breath. However, the fact that it was readily available, making it on occasions tempting irrespective of the strict regulations on campus, the thought was never far from her mind, that should Angie get caught up in the "good time" syndrome, she would have to be sent home. If this happened, her studies could be affected if she was forced to depend on an unreliable babysitter. Similar situations were already evident on campus.

Meira had an assignment to finish but she would require to access some further information at the college library before she could attempt a conclusion. As she emerged from the path among the trees and proceeded across the snow covered field, she was aware of someone behind her. Turning around she faced a tall man with long plaits. For a moment her heart missed a beat because he reminded her vividly of Trolin. He smiled and asked her if she wanted to be accompanied across the field as he was heading for the library. Meira replied that she had no objection as she too was going in the same direction. From the conversation she had with him she ascertained his name was Maury and he was a first year student in the Renewable Resources Technology program. When they arrived at the library they each went their separate ways. It took Meira rather longer than usual to complete her notetaking and she was still sorting through the books in front of her when Maury stopped beside her. He proffered an invitation to accompany him to the student activity centre for coffee and a chat. Meira paused for a second before replying. She looked at the book pile, the unfinished page, and declined. She could detect a look of disappointment on his face and in his voice as he replied "Some other time then."

Before she continued with her work, she dwelt on what had just transpired and wondered if she would have accepted the invitation if there hadn't been such a pressing need to complete the assignment. Since Trolin's sad passing she had devoted herself entirely to Nuniye and readying the both of them and Angie for removal to the college. Since she arrived, she had been kept busy and hadn't really involved herself in any of the social activities offered at the college. Presently her mind was focussed in one direction and she had no wish for any distractions. She remembered seeing Maury at the general assembly of staff and students because he had stared at her several times. His appearance had been different then. His hair had been swept back into a ponytail and he hadn't been wearing a headband. The jolt she received this evening had been the two plaits and headband which transformed him into a vision of Trolin. She shook her head negatively which answered the question she had just pondered on.

Meira had just entered the trailer when Angie announced that Nuniye had been sick and feverish. Meira felt his forehead which was quite hot and immediately prepared him for bed. She administered half an aspirin with a teaspoonful of honey followed by a hot drink. Angie announced that a stomach flu was presently attacking the children in the elementary school. She thought Nuniye may have picked it up when she took him to visit Dora who had two kiddies for whom she was responsible, one of them attending the school. Although Meira wasn't unduly concerned about Nuniye's fever, she became more worried after midnight as his temperature began to soar. She commenced applying cool cloths to his forehead and body and was about to transport him to the hospital, when the fever began to subside and the thermometer registered a satisfactory reduction. Meira sat with Nuniye for another half hour before he fell into a deep undisturbed sleep. She felt very tired and decided to rest for a few hours before finishing her assignment. When the alarm went off, Meira dragged herself out of bed and after checking that Nuniye was resting comfortably spent two hours completing the unfinished work. Still feeling weary, she dragged herself into the kitchen where she poured a dish of cereal. After a few mouthfuls, she set it aside and commenced to drink some coffee but even that appeared to be too much for consumption. Meira realised that she would have to do something about her declining appetite and alarming weight loss. She decided to attend the Health Centre after the first lecture. Before she left for class she again checked on Nuniye and was pleased to note that he had recovered from the undetermined malady.

Meira was engrossed in a magazine as she waited to be called when Maury seated himself beside her.

"Hi again, Meira. Have you caught this nasty bug that's attacking everyone indiscriminately?"

"Hi Maury. I think I may have succumbed but I won't know until I see the Doctor. I found my boy was quite ill when I arrived home last night. He had a raging temperature and was very sick, but thank goodness, whatever it was disappeared in the early hours and he's fine this morning. It's just as well I went straight home instead of accompanying you to the library or recreation centre. It's difficult trying to complete assignments and look after a sick child."

"It must be. At least I don't have that added responsibility. Do you have only one child?"

"Yes, one child who will be eligible for Kindergarten next year."

"I had two boys but lost them two years ago, along with my wife, from smoke inhalation when the house went on fire. I have many scars on my body from trying to enter the burning house."

"I'm sorry to hear that. I too lost my husband in tragic circumstances. He was murdered by his own brother."

"We have something in common Meira both of us having suffered family fatalities."

"It would appear so."

At that moment Meira's name was called by the hospital clerk who ushered her to the Doctor's room. After a thorough examination, Meira was sent for a blood and urine test. As she passed through the waiting room she noticed that Maury had gone.

Meira went directly to the drug store with the prescription she had been given and again she confronted Maury who was rifling through some magazines as he waited for his medication.

"We meet again Meira. It must be fate. How did your examination go? Nothing serious, I hope?"

"No, I'll live. What about you?"

"I just had some stitches removed. No big deal and I've been given some medicine for my hacking cough. I'm sure it will taste foul."

"I prefer tablets. Easier to swallow and tasteless."

"Are you going back to class, Meira?"

"Yes. Are you?"

"I am. I'll walk part of the way with you."

"I haven't received my prescription yet."

"It's OK. I'll wait."

It was some time before they were able to continue on their journey towards the college. As Meira veered off towards her destination Maury asked her if she would like to go for a drink in the evening. When she replied that she didn't drink or frequent bars he again asked her to accompany him to the recreation centre. Her response that she had other plans for the evening didn't seem to deter him as he replied

"Just my luck. OK, Meira, see you around."

Maury walked away and Meira felt sorry that she had been so abrupt with him but it was the mention of a drink at the bar that had affected her attitude. He seemed a nice enough person but she had no wish to be involved with people whose social activities were confined to bar entertainment.

She was glad to see Nuniye was once again his chirpy self and none the worse for the previous night's episode. She bathed him and put him to bed before she settled down to watch television. Being Friday, Angie had gone out with Dora so Meira was looking forward to a quiet evening. She had no sooner switched on the television when there was a loud knock on the front door. Meira was surprised to find Maury on the doorstep with a large box in his hand which he pushed towards her.

"Here, Meira. I've brought you and the boy some Kentuckey Fried Chicken."

"Where did you get it, Maury?"

"Direct from Yellowknife. One of the guys brought a few on order."

Maury was still standing at the open door and Meira invited him in.

"That's very thoughtful of you Maury. Have you eaten yet?"

"Yes. I had a good meal in the Cooking Instructor's house."

"I won't eat this chicken now. I'll save it for later. Nuniye already had his supper and is fast asleep."

They sat for a while both engrossed in the television program.

"I thought you were going out Meira. Didn't you tell me you had plans for this evening?"

Meira felt a bit confused that her little white lie had back fired. She quickly answered that she was waiting for her niece to come back before she went to visit her friend. Being a highly sensitive person, with a caring attitude that would not allow her to crush another person's feelings, she opted for a friendly approach to his visit and hoped for an early departure. Maury's kindness would not merit a brusque departure and she decided to handle it diplomatically. They continued conversing while Meira's mind was working overtime trying to concoct an excuse for the non appearance of Angie. She announced that she would have to get ready, with the hope that Maury would leave, but he told her to go ahead because he wanted to see the end of the sitcom which was being shown. Disappointedly, Meira went to her bedroom and changed her sweater. She then decided to try a different tactic. When she entered the living room she immediately went to the entrance porch, put on her boots, and brought her parka over her arm towards the settee. She threw it down giving the impression that she would be donning it once the babysitter arrived but Maury was still looking at the television. He seemed to be transfixed and oblivious to her movements and discomfort. Finally, she sat down on a chair beside the table and commenced to leaf through the News of the North. When the sitcom finished another one followed.

"Friday is a good night for this funny stuff Meira. What time is your niece supposed to be here?"

"Any moment now."

"I'll just wait then. I can see you safely to your friend's place. Is she also at the college?"

"Yes, and she is my sister-in-law."

"That's good you have family here. It makes it easier to settle."

Maury, once again, became mesmerised by the television program and Meira began to fidget. After a short while, he looked at the clock, turned towards Meira and announced that he would house sit until her niece arrived. Meira had no option but to concede to his suggestion and she left the trailer feeling greatly distressed. She didn't know much about Maury's background except for the few scraps of information he had divulged. He seemed to be a kind person and had been a family man. Trolin's words rang in her ears, "Kind actions can be a forerunner to more sinister ones." She made a fast decision to enlist the aid of Rachelle and quickly made her way to the house only to find a fourteen year old in charge of the children, Rachelle and Magda having departed an hour earlier. The minder announced that Meira would probably find them in the hotel bar. She became more upset when she knew that the only option left was to pay a visit to the bar and seek Angie. When she entered the smoky crowded raucous atmosphere she was assailed by several students who asked her to join their table

Meira politely refused and enquired if anyone had seen Angie. Receiving negative replies she withdrew and went to the next drinking venue which was even more crowded and smoke laden but there was no sign of Angie. She observed Rachelle and Magda in a far corner surrounded by three or four cronies and quickly made a getaway before they managed to get a glimpse of her. She realised precious time was being wasted searching for Angie and decided to go back to her residence and inform Maury that her sister-in-law wasn't feeling well and she was forced to return. Another of Trolin's sayings entered her mind. "One small lie can easily become a gigantic snowball," and this was happening. When Meira entered, surprise registered on Maury's face.

"That was a short visit, Meira."

In an instant Meira quickly changed her story.

"I wasn't feeling too well. I think it might be the medication I took this afternoon. It suddenly dawned on Meira that she could have made this excuse without venturing out at all. "I am going to get a good night's rest and I'll probably feel much better tomorrow."

"Are you sure you'll be OK here alone?" Maury said as he jumped to his feet.

"I will be fine thanks."

"I'll just leave then. I hope you enjoy the chicken though I can't imagine you'll eat it tonight."

"No. I don't think so but thanks all the same."

"I'll be off then. See you Meira."

Meira heaved a sigh of relief as she closed the door behind Maury. She thought long and hard on the evening's antics. It appeared that Maury had more than a friendly interest in her but she was not prepared to enter into any close relationships with the opposite sex. Nothing was going to deter her from achieving her goal. If he wanted her as a friend she might entertain that idea but romantic involvement was taboo. Meira had been disappointed to observe that Rachelle and Magda had not abandoned their favourite haunts. She strongly disapproved of a fourteen year old girl being held responsible for a mentally handicapped child, as well as two others aged respectively seven and eight years. She realised she was developing a puritanical attitude to alcohol but the more she thought about it, Meira became so incensed that she decided to share her concerns with one of the college counsellors.

Meira checked on Nuniye and his quiet steady breathing indicated that all was well.

CHAPTER 13

For months Eric had been grief stricken, his mind in turmoil, and on the verge of becoming addicted to anti-depressants. Valerie's parents had requested that she should be cremated. He had made the saddest journey of his life when he transported the ashes to Britain. On arrival, he had once again found himself being forced to attend another funeral service and reliving the pangs of mourning and inconsolable sorrow. The visit, which should have been a precious moment in time, became one of despair. Memories of Valerie were refreshed as her family clamoured for tales of their daughter's life as the Public Health Nurse in a far northern settlement where the summer sun's golden rays sparkled and gambolled across the living tundra night and day before disappearing into winter hibernation.

Eric spent a dismal week with Valerie's parents before joining his sister and family at a cousin's residence in the Cotswalds. Everyone handled the situation with great diplomacy knowing that Eric's grief and pain was still raw. He found solace in his private memories as he roamed alone through the beautiful countryside. During many of these solitary walks, his thoughts turned to reincarnation from which he derived even more comfort as Valerie's words, "We are soul mates and will always be together," kept revolving in his tortured mind. He realised that on his return to Canada he had a big decision to make. He could resume his former duties as Director, and live in the accommodation provided, until the tenancy of his rented house expired, or accept a renewal of the contract offered by the

Canadian government. He doubted that he would be able to face the heartache of living in familiar surroundings where Valerie's shadow would be forever present.

When Eric arrived in Vancouver, he discussed the situation with Charles with whom he resided for a few days. The Stratton family were equally as sensitive as his cousin's family and avoided referring to Valerie during the many grief stricken conversations Eric introduced. Charles' advice that he should not run away from bereavement, as he had done when Tamalyn died, but face it so that healing could begin immediately was sound and he accepted it. He phoned Yellowknife to confirm that he was prepared to return, only to be informed that he would be required to work on a new project in the Wood Buffalo National Park on the border of the Northwest Territories and the Province of Alberta. Eric accepted and Charles and he raised a toast to a successful healing year.

The first snowfall had already left its calling card on Halloween and the wind felt chilly as Eric stepped on to the icy tarmac at Fort Smith The small airport was crowded with people waiting to go further north. He was met by a very affable Parks Canada official, named Terry, who transported him to a well furnished duplex. Eric inspected his accommodation and nodded approval.

Since it was Saturday, Terry stated that he had time to give him a tour of the town and take him to the grocery store. As they sped past the elementary school, Eric briefly noticed a tall native woman in the company of a young girl and small child, who was snugly wrapped in a blue parka and woollen scarf walking in the same direction. The thought struck him that the graceful posture of the woman reminded him of Meira just as Terry directed his attention to the location of the drug store. The neat looking houses appealed to him as did the well stocked stores and he expressed surprise that such a small town should have a large Cathedral. Terry informed him that Fort Smith was at one time chosen to be the capital city, hence the Cathedral, but the idea was abandoned and Yellowknife replaced it as the main seat of affairs. Eric agreed it was more practical to have headquarters farther north instead of bordering on the Province of Alberta.

Terry then stated that should he ever need medical treatment the centre was adjacent to the cathedral. Momentarily, Eric was drowned in a feeling of anguish.

As the truck swung on to a high ridge of land, he was struck by the beauty of the area. The frozen river, banked on either side by boreal forests of tall trees their branches bowed by ermine blankets of snow, painted a pretty picture. He made the remark that it was another unique part of the Northwest Territories with its own particular loveliness and appeal.

Terry helped Eric to carry the groceries into the house and stated that he would have invited him to eat but he was going out of town for the weekend. The idea of being able to travel by road for long distances in this fascinating area appealed to Eric. Having his own transport would enable him to explore farther afield. The car he had in Vancouver was more suited to an urban paved road mode of travel, but a more sturdy vehicle would be required on the gravel highways, in the rural scenic area he was now inhabiting. He mentioned to Terry that he wished to purchase a vehicle and began to scan the local newspaper which he had just removed from the grocery bag. He failed to find anything suitable but Terry, who had been perusing The Hub exclaimed that there appeared to be a couple of good deals in Hay River. Since he was leaving shortly to visit the area, he would be glad to transport Eric to inspect the vehicles advertised. Eric suggested that perhaps he should telephone first so as to make sure he wouldn't be going on a wild goose chase. The result of the calls sounded promising and they set off after they had eaten Eric's makeshift meal of salami sandwiches and coffee.

During the journey, Eric remarked on the charred areas where fire had evidently swept through. Terry replied that during the summer season the fire hazard could be quite high and it is a busy time for fire crews and pilots. Farther along the highway, Terry pointed to the lookout tower, which he added is also manned for three months during the fire season. The conversation then switched to survival techniques on highways where there is no habitation for hundreds of kilometres should a driver have an accident or break down in the season of frigid temperatures. Terry advised Eric, if he purchased a vehicle, to stock it with a sleeping bag, flashlight, shovel, candles, chocolate, nuts, first aid kit, a can of gas and sand or cat litter for traction.

"It always pays to be prepared. To find yourself stranded without the necessary essentials and no sign of another vehicle for hours could mean hypothermia, resulting in death."

Eric replied that having lived in the Arctic for almost two years he was aware of the hazards of travel in such perilous areas but thanked him for the advice.

Neither of them was impressed with the first vehicle viewed but when they went to the car dealer, who Terry knew personally, and viewed the Ford truck, Eric was pleased, after a short drive, with the performance of the vehicle and the price. Terry then left him with a jocular remark that he hoped Eric didn't get lost on the way back to Fort Smith. With Terry's advice in mind, Eric shopped around for the survival items. When he had procured them and eaten a hot meal he set off on the long journey to his destination. He had barely left Hay River when it suddenly came to mind that a momentary distraction in the store had caused him to forget the cat litter. He uttered an emotional exclamation and hoped the substance wouldn't be required.

He was glad that he had requested a tape player and radio to be fitted while he shopped and dined. He had no difficulty making his way out of the town and on to the highway. As he travelled at an easy pace along the frozen road, highlighted by an incandescent moon, he observed the headlights of a vehicle approaching at a fast speed in the opposite direction. As it drew almost level with Eric's truck, it skidded towards it, before righting itself, causing Eric to swerve violently into a deep snow bank. By the time Eric had recovered his senses, realised he was unhurt, and floundered around knee deep in snow to inspect for damage, the driver of the other vehicle, and its occupants, was speeding towards Hay River without thought for the mishap to which he had contributed. Eric retrieved the shovel and proceeded to remove the snow. It was hard work and he laboured strenuously for some time before a clear path was visible. He made several unsuccessful attempts to extricate the truck but the ditch was too deep and the wheels wouldn't grip. He was beginning to feel cold so he sat for a while, with the engine running, trying to figure the best possible way of getting out of the dilemma he found himself in. He felt annoyed that the culprit, who had been responsible for his predicament, and must have been aware of it, had failed to stop. He remembered Terry telling him that he could be stranded for four to six hours, and maybe more, before another vehicle would appear. He decided to make another attempt at snow removal and had just picked up the shovel when headlights in the distance heralded a possible rescue. As the vehicle drew near he observed it was another truck. The driver, a tall native man, who reminded him of Trolin, accompanied by a younger man, soon had Eric towed out of the deep ditch and on his way, thankful that he didn't have to spend the night relying on his survival accoutrements. His rescuers, both students at Thebacha College, were also heading in the same direction. He found their dispositions most friendly and generous. They were returning from Hay River with a load of wild meat and offered some to Eric, after hearing that it was his first day in the southern part of the Northwest Territories. This kind gesture assured Eric that there were still some less scrupulous people around.

As he drove more cautiously along the highway, he hoped that he wouldn't encounter another daredevil speed monger. The thought occurred to him that bad luck seemed to be dogging his footsteps and a feeling of uneasiness engulfed him. The ink was barely dry on his contract and already he was the victim of a callous road hog. His thoughts then reverted to the truck driver who helped him and his strong resemblance to Trolin. This caused an immediate deflection to the woman resembling Meira, he had seen walking along McDougal Road, and he wondered how she and Nuniye were getting along. Since he sent the letter of thanks and returned the poem he hadn't heard anything but under the circumstances he didn't really expect to enter into correspondence. The short duration of association, which was to have been based entirely on a work relationship was circumvented by Trolin to extend to a more informal type of professional liasion. This resulted in Meira co-operating voluntarily in assisting her husband to make the visit more friendly. Eric had held them in great esteem because of their combined efforts to facilitate him professionally and socially.

Eric had faith in Charles' philosophy. He admitted to himself that once he became totally involved in his daily occupation and participated in some leisurely activities, all the sad memories would become less sensitive. As all these disjointed impressions pervaded his mind the journey's length diminished. Soon he found himself on the outskirts of Fort Smith his headlights depicting a magnificent wolf as it speedily vaulted over the high snow banked ditch.

Eric's Bison research kept him so busy that his socialising skills had become obsolete. Several times he turned down dinner invitations, when he suddenly realised, if he kept refusing, people would stop inviting him. With this in mind, he agreed to attend a function in the British Legion. Here he befriended a young couple from Toronto who, like himself, were newcomers in Fort Smith. Derek was a pilot, who had secured a position with a local airline company and Mimi, his wife, an attractive brunette with a background entrenched in the Arts. She was a gifted person, who made exquisite jewellery, and painted outstanding pictures and portraits. Mimi hoped to use her talents by promoting Evening classes which had met with enormous success in other areas of the country.

The trio's immediate rapport led them into an evening of scintillating conversation and jovial anecdotes. Derek and Mimi had just procured a husky pup. They were so enthralled with the new addition to their household that they decided to leave the festivities early. They managed to persuade Eric to accompany them for a nightcap. Their living accommodation was a large trailer near the Queen Elizabeth Park, aptly named after the royal personage who had visited the town a number of years previously. Mimi lifted the little furry bundle from its bedding and deposited it on Eric's knees. He was smitten with the capricious puppy as it licked his hand and attempted to chew the tassel on the end of his sweater zipper. Mimi, having been attuned to Eric's sorrowful past, observed how he reacted to the pet's playfulness. She remarked that he should get the remaining pup of the litter, emphasizing that it would have a therapeutic value. At first, Eric was reluctant to entertain the idea, but as the evening progressed his resolve began to weaken and he arranged with Mimi to go next day and purchase the pup.

When they arrived at the home of the dog breeder, Eric was surprised to find the young man who had come to his aid when he had found himself practically upended in a snow ditch. Maury expressed pleasure at meeting Eric again and very soon he, Mimi, Maury and the owner of the pup were all chatting cosily over coffee and cookies. The conversation varied from dogsled racing to the consequence of the inevitable division of the Northwest Territories.

Eric was asked by Mimi what name he was going to append to the playful animal which was frolicking around his feet. He replied, Nuniye, because it was the name given to a child of some very special people he knew, one parent having since died under very tragic circumstances. Maury's ears pricked up at the name chosen for the animal and the circumstances surrounding the death of one of the parents in the family. He was about to comment on the coincidence but changed his mind.

Everyone agreed that the name would be most suitable for such a frisky little pup which had captured Eric's affection as soon as he had picked him up.

Derek and Mimi had suggested cross-country skiing and Eric, being a downhill skier decided to give the more strenuous aspect of skiing a try.

The ski trail had already been well used which made it easier for Eric to move skilfully through the forest of silver frosted trees. He was totally impressed with the charm of the area and the feeling of solitude which dominated the tranquil scene, even though there were others on the trail. Eric thoroughly enjoyed the afternoon and he decided to give cross country skiing top priority on his list of outdoor activities. After partaking of some mulled wine at the home of Derek and Mimi he returned to his house to find that Nuniye had chewed several pages of the novel he had been reading. He was becoming fonder of the little animal and spent quite a lot of time grooming, walking and playing with him. Huskies, being outdoor animals had prompted Eric to arrange for a kennel to be built which would be used when Nuniye attained the age of three months. As Mimi had predicted, Nuniye was proving to be a loving companion and he looked forward every day to being greeted affectionately and enthusiastically by his lively, fur-coated, blue-eyed friend.

CHAPTER 14

Maury was becoming more attentive. No matter how many times Meira rejected his advances, he kept pestering her. It had reached a stage where she was reluctant to answer a door knock and then find some time later a gift of meat or ptarmigan on her doorstep. She avoided going to the recreation centre and was beginning to feel stifled spending so much time indoors. Skiing had been arranged for the first year students followed by an outdoor barbecue and she was looking forward to this activity. Angie had taken Nuniye to a birthday party so she felt a sense of freedom as she stepped outside. She almost crashed into Maury.

"Hi Meira. Going out?"

"Yes, Maury. I'm skiing with my classmates this afternoon."

"Too bad. I came at the wrong time." He pushed a small box into Meira's hand.

"This is for the boy. I was in the drug store, saw this, and thought he might find it amusing."

"Thanks Maury but I wish you wouldn't keep bringing things."

"You don't have a man to look after you and the boy anymore so I have taken on the role. I enjoy doing it."

"But I can't repay you Maury in the way I think you expect."

"Not to worry. I'm a patient man, Meira. I know how much the Teacher Education program means to you and when you are finished you might change your mind."

"You're incorrigible Maury."

"I'll not detain you. Can I give you a ride to the College?"

"No thanks. The walk will help me limber up. Thanks for Nuniye's gift."

As Meira made her way towards the College she thought about all the gifts which had been handed to her or left on the doorstep. She made up her mind to be less obligated by making a pair of mukluks for Maury.

It was a beautiful afternoon, the temperature having risen, and the winter sun throwing its weakened rays across the sparkling landscape. As Meira glided along the ski trail she observed that one of her skis needed some adjustment. As she moved off to the side to attend to it she was pounced on by a frisky husky puppy trailing a leash behind it. From the depths of the bush she heard the name Nuniye being called. Startled, she looked around to see a tall man emerging from the trees in her direction, whistling loudly. As he got nearer she recognised him, as well as the mukluks.

"Dr. McClure, I never expected to find you wandering through the Fort Smith bush."

"Meira? So it was you I saw walking along McDougal Road a few months ago.?"

"It probably was. I am a student in the Teacher Education program. I'll be spending the next two years here. So this is your little dog and you have named him Nuniye."

"I have Meira I think it is a lovely name. I was told it is a Chipewyan name meaning wolf. Incidentally, I sent your poem back to you. I hope you received it."

"I'm sorry about that Dr. McClure.

"Just call me Eric. It's less formal."

"OK Eric, as I was saying I forgot to remove the poem from the mukluk. At the particular time I was preparing the parcel for posting, I was distracted by Nuniye who had injured himself. I am glad to see that the mukluks are a good fit."

"They are perfect, very comfortable and warm. As I stated in my letter it was very kind of you, Meira."

Nuniye was about to dash after another skier and Meira and Eric collided as they both made a grab for the trailing leash. The incident caused them to break into uncontrollable laughter as Eric managed to capture the recalcitrant pup.

"Has your research brought you to this part of the Territories?"

"Yes, Meira I lost my fiancee in a plane crash. We were to be married a few months ago.

"Oh, I'm sorry to hear that. You have also suffered a big loss in your life."

"C'est la vie, Meira Nothing for it but to get on with life. In a way, I'm glad I didn't go back to the Arctic. There are too many sad memories there to bruise the mind."

"Well the reason I am in the in the Teacher Education program is to carry out one of Trolin's dearest wishes. He always wanted me to become a teacher."

"That's an excellent profession for you Meira. How is Nuniye?"

"He is growing so tall Eric, going to be like his father in height and temperament, but so like my dead brother in features."

"I often think of your delicious stews and wish I could be as accomplished in the kitchen."

Meira laughed and replied that she would be happy to invite him for a caribou stew whenever he had some free time. Before she went on her way it was arranged that Eric would accept the invitation for the following Saturday evening.

As Eric led Nuniye away from the ski trail he felt happy that he was able to renew the acquaintance. He was looking forward to spending an evening with Meira and her child.

Meira asked herself a question as she continued along the trail. Why did she, without any hesitation, invite Eric for a meal. The answer which came to mind, that Trolin would have considered him as a welcome guest, satisfied her.

Next evening, she went curling with her classmates and at the rink she again met Eric who introduced her to Derek and Mimi. It was a carefree time with lots of camaraderie and laughter.

On Saturday evening, as Meira prepared supper, Maury arrived. She had the table laid for two which he was quick to observe.

"Expecting company, Meira?"

I am Maury so you will have to excuse me, I have so many things to prepare."

"Well, I won't get in your way. Just called to let you know I have two tickets for a concert in the elementary school on Wednesday evening. Would you like to accompany me Meira?"

"I can't Maury because I have an important test Thursday morning and you know how I feel about keeping up my grade levels. I'll be swotting all evening Wednesday, but thanks for asking."

"I'm very disappointed. Your devotion to your studies is commendable. I wish I was as equally ambitious Meira. Anyway, no harm done. I'm sure I'll find someone else."

Nuniye was playing on the floor with the helicopter which Maury had previously bought for him and Maury joined him. This action on Maury's part led Meira to believe that he intended spending longer than anticipated in her living room. She had no option but to intervene by asking Nuniye to put his toys away and calling on Angie to prepare his bath water.

"What a shame Nuniye, but we will play another time," Maury said as he patted the child's cheek. "I'll be off then Meira. Have a nice evening."

As Maury departed Meira heavily exhaled a flow of breath and resumed the task of stew making. An hour later, Eric's light tap on the door announced an early arrival.

"Hi Meira. I know I am a bit early. I went to Mimi's place first but there was no one at home so I hope my arrival at this time doesn't inconvenience you.

"Not at all. Just remove your parka and have a seat. I can offer you orange juice or coke. Which do you prefer?"

"Coke, please. Where is Nuniye?"

"He is just being bathed and changed. He will be ready in a moment or two."

"I think this is a very nice spacious trailer. Does the furniture come with the accommodation?"

"It does. I brought only bedding, television, dishes and cutlery."

"Me too, Meira. I bought my bedding etc. at the store but I never bought another television. Anyway, I wouldn't have time to view it. My research keeps me busy enough, as well as my outdoor activities."

"I'm sure Nuniye also keeps you busy. He seems to be a bundle of fun. Has he quietened down yet?"

"No, he is as fiesty as ever."

"You should have brought him with you. I was telling Nuniye that you have a puppy named after him."

At that moment, Nuniye appeared and asked Eric could he see the puppy.

"I left my puppy at home, Nuniye, but you and your mum can come any evening to my house and see him. How does that sound?."

Nuniye looked at his mother for a suitable reply. She responded by saying that she would arrange with Eric to take Nuniye to visit the puppy next weekend.

Eric learned all about the College and the various programs offered. He was particularly interested in Meira's program and remembered having a conversation with Trolin on the employment of more native teachers. He was also impressed with the wide variety of skill programs offered and agreed with Meira that the College was the best thing that ever happened in the Northwest Territories. Meira stated that northern aboriginal people were reluctant to leave their families and travel to a southern institution, either to be educated or receive medical treatment. The implementation of a College and hospitals was a blessing. She informed Eric that once she graduated she would pursue her education further and attend University to obtain a B.Ed degree. This, of course, would mean that she would have to reside outside the Territories once she became a University student. She felt she could tolerate the alienation in order to achieve the ultimate goal. Meira emphasized that the next important step should be a Northern University, once the divisions were in place, and the Territories self governed, devoid of controlling external influences. She then quickly retracted the statement by adding that there could be problems regarding the site for such an institution as the east appeared to be in fierce competition with the west. Eric couldn't help but admire the tenacity with which she approached her own future and that of the Northwest Territories. He complemented her accordingly.

Meira listened with interest to Eric's dialogue of exploits in the Arctic region, and of his love and anguish for Valerie. She felt great sympathy for him. The fact that they had both shared a few close moments together, fused in shock, disbelief, and sorrow, when Trolin was murdered seemed to have created a special bond of friendship.

As Eric drove back to his house he also felt that he had renewed and cemented a very special relationship.

Meira was worried. It was 3:00 a.m. and Angie hadn't come home. She had always appeared around 1:00 a.m. or shortly thereafter. Meira had gone to bed early but she was restless and on getting up to make some tea discovered Angie's empty bed. She had just finished rinsing the teacup when she heard a car door slam. Angie, in a dishevelled state, stumbled through the door sobbing. Meira enfolded the distressed girl in her arms and it was a full ten minutes before she could compose herself to tell her harrowing tale.

Angie and her friend had been enjoying a night out in the hotel bar, with some friends, when they decided to accept an invitation to a house party. The three males, who had issued the invitation, escorted them by cab to a house in the Indian village where they plied them with spiked coke. The girls, realising that they had been inveigled into accepting a bogus invitation, made several attempts to escape but their rigorous efforts to do so were utterly futile, and each of them ended up in the basement where they were repeatedly raped.

Meira immediately contacted the Royal Canadian Mounted Police. The woman constable, after taking a statement, accompanied both of them to the hospital. It was breakfast time before either of them could come to terms with the distressing incident. Angie kept insisting that she didn't want to stay in Fort Smith, causing Meira to confront the situation which had occasionally crossed her mind. She was now being forced into a position of relying on Day Care or seeking another child minder. When all the legalities had been systematically put in place, Angie, in spite of the advice given by the lawyer and Meira, refused counselling. She remained adamant in her desire to return to her mother and Meira would not see her again until a week before the court hearing.

CHAPTER 15

Meira had made a quantity of fresh bannock and she decided to take some to Rachelle along with a pot of stew. She was concerned that the children in Rachelle's household were not being fed properly. Meira had voiced her concerns to the College counsellor but she wasn't aware of the outcome of her complaint. Despite Rachelle's active social life she appeared to be successfully passing all tests administered in the classroom.

When she reached the house, she was disappointed to find that Magda and Rachelle had gone out the previous evening leaving the children in the care of a young babysitter. The teenager was glad to see Meira because she had been expecting to be relieved of her duties in the early hours of the morning. It was now noon and neither Rachelle nor Magda had put in an appearance. Before the babysitter left Meira paid her. She then commenced to feed and wash the children.

It was an ideal afternoon for sledding and Meira decided to take them to Axehandle hill where they could participate in the sport with Nuniye. In the midst of their exhilarating exercise a young husky appeared and commenced to run down the hill after the sleds. Nuniye, who had become acquainted with his namesake, recognised the animal and informed Meira that it was Eric's dog. It responded obediently to its name and certain commands. When Meira inspected its collar she realised the dog had escaped from Eric's yard. Maya seemed to be enthralled by the dog's antics that she decided to let it remain with the children meantime. When it came time to leave the hill, Meira attached a belt to the collar and the dog walked towards Rachelle's house, being led by Maya.

Meira was relieved to find Magda and Rachelle at home. There was no consternation that the children were not in the house because they assumed that the babysitter had taken them out. They had failed to return earlier because they had been sleeping off the effects of too much alcohol. Meira knew her remarks would be scathing. The situation reminded her so vividly of a similar phase in her life which she would never forget. As she and Nuniye were about to leave Maya began to make a fuss because she wanted to keep the dog. It was some time before Meira was able to pacify her by promising to take her sledding with the dog again, very soon.

Eric sat at his desk leafing through a report. Out of the corner of his eye, he detected a movement near the window. He stood up to get a better view of the yard and observed Meira attaching Nuniye to his chain. She turned to leave, saw Eric and waved. He immediately went to the back door and invited Meira and her son into the house.

"That is the second time this week that Nuniye has escaped the confines of his chain and disappeared Meira."

"You will have to make the chain more secure Eric otherwise you might lose him."

Nuniye intercepted by saying that they had so much fun with the dog, while sledding and Maya didn't want him to leave.

"Who is 'they' and 'Maya,' Meira?

She then proceeded to tell Eric the story of Magda, Rachelle and their family. He replied that anytime she wished to take Nuniye, she could do so, since he appeared to give so much pleasure to the children.

Eric enquired if Meira had done any more skiing and on learning that she had not been out for some time Eric invited her to join him, Derek and Mimi, the following afternoon. Her hesitancy in replying disconcerted him until she stressed that there might be a problem finding someone to look after Nuniye. She informed Eric that she would telephone him later after she had ascertained the child minding situation. After partaking of tea and cookies, Eric drove them both home and was pleasantly surprised to hear an hour later that she would be delighted to join the ski party.

For two hours, the skiers had weaved and glided through the snow clad forest of conifer, spruce and pine before they arrived at the home of Derek and Mimi, rosy cheeked and hungry. It wasn't long before Mimi had a hot meal on the table and the men tucked into the food voraciously. Meira enjoyed the repast, and was pleased to note that there wasn't excess indulgence in alcohol. It had been a very enjoyable afternoon and she found the company congenial. She would like to have remained a while longer but she had Nuniye to think about. When Eric left Meira at her trailer he made the comment that she might like to accompany them on the following Sunday for another afternoon of skiing. She replied that she would get in touch with him before then and disappeared with a wave and a smile which denoted pleasure at the invitation.

While Eric waited in the living room for Meira to change into her skiing apparel he couldn't help noticing an open scrapbook on the dining table. He read a handwritten poem titled 'The Call of the Loon'

> *I'm aroused from my sleep by a haunting tune*
> *What creature is this that pervades my dreams?*
> *Is it the nymph that scatters all the moon's beams*
> *No, it's only the call of the loon*
> *The chatter of jays in the trees at noon*
> *Ne'er intrudes upon my train of thought*
> *But this whimsical note that my ear has caught-*
> *Why, it's only the call of the loon*
> *The lake will be calm and silent soon*
> *As southward bound the flocks will fly*
> *And as windswept trees shed golden leaves,*
> *I'll sigh, for that haunting call of the loon*

When he had read it and several other poems Eric meditated on their contents and realised that Meira had the intrinsic soul of a poet attuned to the universe and its idiosyncrasies.

Her writings signified hidden depths of compassion suited to her resolute beliefs which complemented her composure and sunny temperament. When Meira entered the room embarrassment engulfed her as she observed Eric absorbed in the scrapbook scribblings. He noted her discomfort and apologised for being so intrusive.

"Meira, you should have this poetry published. I find it very appealing and demonstrative."

"I might do that someday Eric but not everyone likes poetry. I enjoy writing for my own pleasure and have never thought of sharing it."

"If you don't mind Meira I would like to take this scrapbook and read some more of these delightful odes."

Meira nodded in agreement and Eric announced that he would pick it up when he brought her back to the trailer.

Eric's admiration for Meira, which was purely platonic, remained as a link in a supportive chain. On numerous occasions he had undertaken the job of caring for Nuniye when Meira couldn't rely on the usual sitter. This gave Nuniye the opportunity of bonding with the dog. The three of them quite often hiked to the Rapids, and Nuniye and his namesake always kept Eric entertained along the way with their constant frolics. He felt that Meira treated him like a brother and he was quite happy to fit into this family role. He played his part like a caring brother should by being helpful and attentive when required.

Eric learned indirectly that Meira's birthday was approaching and he decided to have her poems published. The unique gift would be one to which she could refer years later and leave to her descendants. The thought also struck him that a dedication to Trolin, on the flyleaf, would be appropriate. The words "Dedicated to Trolin, a humanitarian, who made pearls from raindrops and sunshine from ominous clouds," sounded like a fitting and perfect inscription.

In collusion with Mimi, a surprise birthday party was arranged. Mimi's organizational skills, down to the last candle on the birthday cake, and scrolled invitation cards, resulted in an afternoon of joviality. It included fun and games for the many children who attended. When Eric presented Meira with the poetry books she was absolutely flabbergasted. As she read the dedication her eyes momentarily filled with tears. It was some time before she regained her composure and assigned herself the task of signing copies for her friends. Eric's copy bore the inscription "With deepest gratitude for always being there when needed."

Meira arrived home in a state of euphoria. It had been a wonderful afternoon. She had received many gifts but the poetry books were the piece de resistance. She began to wonder how she could repay Eric because she considered the gift was too extravagant, even though the thought behind it was a benign one. Her train of thought was disrupted by a loud knock on the door and the entry of Maury who immediately concentrated on the books neatly piled on the table.

"Meira you are a celebrity. I didn't realise you had such a special talent," he said as he leafed through one.

"I never considered it very special until my friend mentioned it. He thought it worthwhile to have the work published and presented the books to me as a birthday gift."

"That's why I am here. I heard about the birthday party a week ago but never received an invitation. I brought you a present."

Meira unwrapped the paper and uttered a cry of delight when she removed the exquisitively decorated waistcoat.

"It's beautiful, Maury. Thank you so much. I'm sorry you did not receive an invitation to the party but it was a surprise, over which I had no control."

"So I now have a competitor. Who is this Don Juan?"

Meira observed Maury's facial expression change from smiley to dour and quickly replied, "He is a very good friend and most helpful. My late husband associated with him on a government project. As for being a competitor Maury, you can rule that out. I'm not a prize to be competed for by either of you. You and Eric are merely friends with no strings attached and I want it to remain like that."

"These books must have cost quite a few dollars Meira. May I have one suitably inscribed?"

Meira obliged by writing "In friendship" and Maury accepted it gratefully.

"When you mentioned the name "Eric" it rang a bell. I remember assisting a guy by that name, some kilometres from

Hay River, who had been forced to swerve into a ditch and was having a hard time extricating his truck. I met him again, at Rudy the musher's place, when he arrived to buy a Husky. Funnily enough, he said he was going to name the dog Nuniye. It then occurred to me that it must be the same guy."

"It is, because he remarked on how appreciative he was of the kindness shown to him by two college students when he was floundering around at the side of the road in frigid temperatures. Your efforts didn't go unnoticed. He sent a letter to the Director of the college praising his rescuers."

"Yes. The letter was posted on the notice board in our classroom. I found him very personable. He works for Parks Canada but I haven't seen him around much. He doesn't frequent the bars. A couple of classmates did mention that they had seen you in his truck on several occasions."

Meira ignored the comment, asked to be excused for a moment, and fetched from the bedroom the mukluks she had made for Maury.

"I made these for you Maury. Just a little thank you for all your many kindnesses to Nuniye and me,"

Maury whistled in appreciation as he examined them.

"Another hidden talent, Meira They are perfect. These will be very special. Thanks a million. I've come to issue another invitation. Would you and Nuniye like to accompany me to the Dog Sled races on Saturday and please don't say No?"

"It's going to have to be another refusal Maury, because Nuniye and I are going with Eric and two other friends to the event."

"Why is it I am always on the tail end of things? I'll have to get my act together. Oh well, better luck next time."

Maury departed, leaving Meira with the impression that he was sorely vexed, because his invitation had once again been turned down. She felt relieved that she was no longer indebted to Maury, and turned her thoughts towards providing something for Eric. It suddenly occurred to her that a couple of framed moose hair tuftings would be suitable. Her tuftings were on display in several craft shops across the North. Meira's foster grandmother had taught her this skill which was becoming a dying art. Only the Slave Indians in Fort Providence produce this type of handicraft. Meira was taught to select the white hair along the centre of the moose hide. The best hair was obtained after December when it had grown six inches in length. She relied on crepe paper and powdered dye for colouring. Meira very much adhered to her foster grandmother's teaching. She used a small stick sharpened to a point, dipped in a flour and water paste, to draw her pictures on either stroud, velvet or moose hide. It was a time consuming job, but she felt that two framed moose hair tuftings, at today's prices, would be more than adequate to equate the outlay involved in having her poems published, as well as compensating for Eric's many childminding services.

Meira and Rachelle decided to take the children on a picnic near the river. There were still large chunks of ice, and smaller lace configurations, floating lazily past them. The sun was valiantly trying to diffuse its strengthening rays across the melting landscape but the children were warmly wrapped. Meira had brought Eric's dog who seemed to be leading Maya and Nuniye, both tugging on the leash in an attempt to bring him to heel. The animal was in a playful mood as it tried to break free from its restraint.

Meira chose a large flat topped rock on which to lay the picnic items. As she and Rachelle engaged themselves in unwrapping the food, the dog managed to escape from the children's grasp and commenced to cavort with them. The tussle lasted for several minutes before he disappeared into the heavy bush behind them. Although they repeatedly whistled and called his name loudly, there was no response. Observing that Nuniye and Maya were both distressed at the loss of their frolicking friend, Meira tried to appease them by saying that they would search for the dog after they had eaten.

While Meira and Rachelle tidied the picnic area, they asked the older children to keep an eye on Nuniye and Maya for a few minutes before involving them in a game. The children had moved some distance from the picnic area where the older ones got into a huddle to discuss the game they wanted to play. Nuniye grabbed Maya's hand and pulled her towards the trees into which the dog had vanished a short while previously. He kept repeating "let's find Nuniye."

They had covered quite a distance when they came upon a trapper's team of dogs securely tied to stakes. One of the animals resembled Eric's missing husky, in colour and size. Maya thinking it was Nuniye ran towards it, sending the team into a frenzy of barking, jumping and rattling of chains. As Maya attempted to put her arms around the dog's neck, it knocked her to the ground and commenced to attack her viciously on the exposed face and throat. Nuniye stood screaming, which excited the team even more. Meira and Rachelle, hearing the commotion ran as fast as they could towards the sound, followed by the other children. The horror that met their eyes was one neither of them would ever forget. They managed, with the aid of stout branches to get the frenzied animal to release the blood covered child, so badly mauled that life was extinct.

Meira took control of the situation knowing that Rachelle was a victim of shock. If she also went to pieces there would be no one to control the screaming children. It was a nightmare trying to organize their departure from the area. Meira placed Maya on the sled and covered the body, concealing the badly mutilated face and neck with the blanket on which all the children had happily sat only a short while earlier. As they made their way towards Rachelle's truck, Nuniye ran barking from the bush, but there was no positive response or reprimand from the despondent group, some sobbing, others traumatized.

When Eric had been made aware of the horrific incident, he began to regret the nonchalant offer he had made to Meira of offering his dog as a playful companion to the children. Meira laid the blame on the older children who had been instructed to keep Maya and Nuniye amused. She also blamed herself for not being totally vigilant and exercising more control over Eric's pet. A verdict of accidental death was recorded and the Royal Canadian Mounted Police disposed of the rogue animal.

The tragedy seemed to have caused a turning point in Rachelle's life which eventually impinged on Magda's daily activities. Meira was pleased to note that they, and the children, were becoming involved in the Pentecostal church which she considered the lesser of two evils. She had constantly listened to Trolin's inexorable memories of his experiences in the Catholic church and the inestimable damage they had caused. However, the Pastor of this church was a woman, whose widespread virtue had already attracted some of the college students towards its lively and cordial congregation. During and after the bereavement, the Pastor had been very attentive and kind to the family. This resulted in an alienation of the drinking establishments to the more sanctimonious ambience of the church. The change of lifestyle was evident in many respects, especially the welfare of the children which had previously been negligible. Meira approved of the immense turnabout and encouraged Rachelle and Magda to pursue their newly found religious convictions.

When the last term ended all the books would be put away. Magda and his family would go out on the land and the summer would be spent harvesting the resources. This pursuit was one that would keep everyone busy, even the children, who would be assigned tasks such as berry gathering and hide scraping. It was an essential part of the native lifestyle which Meira loved. She too was looking forward to finishing the year-end exams and returning to the cabin where she had spent so many happy hours.

Maury's sudden disappearance from the scene led Meira to enquire as to his whereabouts. She was informed that he and his classmates, along with two instructors, were attending an instructional outdoor camp for two weeks. She was glad of the respite from his over zealous attentions. After the tragic demise of Maya he had been very helpful to the family, as had Eric, but Maury had a habit of making a nuisance of himself, while Eric seemed to know when limitations were being imposed and tactfully withdrew.

Eric had not been in touch with Meira since the funeral and she began to wonder if he was still blaming himself indirectly for the tragedy. It was time to pay him a visit and present him with the moose hair tuftings which had been nicely framed in Yellowknife. She deposited Nuniye with her friend and set off in the direction of Eric's residence.

CHAPTER 16

Since the fateful event involving Nuniye, Eric had become very depressed to the extent that he began to dose himself with mild antidepressants. His depressive state prompted him to phone his friend in Vancouver. Eric relayed to Charles the information of the mishap while returning from Hay River and the tragedy involving Nuniye, adding that the dark shadow appeared to be still dogging him. Charles' advice was to forego the antidepressants. Put all the unhappy incidents behind him and forge ahead with the same alter ego and self assurance, evident in the days prior to Tamalyn's demise. His avant-garde attitude, in the face of adversity, must not weaken. Life is full of confrontations, pleasant and unpleasant. It is only the rational and well adjusted mind that will be able to separate the wheat from the chaff. He also advised Eric not to put the blame for the tragedy concerning Maya on the dog. The animal should not be allowed to suffer by being treated differently, in other words, starved of the affection which had been heaped upon it since puppy hood.

Charles ended the prolonged conversation, by inviting himself for a visit since the distance to Eric's present post was nearer than his previous one in the Arctic. Charles settled on a fishing week when the rivers were ice free. Eric whole heartedly endorsed the idea. He informed him that the Northwest Territories was an angler's paradise where great northern pike make the effort worthwhile by fighting ferociously against the fisherman's line. Because of the clearness and coldness of the water the fish can be found close to the surface from early June to late September.

When he replaced the receiver he felt as if a load had been lifted off his mind. Eric went into the kitchen removed the tablets and flushed them down the toilet. Charles was right, he didn't need a crutch. He was perfectly capable of disposing of the seeds of depression without superficial aid and reverting to the contagious enthusiasm for which he was well known. Eric went outside, fondled Nuniye and brought him into the house. There was no doubt in his mind that the dog was a loyal companion with whom he had spent innumerable fun-filled hours.

The animal had only been enjoying his freedom on that fateful day.

Nuniye's bark of greeting indicated that a welcome visitor was at the door. As soon as Eric opened it he too joined in Nuniye's noisy greeting and welcomed Meira.

"Hi Eric. Where have you been hiding?"

"Hi, Meira. I am glad to see you. I meant to call on you but there was an outbreak of anthrax in the park and I found myself involved in the crisis. I have also been feeling a little under the weather recently."

"I expect it is because of Maya."

"You are right Meira. The dreadful incident freaked me out and really depressed me, but after being counselled by my friend Charles I feel better. I was really blaming this fellow here as the instigator of the whole sad affair."

Eric fondled the animal's ears as it stood expectantly waiting for him to attach the leash held in its mouth.

"I thought we had settled that weeks ago. Well, here is something to cheer you up," said Meira with a smile as she handed him a plastic shopping bag.

As Eric peered curiously inside she added, "No, it isn't anything alcoholic. You know my views on that, Eric."

Eric withdrew the two moose tufting pictures and emitted an exclamation of surprise.

"They're beautiful Meira. Actually, I was looking at similar pictures last week in the Yellowknife craft shop and thinking how nicely they would adorn my bare walls. They were very pricey. Thank you. What did I do to deserve this gift?"

"You have no idea how happy you made me when you gave me the poetry books. I am sure they were more expensive than the pictures you priced in Yellowknife, not forgetting the many hours you spent taking care of Nuniye."

"You always feel the need to reciprocate Meira, even a birthday gift." answered Eric with a smile.

Meira shrugged off the remark and changed the subject.

"I am pleased that I have progressed so well in my first year at the college. It has been a lot of hard work but the results have been worth it".

"Congratulations, Meira. You are very dedicated to the program and deserve the laurels merited this year,

"I feel so relieved that the first academic year is over and I am looking forward to returning for my second year. I am taking a couple of extra courses before I return home.

"Excellent idea. How about some refreshment, perhaps a cup of tea?"

Meira accepted Eric's offer and followed him into the kitchen.

"Nuniye and I went with Derek and Mimi to the carnival in Fort Simpson and had a great time. I really enjoy being in their company. They spoil Nuniye."

"Yes, Mimi told me. I was supposed to accompany them but there was so much going on in the office that I couldn't spare the time."

"Mimi also took Nuniye to Yellowknife for a week-end and I certainly made use of the freedom by cramming for the year end exams. Nuniye is leaving next Wednesday accompanied by one of my friends, who will look after him until I return, then we will be joining Trolin's extended family on the tundra."

"I am sure you are looking forward to that Meira."

"I am, Eric, but there will be many sad memories."

"I can empathise having been in the same position twice. I am glad the NWT Government decided to relocate me."

"Life goes on Eric and it is good that we have the precious jewels of memory to cherish and draw upon".

Meira rinsed the empty mug and replaced it in the cupboard.

"I must leave now, Eric. I have packing to do. I hope you have a good summer."

"I'm sure I will Meira. My friend Charles is coming to visit and I have a few things planned. Give my love to Nuniye and I look forward to seeing you both next academic year."

When Meira had gone, Eric hung the pictures then he sat back to admire them. It was apparent that Meira was very talented, an extraordinary woman with a penchant for artistic endeavours. Her words "precious jewels" brought to mind a poem in her book. He withdrew it from the bookshelf and commenced to read :

> *Memories, pearls of reminiscence stored in the*
> *   labyrinth of the mind,*
> *Priceless treasures, fleeting gems of yesteryear,*
> *   long since left behind,*
> *Released from captivity by the mystic fragrance of*
> *   a rose,*
> *The muted strings of a violin, Auld Lang Syne, a*
> *   dusty book of prose*
> *Baubles on a Christmas tree, crisp snowflakes on a*
> *   winter morn,*
> *Raindrops pattering on the roof, a waving field of*
> *   golden corn.*
> *Each fragment stirs the heart string and illuminates*
> *   the brain*
> *For time stands still and with bated breath, we*
> *   relive the scene again.*

The poem stirred up many transitory images rightly described by Meira as jewels. As Eric closed the book, he lingered on the words "Life goes on" and felt that he was now released from captive memories and free to enjoy the precious jewels.

A buoyant Charles made his way across the tarmac, grinning from ear to ear, and received an equally effusive greeting from

Eric and Nuniye. As soon as they emerged from the airport, Charles was immediately attacked by the pesky vampires of the north, the voracious female mosquitoes that constantly search for fresh sustenance. Charles' frantic waving and slapping hands caused Eric much amusement.

"That's your initiation to the north Charles, a mosquito welcome. Here put this on."

Charles donned the bug jacket and applied a squirt of repellent to his exposed face and hands as he grimaced.

"Filthy stuff, Eric. Can't be good for the skin."

"At least it acts as a deterrent Charles. You'll get used to it."

"Is there not a spray eradication program in force here?"

"No. It was tried a few years ago but the farthest northern colony of Pelicans breed here and the spray could affect the breeding program. There is also concern about the nesting ground of the practically extinct Whooping Crane. Every year some eggs have to be removed from the Whooping Cranes' nests and transported to southern United States, where the hatchlings are reared by Sand Cranes. It is the only way to ensure survival."

"Has that scheme worked?"

"So far it has been effective. Therefore, for a few months the population of Fort Smith tolerate the stinging menaces and use their own less harmful methods of eradication. The swarms of mosquitoes here are meagre in comparison with the infestation on the Arctic tundra.

"Well, Eric, that's one place I will avoid."

"Usually, in July there is an onslaught of mosquitoes which attack the grazing caribou, causing them to head towards the coast, where the sea breezes disperse the vicious insects and give them some respite. If they cannot graze, it could be life threatening, as the summer seasons are so short and they need to store some fat to enable them to face the harsh winters."

After Charles had been given a tour of the area, Eric announced that he had permission to use for the week-end, a cabin in a picturesque setting at Pine Lake. It would be a good beginning to the start of the fishing expedition and give them both an opportunity of catching up with past and current events in their respective lives.

"Before that we are going on a rafting expedition Charles."

It was an exceptionally hot day, even the mosquitoes were lethargic, but Eric and Charles joined a group of enthusiastic rafters.

Their rafting companions appeared to be a fun tourist cosmopolitan group. There was much laughter and shrill screams as they plunged through boisterous churning waters, being assaulted by the flying sparkling spray and ending up with squelching footwear. Charles was thrilled, photographing wildly, as he made every attempt to keep his camera dry and out of harm's way

After the exhilarating ride through the Rapids a pleasant interlude on one of the many islands was welcomed. Everyone participated in games and swimming before enjoying a delicious meal. According to Charles it had been a truly wonderful experience which he would again repeat if given the opportunity.

Later, as the truck travelled along the unpaved road in a swirl of dust, Charles commenced to cough and Eric suggested that he should close the window.

"I think I'm allergic to mosquitoes and dust, Eric. A bad start," stated Charles with a gutsy laugh.

"You have been leading too coddled a life in Vancouver Charles. It's time you unwrapped the cotton wool and stepped into the world of true adventure," replied Eric jovially.

"That's why I'm here, boy. It just takes a bit of getting used to."

The banter between the two friends continued until Nuniye's sudden bark, and forepaws placed firmly on the dashboard, caused Eric to slow down. In the distance a herd of Bison were crossing the road. Among them were some small rusty coloured calves. Charles took the opportunity of capturing the scene on camera. As the herd moved very slowly he was able to get several photographs.

"Impressive animals, Eric."

"Yes, Charles, Wood Buffalo National Park is home to the largest free-roaming Bison herd in the world."

"There is quite a variety of wildlife in the Northwest Territories, Eric. I never realised it until I read some material on the plane travelling north. There was an interesting article on Muskox."

"The Muskox is a survivor of the Ice Age. These arctic animals are rather unique in their long woollen skirts. They actually use each other as scratching posts.

"They must be a sight to see in their pristine environment above the tree line. I suppose you have tasted their meat."

"I have and it is quite tasty as is Bison, Caribou and Moose but my preference is Caribou. Valerie was a dab hand at making Caribou stew. I have many albums full of delightful photos of my sojourn in Canada's Arctic which you can look at when we return to Fort Smith. Incidentally, the dish on the menu this evening is barbequed Moose steak."

"I am really looking forward to arriving at our destination Eric and sampling some of the Northern cuisine."

When they arrived at Pine Lake Charles expressed delight at his surroundings. The cabin was situated on a hill, and a swathe of green stretched down to a sandy beach upon which lay a canoe. The lake's magnificent hues fascinated him. He remarked that he had never seen such a resplendent body of water.

After partaking of barbecued steaks and salad they went out in the canoe where Charles was again busy with his camera, which was devouring the film at a rapid pace. In the distance they could still hear Nuniye's barks of disapproval at being left tethered near the cabin.

As evening hastened its descent into dusky night, with a short dip of the sun's golden head, the mosquitoes became quite aggressive. Eric decided to keep Nuniye in the cabin where several mosquito coils were burning.

After a few hours they were immersed in peaceful slumber. As dawn was beginning to make a pearly appearance, they were both awakened by Nuniye's loud rowdy barking and thumping as he lunged against the door. On wrenching back the curtain, Charles was aghast to find himself face to face with a bear standing on its hindquarters, snout pressed against the glass pane. The sudden appearance of Charles caused it to retreat. He bemoaned the missed opportunity of getting a photograph of the huge face, which seemed to have the same surprised expression as his own startled countenance. He did, however, manage to snap a back view of the lumbering animal before it disappeared into the dense bush

"Bears can be quite a nuisance at this time of the year Charles, especially when residents have their cabins packed with food and barbecue smells linger around the lake. It is always advisable to remove all traces of food when closing up the residence for the winter. Last Fall the cabin next door was almost wrecked by a bear that broke in. It raided a cupboard containing jam, syrup, flour, sugar and tea and left its imprint on a mattress where it had obviously been enjoying the jam and syrup.

"I only hope this doesn't happen here Eric. The bear might come back."

"I don't think so Charles. One look at you and he took off," answered Eric, with humour in his voice. "The owner of this particular cabin has hit on an ingenious idea of covering all windows with sheets of wood embedded with sharp nails the heads on the inside."

"One prick would deter any animal Eric. The other cabin owners should follow suit."

"If a bear makes a regular nuisance of himself the wardens will set a trap and transport him out of the area. Now that our sleep has been disturbed let's have a cup of coffee Charles"

Charles nodded in the affirmative and proceeded to calm Nuniye who was still sniffing under the door, emitting low growls, while Eric busied himself at the breakfast counter.

"It is so peaceful here Eric. It would be an ideal place for an author. No distractions except the occasional bear "stated Charles with a gust of laughter.

"I agree Charles. This is an exceptional part of the park."

"Have you made many friends?"

"I have. There is quite a good social life in Fort Smith winter and summer. For such a small place the facilities and camaraderie is excellent. Before you leave you must spend some time in the Northern Lights Museum."

"You appear to have a very good relationship with Trolin's widow. You speak so highly of her and I'd like to meet the woman as she sounds such an interesting person. I enjoyed reading her book of poems which you sent to me.

"Well, that's not possible Charles. Meira and her son have gone home for the summer. They are probably camped out on the tundra now and believe it or not, I miss them.

Charles studied Eric's face deeply before he replied. "I believe you do, Eric. I think you have a hidden depth of feeling for this woman."

Eric remained silent as he thought on this remark and after a few seconds interjected with the word "Perhaps."

Charles did not pursue the matter. He drank the remains of his coffee, set the empty cup on the counter and suggested that they should get another forty winks of sleep before morning, in its flame coloured glory, erased dawn's fading mantle.

As Eric lay listening to Charles' intermittent snores, he ruminated on his remark about the hidden depth of feeling for Meira. He began to seriously analyse the situation regarding the seven month friendship. It was obvious that Meira relied on him in relation to many varied tasks, but his efforts had always been reciprocated, the latest offering being in the form of the two beautiful moose tufting pictures, a gift he would cherish. He would always be there for Meira, but whether this put him in the category of a concerned friend or a prospective suitor remained unclear. Romantic thoughts towards her had never crossed his mind until Charles impinged on the subject half an hour previously. It was then that an overwhelming feeling of affection for Meira suffused him. If it persisted this was something he would have to deal with. He was not certain as to where Maury fitted into the equation but was aware of the fact that he was a frequent visitor at her residence. Meira had always maintained a cool exterior and there was never anything in her demeanour to indicate that Eric was other than a dear and trusted friend. Momentarily, a vivid image of Valerie entered his mind.

The visit had been such a great success that Charles was already talking about another one before the season ended and Eric had enough fish to keep Nuniye happy for a month.

Charles had only two days left, and this would be utilised in visiting the Museum and photographing edifices of interest.

While indulging in a feast of barbecued fish, Charles remarked on the sudden change from sunshine and blue skies to a plethora of dullness. As Eric leashed Nuniye outside, he noticed the atmosphere was thick with smoke making it more heavily overcast, and the strong smell of burnt wood was nauseating. Eric immediately sensed danger and ordered Charles to pack immediately. When they reached Fort Smith, Parks Canada informed him that a fire was burning near Fort Smith and it was cutting off the road as a means of exit. He informed Charles, that it was doubtful whether he would be able to depart the following day, or the day after as the ceiling might be too low to enable the passenger jet to land. Charles replied that he would stay a day or two longer, if necessary. A few hours later, Eric received a phone call informing him that he and his guest should pack a small bag, because the red alert indicated that the inhabitants might have to be evacuated. Military planes were already in place at the airport. This was unsettling news. Eric knew that he could not take Nuniye and the best plan would be to leave him at the river. He had been told to stand by. When a further call came, after Charles and he had consumed umpteen cups of coffee and discussed the ravages of fire on a small community, he was relieved to hear that the fire had changed its raging course. The danger to the town and its distressed residents was no longer prevalent. Both he and Charles heaved huge sighs of relief, Charles stating that it was such a frightening end to a superb holiday. Eric's reply was "Where else could you find such exciting adventure with the threat of fire thrown in.

Charles left Fort Smith with a mind full of wonderful and exciting memories of the Northwest Territories and a box full of undeveloped films.

CHAPTER 17

When Eric entered the office he was confronted by Maury who gave him a cheery greeting.

"Hi, Eric. I am working in the Park for a couple of months. Summer employment will fill my pocket with a few dollars and my head with more knowledge. I have been assigned to assist you for a few weeks."

Eric was already aware that a student from the College had been hired to assist him but he never suspected that Maury would be the chosen one. Eric's research was associated with the Wood Bison population, in the Slave River Lowlands and the Park which was infected with bovine tuberculosis and brucellosis. In order to protect the healthy Bison herds, in the Mackenzie and Nahanni regions, a Bison Control Area had been created from the border of the Northwest corner of Wood Buffalo Park to Trout Lake. Bison seen moving in this area are treated as suspect and require to be removed and tested in order to reduce the risk of transmission of these diseases. In conjunction with the Alberta and British Columbia governments the Northwest Territories has worked to re-establish the two disease-free herds making the recovery program, so far, successful. The active participation of the public and various agencies also go a long way towards making the Bison management a success.

"There is a lot to be done in this department Maury so you will be kept busy," said Eric in a cordial voice as he produced a box of slides. "Let's begin with these."

They worked together assiduously until coffee break.

"How do you like the work, so far, Maury?"

"I find it quite interesting and expect to gain a lot of info which will be helpful in my final year."

"You have chosen a good career Maury."

"What are your plans when your contract expires Eric?"

"I haven't thought so far ahead yet. My experiences have taught me that it's better to take one day at a time."

"I have big plans in mind. I hope to find permanent employment, marry again and have a family. I miss my wife and boys."

"I know how it feels Maury and I hope your plans come to fruition."

The conversation between Eric and Maury dissolved as they were joined by other members of staff.

Both men, having involved themselves in an extraordinary amount of mental activity all week, decided to have a few drinks in the British Legion on Friday evening. During the course of conversation it transpired that Maury had a very checkered background in the career field. Trading posts for the Hudson Bay Company and Northwest Trading Company were established in various settlements. Although Maury had always lived the traditional lifestyle of hunting and trapping and following in his father's footsteps living off the land, he commenced working for the Hudson Bay Company. Then he discovered that more money could be made in the Beaufort oil expansion boom. The wealth brought alcohol addiction and other problems of a nefarious nature which resulted in broken relationships between him and his wife, children and parents. The new lifestyle had also been detrimental to his health and he became a patient in a drug rehabilitation centre on more than one occasion. Later he became involved in mining exploration, followed by a carpentry course which enabled him to secure a position as a builder's helper. The horrific episode of attempting to save his family, with whom he had been attempting to effect reconciliation, from the house fire, was the critical moment in time when Maury realised that money could never replace such an incalculable and distressing loss. It resulted in his return to the traditional lifestyle he had forsaken, with an ardent desire to acquire more knowledge in relation to preservation of the land and its resources.

From Maury's invective on the government's handling of the oil and gas exploration more than a decade ago, Eric gained some acumen into the oil speculation in the Northwest Territories which held at least twenty five percent of Canada's remaining recoverable resources. The oil boom in the 1970s was strangled by a Federal government moratorium, after hearings in communities all over the territories. The political development involving Land Claims and Division was a big setback dampening the enthusiasm of oil prospectors.

The moratorium remained in effect for quite a while before companies began again pledging to invest millions as determined by their leases.

Besides resembling Trolin in stature, Eric concluded that Maury also expressed inwardly and vocally, the same sentiments in relation to the Canadian government's controlling influence on the Northern aboriginal population and the rich resources abounding in the land. His provoking attitude induced Eric to repeat the nuances he had, on many occasions, previously echoed in defence of the government's actions. The lengthy discourse, which could be considered at times as being fiercely argumentative, ended amicably with Eric agreeing to accompany Maury on a trip to Fort Resolution the following day for the purpose of transporting a relative to the settlement.

The fire hazard was still looming and the thick smoke laden atmosphere was obscuring the sun when Eric, Maury and his cousin Dave set out on their journey. Prior to approaching the turn-off towards their destination, a wobble in the steering indicated a flat tyre. While Eric and Maury busied themselves with the wheel change, Dave went into the bush to relieve himself of the copious amounts of beer he had been consuming on the journey. Because the proper wheel-jack hadn't been in the trunk of the vehicle when Eric purchased it and this being the first occasion for its use, it took quite a while to set the change in motion. The task finished they then realised that Dave had failed to return to the vehicle.

After calling his name several times and receiving no response, they proceeded in the direction he had taken. Forty paces brought them to a fork at the end of the road. Glancing at his watch, Eric observed that they had been working for a full thirty-five minutes and assumed that Dave's departure and return shouldn't have taken more than five minutes of that time. At the end of the path they went their separate ways calling loudly on Dave as they glanced right and left searching for him.

The bush became more dense and the mosquitoes more voracious. Eric hadn't applied any deterrent to his skin so he decided to return to the vehicle. He turned around and ambled along a path which he presumed would lead him to the road. After covering some distance he knew he had taken a wrong turning. He followed one path then another until he became completely disorientated. It was impossible to use the sun as a guide because of the heavy smoke.

Eric had been trekking through the bush for ages completely exhausted and covered in stinging bites. He sat down on a fallen tree so that he could rationalize the situation. As he swiped viciously at the attacking mosquitoes and flies around his head and ankles, he spied a cardboard box wedged in the undergrowth near where he was seated. He pulled it out and decided to make use of it against the onslaught of the biting insects. Using his penknife he cut two holes and a slit, then placed the box over his head. It reached to his waist and also afforded protection to his arms which were also engulfed. His voice was hoarse from shouting. This disposed of one irritating aspect of his dilemma. The more crucial aspect was finding his way out of the maze in which he was totally lost. He was also intensely thirsty. The heat of his body enveloped in the enclosed cardboard carton, while having a protective quality, was causing him to perspire heavily. Dehydration was a worrying factor and if he failed to find his way out soon the situation could become perilous. Eric lowered himself to the ground and fell asleep cushioned against the tree.

When he awoke the northern night had already been liberally sprinkled across the land. As well as being thirsty, hunger also gnawed at his inners. The strong smell of smoke still permeated the air which meant that he could not rely on the heavens as a means of escaping his solitary confinement. At the first sign of light, he stretched his cramped body and decided to follow another path using his mind as a compass. When he arrived at the uprooted tree trunk, on which he had deliberated an hour earlier, he realised that he had walked in a wide circle. Momentarily he became frightened, but he quickly dispelled the feeling by telling himself that a walk in the opposite direction would probably lead him to the road. After a few more aimless steps Eric realised he was hopelessly lost. He resigned himself to the fact that a search party would have to find him because he could not rely on his own sense of direction.

Eric had become so dehydrated that he was beginning to hallucinate. He imagined he saw a bear a few feet from where he lay, then Valerie appeared in front of him with outstretched arms. As he reached out to touch her she disappeared. A cry of disappointment which escaped his swollen and cracked lips jolted him into reality. There was no Valerie only he and the creatures that inhabited this vast wilderness. The lethargy which enveloped him caused another relapse into a world of fantasy.

Eric was walking on the Salt Plains. He had a small child by the hand and they were tracking the foot prints of a black bear. "There. There," shouted the child excitedly pointing ahead of him. In the distance he saw the bear's outline but as he and the child drew nearer, he observed it was Meira her long blue black hair, tossed by the wind, flying like a cape behind her. She smiled, came towards him, and grasped his hand. He was aroused from his stupor by the strong clasp of Maury's hand and other hands assisting him. Eric was transported to the hospital. He remained for a day and a half before being discharged, none the worse for his sojourn in the vast uncultured tract of land that had held him captive for two days.

CHAPTER 18

As Meira and Rachelle prepared a large catch of fish for smoking, Meira announced that she had a weird dream during the night.

"What did you dream, Meira?"

"I was walking through the bush in Fort Smith and became frightened, because it was extremely dark and there was no moon or stars to guide me. Someone grabbed my arm and we remonstrated for some time before I discovered it was Eric. Then we were walking on the Salt Plains hand-in-hand and I was extremely distressed because I couldn't find Nuniye."

"That certainly is weird Meira. What do you think it means?"

"I have tried to analyse it all morning, without success. Since the terrible incident involving Maya, I have had numerous frightening dreams and it may be that I am still suffering the after effects."

"As you know, I too, as well as the rest of the family was very disturbed. There were nights when I never closed an eye but once I attended the church I found a spiritual contentment which has helped me reduce the stress. I wonder why Eric figured in your dream.?"

"I find it very strange."

"I know you two are good friends Meira but there isn't any romance involved in the relationship. Is there?"

"No, Rachelle. Eric is very dear friend. I am quite fond of him just like one of the family. I think our relationship co-exists because of what happened to Trolin. Eric had a strong shoulder to lean upon at that dreadful moment when I heard the gun shot and we have become more friendly since we met again last Fall."

Rachelle gave Meira a quizzical look. "Well, do you know what I think Meira?

"No, tell me."

"I think you have fallen in love with Eric but you refuse to admit it to yourself."

"Nonsense Rachelle," said Meira in a vitriolic tone of voice. "I have already told you how the situation stands so let's leave it at that."

Rachelle shrugged her slim shoulders and focussed again on the task in hand. There was a lapse in conversation until Rachelle once again became voluble.

"Meira I don't think any of our women should marry a white man. It never seems to work. Take Bessie for instance. Look at the wretched life she and her children lead. The poor woman never has a day's peace. She has been beaten unmercifully and called vile names. The treatment she receives at the hands of her white husband is degrading. If I were Bessie I wouldn't stay, I would take the children and return to the settlement."

"Not all white men treat their native wives so despicably. Some of them are very understanding and make every effort to integrate. It is not only white men, who behave in a contemptible fashion towards their wives and children. It is also very prevalent in the male native population. We don't have too far to look to find this irascible behaviour. It is occurring in our own family. Even you, Rachelle, have been on the receiving end of humiliating scenes by your husband."

There was a very long silence before Rachelle replied.

"I cannot say otherwise Meira. You are right. Bessie just happened to pick the wrong man. If she had chosen someone like Eric things probably would have been different."

"I'm certain they would. Eric is an altruistic, sensitive, loving human being. He has had his fair share of tragedy recently but he once made the remark that it was beginning to make him a stronger person. His favourite saying is 'these things are sent to try us.' Trolin had a good word for Eric and he was a fair judge of character."

"You became friendly with many white people when you attended the college Meira."

"Yes. Eric introduced me to some of his friends and I was treated really well. We had some fabulous week-ends on the ski trails and the curling rink, especially the bonspiels. Similarly, Eric had a good rapport with my classmates at the various functions to which I invited him."

Rachelle, just like a rapacious dog with a bone, persisted in an intransigent crunching diatribe on the pros and cons of native and white relationships in an attempt to elicit Meira's true feelings towards Eric. Her attempts were utterly futile. Meira never wavered from the concepts previously expressed.

The constant hum of mosquitoes around her head did not distract Meira from berry picking. The crop was bountiful. It was a good season, and in Meira's mind the Great Spirit was beneficient as manifested by the colourful carpet which swept like a floral tide across the tundra. As her fingers expertly plucked the luscious fruit Rachelle's comments came to mind. Maybe Rachelle was correct in her summing up of the relationship with Eric. He was, as she had correctly described, a compassionate man with a big heart who knew no bounds when it came to helping a person in need. He had demonstrated this characteristic on many occasions not only to Meira but to others in their close circle of friends. Whoever was lucky enough to capture Eric's attention as a partner would be a fortunate woman. She had to admit that Eric had been in her thoughts many times since she left Fort Smith, but they had only been thoughts of a solicitous nature concerned with his general welfare. When news of the fire reached her she had been anxious for his safety, but the safety of Maury had also troubled her. To Meira fire was a word that always incited great agitation. Having experienced its dreadful and appalling consequences it made her nervous when she learned that two of her friends were surrounded by it.

The can began to fill with red berries while Meira kept ruminating on some of her actions which could readily be construed as being reserved for a loved one. No wonder

Rachelle was confused. Eric, more so than Maury, had been the recipient of these attentions. Not all of them could be considered as reciprocations for little gifts or kindnesses which had been bestowed. She enjoyed surprising Eric, whether it was in her kitchen or using a needle and an intense analysis caused her to admit that actions certainly do speak louder than words. She was attempting to suppress her true feelings, but the more she thought about it intense emotions surfaced until her mind felt swamped. It caused her to abandon the berry picking.

Eric and Maury sat in Mimi's living room, enjoying an after dinner drink, while Derek busied himself loading the dishwasher in the kitchen. The topic of conversation was the drama incurred by Eric.

"I would have suffered claustrophobia Eric if I had found myself in your shoes," said Mimi with a violent shiver. "I doubt if I would have survived such an incident."

Maury then intercepted. "If Dave hadn't fallen into a drunken stupor and lain down the whole scene could have been avoided. After I had found him and escorted him to the truck I went to search for Eric travelling the path he had taken. I realised he was well out of hearing when he failed to respond to my calls. Things became serious after an hour and I had to seek help."

"The volunteers have to be admired. I am truly thankful that they came to my rescue. I am forever in their debt."

"You're lucky there were no lightning strikes. Then you would have been in serious trouble Eric, stated Maury grimly.

"That would have made the situation more horrendous Eric," interjected Mimi with a grimace. "I shudder to think of the dire consequences. Thank God, you were found."

"Well it's all behind me now and it has become another notch in the belt of experience."

Eric then directed a question towards Mimi. Have you heard from Meira?"

"No I haven't, Eric but she is really isolated and there are no postal facilities on the tundra," answered Mimi with a giggle.

"I realise that Mimi but I thought you might have heard from her before she finished her extra courses."

"Not a word but I expect she was too busy studying. As you know this program means a lot to her."

Maury then intercepted the conversation. "Now, there is a woman I really admire. You may as well know I have plans for Meira. As soon as she graduates, she and I will be an item. Meira is my type of woman."

"Does Meira know of these plans Maury," asked Mimi in a surprised tone of voice.

"I did mention them several times but Meira will not make any commitments until she has achieved her goal. When she descends from the graduation platform I will approach her again."

Eric who had been listening intently replied "I understand Meira is going to University to pursue a B.Ed Degree. Are you referring to the University platform or the College platform Maury?"

"I didn't realise she was going for a Degree so I guess it will have to be after the B.Ed graduation."

Eric felt disheartened at this information but he managed to smile as he wished Maury luck in his endeavour to persuade Meira to conform to his wishes. It was obvious to Eric that Maury had a deep affection for Meira but she had obviously, not as yet, responded to his overtures. Later, in the privacy of his home, he recalled Maury's matrimonial intentions and had to admit to himself that he felt a twinge of jealousy. However, two years into the future was a long time and he would probably be back in British Columbia by then. He dismissed the feeling of rivalry and concentrated on the paperwork in front of him.

The fire season was almost over and Maury had gone home for a couple of weeks to spend some time with his family before returning to the College. Prior to leaving, Eric had commended him for his hard work and dedication to the many tasks he had been given. Despite the uneasy feeling Eric experienced when Maury had referred occasionally to Meira, they had built a good rapport between them. He was looking forward to Maury's return and to the Moose hunt in which they would participate in the Fall. He was also surprised that he was counting the days until Meira appeared. Meantime there was twice as much work to do now that his assistant had gone.

CHAPTER 19

As Eric ambled along Franklin Avenue a light tap on the shoulder startled him. Turning around he confronted Meira.

"Hi, Eric. I'm glad it's you I tapped and not a stranger. I wasn't sure because of the very short hair style. A backward view can sometimes be deceiving as well as embarrassing."

"It's good to see you Meira The hair was much shorter a few weeks ago. I found it cooler during the hot weather.

"I heard via the radio that Fort Smith was almost on the point of being incinerated."

"It was a scary situation and to make matters worse my friend Charles was visiting at that particular time but luck was on our side."

"Are you visiting friends in Yellowknife Eric?"

"No, I am attending meetings. I assume you are on your way to Fort Smith, Meira. Where is Nuniye?"

"I will be travelling in that direction tomorrow morning and I am really looking forward to becoming absorbed in Early Childhood studies again. Nuniye will return next week. He is staying with Rachelle and his cousins in the meantime."

"I was just leisurely making my way back to the Explorer Hotel to dispose of the briefcase then have something to eat. Would you care to join me or do you have other plans?"

"Thanks. I'd love to join you. Do you mind if we stop off at the Yellowknife Inn where I am staying? I'd like to freshen up."

The dining room was crowded with Japanese tourists but Eric was fortunate to secure a table in the corner of the room.

As he scanned the menu, he observed Valerie's favourite food and decided to order it. Meira also chose the Arctic Char and while they waited she sipped a mineral water and studied Eric closely.

"You look different Eric. I think you have lost weight or maybe it's the short cropped hair which gives a different angle to your face. Are you feeling O.K?"

Eric replied by telling her that he had spent the summer working long hours. Then he related the two-day event trapped in the bush. Meira's retort was that the incident was also reported on the radio and she voiced Maury's opinion that he would have been in grave danger if fire had erupted. She added that the thought was frightening and was glad that he hadn't suffered any serious consequences. Eric was pleased to hear that she had been concerned for his safety.

As the evening progressed they were equally involved in conversation, switching from one subject to another and completely at ease in each other's company. Any of the diners at adjoining tables, observing their attentiveness towards each other, would have considered them as being long time friends, concentrating on a spontaneous reunion in the capital of the Northwest Territories.

Yellowknife, like any other capital city is very cosmopolitan. It was the first official city in the Northwest Territories in 1970 and three years later became the capital. It is a frontier city in the middle of a wilderness populated by a small percentage of Dene, Metis and Inuit people from all areas of the north. The larger percentage of the population combines people from across southern Canada and all parts of the globe. The wilderness, which is practically on the doorstep, is home to bears, beavers, foxes, lynx, muskrat, wolves and wolverine. Extensive river systems and lakes abound with fish and its unique situation is an enticement for people who wish to cast aside a convoluted lifestyle for a more pleasurable one.

As Eric and Meira discussed Yellowknife's many attractions they were approached by Karl, a Biologist who had spent a short time working in Fort Smith. Eric had socialized with him on a number of occasions and as he was staying in the same hotel and dining alone he asked if he could join them. Although Eric was disappointed at having to forego the delightful time he was having, alone with Meira, nevertheless he adhered to Karl's request. He had been studying the behaviour of wolves on the tundra and immediately took the opportunity of launching into an oration on the northern wolf. The subject fascinated Meira and she began questioning him on these graceful carnivores whose eerie keening had disrupted her sleep on many lonesome winter nights. Eric observing Meira's eagerness to elicit more information encouraged the conversation to continue in the same vein.

Wolves are very social animals with a system of intricate rules which enables them to survive. They live in packs dominated by a mated pair, the alpha male and female. Wolves are rarely seen but can be heard communicating with each other across various distances. The northern wolves have adapted well to their environment by growing thick coats of coarse hair capable of shedding frost. Because of its suitability the fur is used for parka trimming. Meira interrupted the dialogue by stating that wolf pelts were not favoured by the Dene or Inuit as Wolverine was more valuable. He nodded in agreement and continued. The wolf's eyesight is so acute that it can spot prey across immense distances. They have a stamina which allows them to trail Caribou for 6km or more before bursting into speeds as fast as 60 to 65 mph to attack the migrating herd.

Eric then related a story which had been told to him by his neighbour who had a one year old terrier.

"Wolves, when their food source is in short supply, will attack other smaller animals. My neighbour was driving back from the airport on the outskirts of town when his headlights focussed on a wolf being followed by his dog. He stopped his truck and put the dog inside. Obviously the female had been sent into town to lure any dog towards the pack where it would have been attacked and eaten. Their jaws, with a crushing pressure of 680 kilos per square inch and 5cm long canine teeth, can easily penetrate a tough hide."

Karl remarked on this tale by adding that the wolf is a much maligned magnificent creature with an evolved sense of preservation. Wolves have been fiercely persecuted down through the ages so their resilience and ingenuity have to be admired. Meira added that wolves are charismatic animals found in the many legends of the north and they are considered by the Dene as an integral part of the overall bounty given by the Great Spirit.

The three of them had become so immersed in the study of the wolf that they failed to notice the empty tables and the agitated waitresses who were anxious to be relieved of their duties. It was only when Eric excused himself from the table did he realise that time had overtaken them. The dining room needed to be vacated so that their table could be laid for breakfast.

Eric escorted Meira to the door of the Yellowknife Inn. She had no sooner entered when she was hailed by a loud voice. Maury's effusive welcome overwhelmed her as she extricated herself from his clasp.

"It's great to see you Meira. The night's still young so let's go out on the town."

Meira looked askance and replied, "I don't think so Maury. I have just left Eric and I'm rather tired."

It was Maury's turn to look askance and he replied abruptly "I see. So when are you going to Fort Smith?"

"I will be on tomorrow's flight."

"Good, so will I. See you, Meira."

Meira stepped into the elevator as Maury turned on his heel and headed towards the door intent on pursuing a few hours of fun.

Meira lay looking at the ceiling contemplating events of the evening. The time spent with Eric had been wonderful until Karl intervened. Now that Maury had appeared, Meira sensed that the situation could become quite unpleasant because of Maury's inability to accept that she was not romantically interested in him. His obsession with her was making her feel very nervous.

She had no wish to provoke either of them. Even though her affections seemed to gravitate towards Eric she decided to adhere to her former resolution and just treat both of them equally as friends.

In his room in the Explorer Hotel Eric was also mentally churning the evening's events in his mind. From the moment Meira made her presence known to the instant he left her at the door of the Inn had been euphoric despite Karl's intervention. Several times she had looked at him with a coquettish gleam in her eyes, which encouraged him to think that the brotherly relationship might be on the verge of disintegrating. However, he deduced from her pre-dinner conversation that her final year at the College was going to be devoted entirely to her studies with very little time left for recreational activities. This put the ball in Meira's court

He would like to be accompanying her to Fort Smith but he had another day of meetings ahead of him.

Similarly, Maury's prognostication was one of close affiliation with the woman of his dreams and an eventual marital relationship. He had felt miffed when Meira mentioned that she had spent the evening with Eric. He recalled the number of times his offers had been rebuffed because Meira was going somewhere with Eric. Although he liked Eric and they had a firm friendship it still bothered him to think that Meira would choose a white man over one of her own kind. He humoured himself by thinking it would never happen. The best way to ensure a successful relationship would be to reduce the pressure of trying to enforce a more meaningful one. With this plan firmly implanted in his mind he headed towards the bar where he knew he would find some of his classmates.

Since Meira's return to Fort Smith Eric noticed that she rarely required his child care services and learned that Mimi, when she wasn't teaching classes, had acquired this job. Eric felt upset because he enjoyed being with the child. Already two months had passed and he had only seen Meira and the child on two occasions, once when she had invited him for a meal and when the invitation had been reciprocated. There was only a fleeting instance when the spark ignited caused by an incident in the kitchen as he almost severed the top of his finger. Meira had driven him to the hospital and fussed around him for a few hours showing great concern for his injury. Eric had been certain on that evening, if Nuniye had not been present, a new turn of events would have transpired which would have put their friendship on a different level.

Maury was a frequent visitor at his residence, but during the course of conversation neither of them mentioned Meira despite the fact that each was wondering what part the other played in her life. Recently fond thoughts of Meira kept invading Eric's mind and could only be dispersed by close attention to the many significant tasks required to be carried out on a daily basis.

Mimi, sensing Eric's restlessness and connecting it with his feelings for Meira, decided that he needed a new distraction in his life. She invited a new friend to join them.

Donetta, a petite blue-eyed blonde was a new addition to the staff in the High school specialising in Maths and Science. She had a terrific sense of humour which kept Mimi and her husband in fits of laughter.

From the very first meeting it was obvious that she was attracted to Eric. She managed to entice him to accompany her on a cranberry picking expedition. As they scrambled among the bushes near the Ski Lodge, Donetta's gay laughter echoed merrily reaching Meira, Rachelle and the children farther along the trail. Meira was on her knees in a lucrative cranberry patch when Eric almost stumbled over her, as he forced his way through the dense vegetation. She looked up with a startled expression on her face before she sprang to her feet then she gave him a warm smile.

"How are you Eric? Are you walking Nuniye?

She then noticed the pail in his hand.

"Surely not gathering berries? That is women's work," she added with a tinkling laugh.

"Believe it or not Meira; I'm assisting a friend who has promised to make me cranberry muffins, provided I fill the can."

At that instant Donetta appeared and Eric introduced her to Meira. He quickly added Donetta is our new hiking companion since you have deserted us.

"Sorry to be such a spoil sport Eric but I have been very busy. As I mentioned to you in Yellowknife this is an important year."

Eric affectionately squeezed her arm which did not go unnoticed by Donetta, as he murmured "I understand Meira. How is Nuniye? I miss him."

"He is well, thanks. I promise I will bring him to see you soon Eric."

Donetta who had been inspecting Meira's cranberry patch said "You have found yourself a little treasure here Meira."

Meira nodded her head in agreement stating that frost makes the berries more luscious and then glancing at her watch she added "I'd better get back to it because I have a lot of uncompleted class work which requires my attention"

Before she dropped to her knees she turned to Eric "Enjoy your muffins" As they went on their way Donetta remarked "Meira is an attractive girl Eric, a femme fatale. How long have you known her?

"I met Meira and her husband during my Arctic contract work." replied Eric rather curtly as he had no wish to discuss the situation.

No matter how hard she tried Donetta failed to capture Eric's full attention for the remainder of the afternoon. She suspected there was more to the relationship than he had already divulged. While he attempted to remain as pleasant as possible towards Donetta and the cranberry gathering his mind was seared with surreal thoughts of Meira.

Meira felt a sad estrangement from Eric brought about by the introduction to Donetta. She began to question her own motives for not pursuing her true feelings towards him. She sighed heavily as she arrived at the conclusion that she had only herself to blame for his attention to another woman. Why, she thought did she not let the friendship continue naturally as it had the previous year? Was it really a question of dedication to her studies, a desire to prevent an unpleasant relationship between Maury and Eric, or the fact that her heritage and that of her son would be placed in jeopardy, buried in the Whiteman's world, once she became vulnerable and made a commitment. She felt unhappy and instead of using the cranberries as intended she stowed the berries in the freezer. Turbulent thoughts prompted her to write lost Heritage.-

The last of a proud and noble race
Integrating, adopting white man's ways
Abandoning skills and cult of former days
Weep my son, to see an indigenous face
The Great Spirit your forefathers extolled
The earth and living creatures they revered
Now simplicity with greed has been veneered
Weep, my son, for many legends untold
Your inheritance like wind sweeping the plane
Into a state of oblivion soon may pass
Its wealth of tribal wisdom no longer amass
Weep, my son, your heritage is on the wane

As Meira studied the words she had just written, it struck her forcibly that subconsciously she was already submerging her son's traditional heritage in a vacuum. Relegating Nuniye's aboriginal inheritance would be a high price to pay for love. Nuniye needed a father in his life, cut from the same cloth, who would teach him the ways of his ancestors. Such a sacrifice would also be a high price to pay for the loss of love, and she was certain that Eric had an immense love for Nuniye and herself. How easy it would have been if Eric's background had fitted the aboriginal mould.

CHAPTER 20

Eric, Donetta, Derek and Mimi travelled towards Pine Lake being entertained by Donetta. Before commencing on the journey, Eric had noticed a slight bulge on one of his back tyres so he decided to stop and check on it. After carefully examining the tyre and reassuring himself that it would safely transport them to their destination, he climbed into the truck which was resounding with laughter. As he turned the key in the ignition, he observed a dark flash out of the corner of his eye then a terrific thump, on the side of the vehicle, sent it careering to the opposite side of the road. Before everyone could recover from the shock another violent thump followed. To avoid further damage being inflicted Eric quickly accelerated leaving behind a thousand pound Bison standing in the middle of the road shaking its head violently, probably feeling exhilarated that its rival had been dealt with satisfactorily. Eric drove a short distance before stopping to inspect the damage which was considerable.

"During the rutting season the bulls can be extremely dangerous" said Eric as he grimly surveyed the damaged door panels.

Derek replied "If we hadn't been laughing so loudly and been more observant we probably would have been able to avoid the encounter."

"I don't think so, replied Eric. "At the speed the animal came charging out of the bush it could have been more serious if we had been on the move. We are lucky none of us are injured."

However, the incident did not detract from the group experiencing an enjoyable week-end. Although Donetta was a bundle of fun and charming company Eric could not give her the consideration he knew she expected. He felt awkward each time she bombarded him with superfluous questions expecting immediate answers.

The skiing season was in full swing but Meira's excuse for not joining their group was always one associated with study.

As Eric traversed the glistening trails with his effervescent companion behind him his mind reflected on happier times. He imagined he could see the statuesque figure of the attractive woman, who had stolen his heart, gliding in front of him, her hair the colour of a raven's wing tumbling to her waist.

He recalled a conversation he had with Maury, on the subject of mixed marriages, and Maury's adamant statement that such marriages were usually a disaster and never survived. He had stressed that the line between whites and natives was too broad a boundary to be overcome by either party to such a union. Consequently, the children suffer in limbo and straddling two cultures as each parent tries to enforce their own cultural identity.

From Eric's conversations with Meira he gleaned that she was extremely proud of her heritage and her marriage to Trolin had been based on sound ethnic values. He asked himself if he had the right to invade these principles with an alien philosophy and deemed that he was allowing his heart to rule his head. He had lifted the phone several times for the purpose of inviting Meira and Numiye but faltered at the last moment Perhaps it was best to leave things as they were but it was a struggle to erase Meira from his mind.

Such intrusive thoughts had lengthened his stride and he found himself alone on the trail, his partner having given up on the effort of trying to keep pace with his vigorous stride. He leaned against a tree and waited for the dainty petite woman who obviously desired his company to reach him. He realised his erratic musings had caused him to neglect Donetta and an apology for his rudeness would require to be forthcoming.

A breathless Donetta arrived looking rather harassed.

"When you disappeared from sight Eric I decided to have a short rest. Cross country skiing is quite strenuous and there was no way I could keep pace. What made you take off as if the Devil himself was pursuing you?"

"I'm truly sorry Donetta. I didn't realise I had travelled so far ahead," replied Eric as he put his arm around her and gave her a quick hug.

The embrace seemed to calm her and they continued at a more leisurely pace. A short time later Derek and Mimi caught up with them and the quartet reached the Ski Lodge in time to participate in the barbecue.

Eric left Donetta at her residence as she had to concentrate on some school work. He then proceeded to the home of Derek and Mimi where he had been invited to partake in a few drinks and some niblets.

"The usual, Eric?" enquired Derek. "I have some beer in the fridge."

"Do you have anything stronger Derek? I feel like a shot of Scotch."

"No problem. Just a sec."

After the third Scotch and Eric's repeated reference to Meira and times past, the Latin phrase 'in vino veritas' (in wine there is truth) was applicable. He laid bare to his friends his true feelings.

"I have suspected for a long time Eric that you are in love with Meira" said Mimi, "and she loves you Eric."

"I am very much in love with Meira but since she returned I am not sure of her feelings towards me. I very rarely see her and she no longer brings Nuniye to visit."

"I think Meira is afraid to recognise her feelings for you Eric. That's why she is avoiding you."

Derek intercepted in no uncertain terms, "If you want her, man, take the bull by the horns and go for it. You will have to make the first move Eric. What's holding you back?"

"Meira is a true native and she may not find it easy throwing her lot in with a white man."

Well, you won't know until you try." stated Derek as he grabbed Eric's keys. "Come, I'll drive you home. Mimi can follow in her car."

Eric rolled into bed, a little worse for overindulgence in alcohol, and failed to hear the ring of the telephone. Donetta, irritated at her failure to get a reply, replaced the receiver with a disappointed sigh.

Next evening, Maury who had been out on field work arrived at Eric's residence with a load of fish.

"For you and Nuniye," he announced as he threw the bag into the kitchen sink. "Any beer, Eric?"

"In the fridge, Maury. Help yourself."

Maury with a can of beer in his hand sprawled lazily on the settee.

"What's been happening around town Eric? I have been out for a week."

"Nothing very much. I have been busy and spent the week-end skiing."

"With Meira, Derek and Mimi!?"

"Derek and Mimi but Meira hasn't been on the trail with us this year. I think she's busy."

"She is. I just left her place half an hour ago and she was deep in the books. A fantastic woman who knows where she is going in the academic field."

Eric squirmed as Maury reiterated his preconceived ideas regarding Meira Several times Eric attempted to change the subject but Maury prattled on until the telephone rang and the caller engaged Eric in a lengthy conversation. When he replaced the receiver he remarked that one of his colleagues in the office had just received bad news. His mother had been informed that she had terminal cancer and his father had died of the same disease six months previously.

"Where do they live, Eric?"

"In the Great Slave Lake area as far as I am aware."

"That certainly doesn't surprise me. You would think the Northwest Territories; an isolated area, would be a safe place to live. The dangers are the nuclear reactor cores of satellites. A few years ago the Soviet cosmos 954 crashed on the Territories.

Although on re-entry most of the core burnt up, nevertheless, particles drifted to earth. Luckily the Caribou herds were wintering further south but radiation could still have entered the food chain once the snow melted and contaminated it causing this sickness. In fact residents in Fort Resolution were warned not to use the top layer of snow for tea making and forbidden to use Caribou bones until the area had been thoroughly tested.

"I heard about the incident Maury but no matter how remote we are there is still a risk from the junk that floats through space."

"A lot of people have been dying of cancer since that disaster and my belief is that the area is still contaminated. Our ancestors were never prone to this disease. The north is a very fragile environment and our small population and economy could be placed in peril if these space projects keep exploding."

"We are living in a nuclear world Maury so these types of accidents can still occur. I understand Ottawa acted quickly by sending in scientists and the military to deal with the problem."

"Not only scientists and the military. There was a world wide deluge of journalists. In fact there wasn't a room to be had in Yellowknife. Nothing like it since gold was discovered there in the 1930s. There's something to be said for the old ways. In my father's early life, the only lights in the sky were the stars, the lights of our ancestors dancing across the sky which you call Northern Lights and the sun and moon. We didn't need satellites. Our lives were simple and we were happy.

"Time doesn't stand still Maury. Man is an inquisitive being and his quest for knowledge is insatiable. We are the precursors of our own destiny."

Maury only shook his head and shrugged his shoulders in response to Eric's statement.

After a few more sips of beer Maury raised the topic of dog sled racing. Eric was already aware that he had owned and raced several teams of dogs.

"A friend of mine once had six huskies without tails."

"Without tails!" replied Eric in amazement.

"Yes, the bitch had wound her chain around a tree and it was minus 35 centigrade. Her pups were born out in the open in that temperature and she couldn't untangle herself. When he discovered the pups they were frozen stiff so he brought them into the cabin and put them on a shelf above the stove. He couldn't believe it when they thawed out but all their tails fell off."

"It's amazing that they even survived, Maury."

"A husky is as strong as a wolf with the same instincts for survival."

"You know, Eric, mushers are also a rare breed of people."

"How is that Maury?"

"They observe each other closely, sizing up mind strengths of their opponents and quality of the teams. There is more science to it than just following behind a team of dogs. Good mushers know what their dogs are capable of doing and will not be psyched by another musher extolling his team's extraordinary fast training run. This is a deliberate statement intended to undermine the opponent's power. Some mushers might take such a statement seriously and lose confidence in their own ability and believe it or not the team will pick up the vibes. There are some mushers who may surreptitiously time their opponents during training. If one happens to become aware of this happening a little subterfuge can be interjected by slowing down the team and giving the impression that there is no threat."

"I think the most difficult contest of all Maury is the Ididerod. It's a gruelling race for both mushers and dogs pitting their wits and stamina against the unforgiving harsh environment. In fact it's cruel and should be banned.

"The team for that race Eric is specially chosen. It takes a special breed of dog, a hardy animal, to compete in the Ididerod. It's costly as well. I've often thought I'd like to try it. Huskies are working dogs and are bred to do just that. They were the only means of transport in my grandfather's time. He could always rely on his team to get him from A to B. They even brought the mail. Now we have snowmobiles and other vehicles.

"That's progress Maury."

"Progress may not always be reliable. If a machine breaks down on the way to the trap line at—45 centigrade you could find yourself in a right pickle. I must agree though, to live in a time warp is not advantageous. Today a man's wealth is not counted by the number of dogs on his property but by the number of machines. My Dad still uses his dogs and the snowmobile which I bought him still sits uncovered, unused."

"The old timers feel more comfortable with familiar things around them. Some people are frightened and react to change while others welcome it Maury."

"Change in the Territories has been too fast. Overnight our primitive lifestyles were swept aside to make way for a more modern society. My Dad described it as clinging to a tree waiting to be swept away as the force of water surrounding it increased in power. I doubt if either of my parents will ever discard their uncomplicated lifestyles. They saw the change as harmful, driving their sons into its web of deception, filled with iniquities, which they could not withstand. Look at me, still drinking, but not excessively anymore. When I am with my parents I never touch the stuff. They are good people, Eric."

"I am sure they are Maury, and they must feel proud of your turnabout and desire to return to the land as a Wildlife Officer."

"The next week-end I go home, I'll take you with me. I'd like you to meet them."

"I would be delighted Maury. Just give me plenty of notice."

The visit ended on that note. As Eric attended to the fish and disposed of the empty cans he mulled over Maury's expectations regarding Meira. He still wasn't sure about the relationship between Maury and Meira but he was obviously still a visitor at her residence In Eric's estimation he was a fine thoughtful man also a good friend, therefore, he had no wish to throw a spanner in the works by intruding on the relationship. The idea of inviting Meira and Nuniye for a meal was now scuppered, irrespective of Derek's advice.

CHAPTER 21

Distant relatives of Meira's adopted parents had invited her to visit them in Hay River. They had a child in the same age range as Nuniye as well as younger and older children. She decided a week-end with them would be fun for Nuniye and she would be keeping her promise regarding the visit. It also occurred to her that a few months ago she had promised to take Nuniye to visit Eric and she must also fulfil that one. As she rummaged in the freezer she came upon the unused cranberries she had gathered and on a sudden impulse brought them out, defrosted them and made a batch of muffins. The plan she formulated in her mind was to visit Eric for a short space of time before setting off on her journey to Hay River. The muffins would be shared between Eric and the relatives.

Eric was waxing his skis to suit the temperature when Nuniye's loud barking drew him to the window. He observed Meira and her child fondling the dog whose excited welcome matched the feelings he was also experiencing. He opened the door and stood on the step, a ski in one hand and the wax in the other, as Meira and Nuniye approached.

"I've kept my promise Eric and brought Nuniye. I've also made you some muffins," she said mischievously.

"How wonderful to see you both. You are very welcome. Come in and we'll have some tea and muffins."

Nuniye then declared that he wished to stay in the yard and play with the dog for a while. Meira consented to his request stating that it would only be for a short time as they were on their way to Hay River.

Eric tried to hide his disappointment by turning his back, laying down the ski equipment and filling the kettle. Meira commenced to help him by setting the mugs, milk and sugar on the tray.

"I see you are preparing for a ski outing Eric."

"Actually I'm again attempting the annual Fitz-Smith Ski Run tomorrow morning. I thought you might have participated again. We had such fun last year."

"Are Derek and Mimi accompanying you?"

"Mimi and Donetta because Derek has to work. He is disappointed that he cannot join us. Donetta isn't all that keen. She thinks she will call it quits at Half-way House but Mimi and I will try and prod her into finishing."

"Well, thirty seven kilometres is a long haul if you are not really enthralled with the sport."

"Your staying power last year was admirable Meira. Not even a weary bone in your body as you tucked into the Pot Luck supper."

"My energy was a little bit depleted by the time I reached the Ski Chalet but I perked up after eating.

"I often think of the fun we had together in the kitchen, preparing the stew and bannock for the Pot Luck, only to have the stew ruined when you accidentally poured half a packet of pepper into it."

"I remember it well. Nuniye distracted my attention at that particular time. However, we made up for it by defrosting one of my chicken casseroles which everyone seemed to enjoy."

"I hope you like these muffins. They are made with the cranberries you saw me picking."

"It seems such a long time ago Meira. I've missed your delightful company and that of Nuniye."

Meira did not reply. She lifted the tray but as Eric took it from her their hands touched and he felt as if he had been struck by a bolt of lightning. She quickly made her way to the back door and beckoned Nuniye to enter the house.

Eric was glad of the distraction when the child entered. He sampled the muffins and expressed great satisfaction with the flavour and consistency. He remarked that cranberry was his favourite muffin. Meira was pleased that her efforts were rewarded and stated she would get around to making him some more, once all the exams were out of the way.

Several times Meira felt Eric's intense gaze devouring her and it made her feel uncomfortable. She avoided looking directly at him and gulped her tea quickly, making the excuse that she had to be on her way as Nuniye and she were expected in time for supper.

As Meira was about to close the door of the truck Eric took her hand in his.

"Meira we have all missed you, especially me. Don't let it be so long before you and Nuniye visit me again."

As he held on to her hand she looked directly into his eyes and saw a great depth of love. She immediately placed her other hand over his.

"I'll visit you again next week Eric," she replied as her heart pounded in her chest.

"Drive carefully, Meira. Have fun, Nuniye." said Eric as he released her hand.

"We will Eric. I hope you enjoy the ski run."

Eric stood on the step until the truck rounded a bend and disappeared from sight. When he entered the house he poured himself another mug of tea. He felt as if he were on Cloud Nine. The spark had again ignited, only this time with a bang. His elation was uncontrollable. He felt like shouting from the roof top.

Meira still felt shaken. When she looked into Eric's eyes she had floundered in their depths and the heat from his hand had sent a tremor through her. Her resolve to maintain the relationship on a friendship level had dissolved into pieces. The fragments could never be put back together. She knew that her life would be inextricably entwined with a man whose aboriginal skills and beliefs were alien, but whose love was deep and wide enough to compensate for the short comings.

Meira's thoughts were so taken up with what had transpired that her attention towards Nuniye had been lacking. He had been leafing through a book Maury had given him.

"Mum, look at the yellow duck," he shouted as he thrust the book in front of her. Momentarily, her eyes were diverted from the road to the book and suddenly the truck hit an icy patch and began to slide violently. Nuniye, feeling frightened jumped on her knee the force causing her foot to hit the accelerator hard. The huge burst of speed caused the vehicle to roll over several times before it landed on its roof. Nuniye had been flung from the truck on to the road and it now lay on top of him. Meira was wedged between the seat and steering wheel engulfed in pain so unbearable that she finally lost consciousness.

Eric answered the phone cheerfully to hear Donetta on the line.

"My goodness, you sound in good spirits Eric. I am just on my way with a meat pie. I hope you haven't eaten."

"That's very thoughtful of you Donetta, and no I haven't eaten. I have left some meat out but it hasn't defrosted yet."

"Put it in the fridge. You can use it tomorrow."

"OK, Donetta. I expect to see you in a few moments."

Recently, he and Donetta had been dining once a week at each other's residence. Donetta was consistently doing her best to capture Eric's attention and put him in a more romantic frame of mind by doing all the right things. She pandered to his every whim regarding wine and food. The ambience, when it was her turn to entertain, was perforated with perfumed candle light and soft background music. Even her dress sense lost its demureness to be replaced by more revealing garments and at times the scene became quite intoxicating. It eventually reached the stage when Eric, rather than succumb to a relationship which would be nothing more than a sex boost on his part, changed the pattern. He insisted that Donetta should bring the cooked food to his residence where the evening would be bereft of all the romantic trimmings. The situation appeared to be getting out of hand again because this would be the third night inside a week that Donetta had produced appetising food. He had it in mind to speak to her about reverting to the once a week arrangement but since experiencing the scintillating episode with Meira, he now deemed it unnecessary. Once he and Meira's relationship spiralled to heavenly heights Donetta's ardour would be dampened. He intended spending every available moment with Meira and Nuniye.

Eric emitted a sigh of relief as he escorted Donetta to the car. It had been a hazardous three hours as Donetta kept referring to his cheerful personality. She remarked that a good fairy must have waved a magic wand over him and added that the result was pleasing. Several times she attempted to force him into an uncompromising position but he had handled the situation with great diplomacy. He felt relieved that the endurance of such unwanted behaviour was at an end.

Eric laid down his book and as he put his hand out to switch off the bedside light the telephone rang. He imagined Donetta on the other end of the line waiting for her usual bedtime chat and decided not to answer it. It rang constantly until he was forced to pick it up.

"Eric, Maury here. Have you heard the news?"

"No, Maury. What news?"

"Meira and Nuniye were involved in a terrible accident. Nuniye is dead and Meira mightn't make it."

Eric vaguely remembered going through this type of telephone call before and speech left him. He lay with the phone in his hand, stunned, unable to make any response to Maury's "Hi, Eric are you listening?"

Eventually he forced himself to reply. Maury's quivering voice didn't help the situation.

"When did this happen, Maury?"

"About eight hours ago. Some of the guys were returning from Hay River and came across the terrible scene."

"Was there another vehicle involved?"

"No, they didn't think so. The truck had rolled and was on top of the boy. Meira was inside, badly mangled. She has been medevaced to Edmonton. Rachelle and her husband have already set off in the truck. I'm devastated, Eric. I have an exam on Monday; otherwise I would have gone with them."

"Thanks for telling me Maury. I am just as shocked as you are and the only thing I can do is phone the hospital. Which hospital is it?"

"I understand it's the University Hospital."

Eric again thanked Maury for the information before he replaced the receiver. He made coffee, and added a large helping of brandy. He dispelled the thought of sleep and decided to take the plane, next day, to Edmonton.

Eric phoned Mimi and relayed the terrible news. When he told her of his intention to travel to Edmonton, she replied that she would have been pleased to accompany him, if she hadn't been substituting for a teacher who was on sick leave. He informed Mimi that he would keep her posted of Meira's condition once he had telephoned the hospital in the early morning. Mimi invited Eric to her house knowing full well how upset he was but he declined the invitation. He wanted to be alone. It was hard to digest that Nuniye, who only a few hours previously had been playing with the dog in the yard, was no longer alive and the beautiful, talented woman, who had captured his heart. was at death's door. Eric, his elbow on the arm of the chair and his hand lying against his cheek stared aimlessly into space. He remembered praying to God to save the lives of Valerie and Daniella but it had been unanswered. He certainly wasn't going to repeat the performance to end up with the same result. He began to wonder if God really existed. When his prayers had been ignored it was difficult to accept that an invisible force could be called upon to grant favours and change circumstances. Many people swore that Divine intervention had saved lives, cured diseases and wrought changes which gave them peace of mind, but it was all due to an intense belief in the power of the Supreme Being. His prayers during Valerie's catastrophe couldn't have been any more intense, yet they brought only pain and suffering to her family and him. He was obviously not one of the favourite ones to be rewarded for performing well in the great scheme of things, so he decided to refrain from making any further pleas to the Deity. Anyway, they would probably fall on deaf ears. It looked as if love was once again going to elude him and he compared himself to a guinea pig caught up in the constant motion of the wheel and going nowhere.

He had already lost a wife and fiancé under traumatic circumstances. Now another woman, with whom he had fallen in love, was lying critically injured, possibly another statistic on the accidental deaths register. It appeared that any woman, who was foolish enough to penetrate his aura, was putting herself in grave danger. On a hilarious note, he thought Donetta should consider herself lucky that he hadn't taken advantage of her constant offers to become romantically involved. The whole sequence, from when he had married Tamalyn to the present time, was like a film script—unbelievable, unimaginable. Eric negatively shook his blonde head and closed his eyes. On second thoughts, perhaps he should pray to the Invisible One to ask for relief from whatever was jinxing him and complete recovery for Meira, although the loss of her son would be a hard cross to bear. This time he would go to the House of God, where he might have a better chance of being heard, instead of performing a silent prayer in his own home. Tomorrow morning, after telephoning the hospital, he would do just that, provided the report was favourable and Meira hadn't already lost her fight to live.

He constantly dissected the ominous thoughts which crowded his mind for most of the night. When dawn broke he reached for the telephone. The report wasn't good but at least Meira was clinging to life. He phoned Mimi and imparted the news which gave them a glimmer of hope. Eric then made some fresh coffee, and a few more telephone calls before he prepared for the flight to Edmonton. On the way to the plane he spent a long time on his knees in the Cathedral fervently asking for Meira's life to be spared.

Eric was not prepared for the sight that met his eyes in the Intensive Care Unit. He was allowed only a few moments but it was enough to convince him that Meira's chances of survival were slim. He joined Rachelle and Magnus who informed him that Meira had serious internal injuries and her spleen had to be removed. Her left arm and leg had been broken. She had severe bruising on her face and a fractured skull. Nuniye never had a chance. He was killed instantly. Until Meira came off the life support system the prognosis was indeterminable. If she did survive, it would be a long time before she would be fit to be discharged. Meantime a funeral would have to be arranged for Nuniye. The three of them were very distressed and spent the week-end flitting in and out of the unit waiting for a change for the better but Meira remained impervious to what was happening around her. Eric purchased tickets for Magnum and Rachelle to enable them to attend Nuniye's funeral. He decided to remain at the hospital in case Meira regained consciousness.

The day after Rachelle and Magnus left, Meira finally opened her eyes while Eric was at her bedside. She smiled at him and uttered the name Nuniye. Eric, not wanting to distress her, told her not to worry, everything was fine. She gripped his hand tightly and replied haltingly . . . . Nuniye . . . . has gone . . . . he is with his dad . . . . I know . . . . I saw them . . . . they were happy together." Her tear-filled eyes stared into Eric's, and he swallowed hard because he could not respond. At that moment, the Doctor entered and Eric was glad to be relieved of the strain of coping with the situation.

It was three more days before Meira's condition improved enough to remove her name from the critical list. Eric had already spent a week in Edmonton and he knew he couldn't spend any more time. He was under contract and would have to return. When he entered the ward, on the evening before he left, he was amazed to see Meira with short cropped hair.

"Why is your hair so short Meira. Are they going to be carrying out some medical procedure?"

"No, Eric. I am in mourning for my son. I acted in the capacity of both mother and father to him and if his father had been alive he would have done the same thing. I asked Rachelle to do it for me."

"I understand" replied Eric as he nodded in agreement.

Eric promised to visit Meira every alternate week-end. As he was about to leave, she put up her hand and stroked his face.

"You have been so kind and helpful, Eric. I am eternally grateful."

Eric caught her hand, moved it towards his lips and kissed the back of it before he placed it gently on the bed. He noticed a glint of tears in her eyes as he left the bedside. As he made his way along the corridor, he muttered under his breath "Thank you, God, for answering my prayer." He then wondered if all the ill luck which was befalling him had also been vanquished.

CHAPTER 22

Eric was seated alongside Donetta, across the table from Derek and Mimi. Mimi had met him at the airport and insisted that he should join them. He described in detail the horror he felt when he first entered the Intensive Care Unit and looked at Meira.

"I'm surprised Meira survived. Neither Rachelle, Magnus or I thought she would see morning and the medical staff had the same opinion."

"I'm so glad she is making a recovery Eric but the death of Nuniye may not have fully impacted yet," replied Mimi.

"I do believe it has Mimi because her first word was Nuniye, followed by he is with his dad. She said she knew he had died."

"She is a very strong minded woman who has had to cope with many tragedies in her life. I have no doubt she will pull through with remarkable courage to face the future and the loss of her child," Mimi answered hopefully.

"I suppose she will be hospitalized for some time," said Donetta looking directly at Eric.

"She may well be Donetta but I have promised to visit her every alternate week-end."

On hearing these words, Donetta knew that any further attempts to lure Eric into a romantic liaison would be utterly futile. She knew in her heart that Eric had eyes only for Meira and answered rather despondently "I'm sure Meira will appreciate your unwavering devotion Eric."

For a moment, Eric reflected on the touch of Meira's hand on his face, before he left her bedside. It was the first time Meira had displayed, openly, her feelings towards him.

Next morning, Eric reiterated to Maury the same information regarding Meira's plight. Maury stated that he hoped to be able to visit the hospital but presently he was under pressure to study for final exams. He had written several letters to Meira saying that he would visit when time permitted.

Maury, accompanied by Eric, was on his way to visit his parents because his mother hadn't been feeling very well.

Eric was surprised to find that Maury's parents lived more primitively than he realised without electricity or running water in a hand-built log cabin. Because they fiercely resisted change they turned their backs on all the modern conveniences offered to them, such as indoor plumbing, instant light and hot running water with a flick of a switch. They rejected the convenience of walking a few steps to a store to pick up, flour, tea, coffee, sugar and canned milk, preferring instead to eke out what remained of a month's supply of these basic staples, until they were replenished by their daughter. This was a monthly chore which she carried out without fail. Their meat supply was found on the land and lakes surrounding them, therefore, protein was the dominant substance in their daily diet. As Eric had already discovered, native women could put the best chefs to shame with their wild meat, wild fowl and fish dishes. They have a knack of turning wild flesh, fowl and fish into dishes, subtly disguised with the land's offering of herbs and spices, which a gourmet would consider exotically appetising.

Even though Maury had informed him previously that his parents were loathe to change their ways, nevertheless, he never expected to find them living in such meagre surroundings and completely isolated. They relied on wood for heat, a creek nearby supplied water, and when frozen, clean snow was used. Their lighting was supplied by kerosene lamps. A wooden hut, a short distance from the cabin was the outside privy. The only means of communication was a local bush radio.

Maury's father's strong handclasp of welcome and the deeply lined face denoted strength and toil. Hardship was also etched on his mother's features as she shyly welcomed him. Bush life is a hard one for the trapper who has to travel immense distances in frigid temperatures to set and check on trap lines. The furs then have to be prepared for market and if the harvest is good the working day is stretched. Maury's mother tanned hides which were used for making jackets, vests, moccasins and mittens These articles were taken by her daughter to the store to be sold. During the long winter nights her needle was busy with embroidery, quill work and beading but such fine, close, work in poor light had weakened her eyes. She resorted to wearing glasses but her eyesight had become very frail and she told Maury that she had been forced to give up the needle. The last pair of moccasins in her possession, beautifully decorated, she presented to Eric. He was delighted with the gift.

In summer, wood has to be cut and stacked for winter use. Fish must be caught and dried along with meat. As well as having sufficient food for themselves, in the event of a poor hunting season, the dog team still has to be fed daily. That was one of Maury's reasons for buying the snowmobile, so that his parents wouldn't have to worry about the care and feeding of the animals. It stood, as Maury had stated, under its thick cover, at the back of the cabin, an icon of the modern age. Despite the self imposed hardships they were a happy couple, each dependent on the other for comfort and support.

Maury's parents were illiterate, neither one having attended school. His respective grandparents had opposed the missionaries' attempts to cloister their children in a building, being subjected to practices totally alien to their culture and uninhibited lifestyle. Despite the fact they couldn't read, they were still able to converse with Eric and he enjoyed listening to tales of bygone days.

His father told a unique story of one of the animals he found in his trap. A magnificent specimen of wolf was firmly entrapped and making a fierce attempt to escape by chewing on its leg. It had obviously been held firm for only a short time before he arrived, definitely an animal in the peak of condition, whose pelt would have fetched a good price. He lifted the rifle to his shoulder but couldn't force himself to fire. It looked at him with such pathetic eyes that he felt hypnotised. In his mind he felt as if it were communicating telepathically the message "I am the leader of the pack and they are dependant on me. Spare me to teach the young." He never experienced any fear as he set aside the rifle and approached the leg hold trap even though he knew the massive strong jaws could crush his arm. The wolf never flinched as he released it. The animal limped a few yards before it stopped, turned around, looked at him for a second, then went into the bush leaving behind a trail of blood droplets on the snow. About a year later he had just finished setting one of his traps when the dogs became restless, leaping and tugging in their traces. As he stepped on to the back of the sled he observed a wolf standing a few yards to the right of him. Instinctively, he knew it was the animal he had released from the trap. It stood motionless and stared at him before it limped away. He had a feeling that the wolf wanted him to know that it had survived despite the injury.

Maury's mother put out some food for the pet dog and instructed Eric to watch the two ravens which were sitting on the spruce tree. The dog was voraciously attacking its food when one of the ravens swooped down beside the dish. Instinctively the dog, on a long chain, sprang at the wily bird it as it ascended a few feet into the air, then it dropped down a short distance away, and waited for the dog to reach it. During this activity, the other raven raided the food dish and flew into the tree with food in its beak. The same antic was then repeated by the raven which had already eaten, enabling the other one to share in the food. After a short time, the dog finally caught on to what was happening and ignored the cleverness of the ravens. Eric laughed, stating that he constantly observed the same behaviour every time he fed his dog.

"Ravens are very ancient and wise," stated Maury's mother. "During my early marriage I had a pet raven and wherever I went it flew above or behind me. One winter I went down to the creek to get a bucket of fresh snow. I was pregnant with my first child at the time and fell on the icy bank twisting my knee and ankle so badly, I was unable to get up."

At this point in the story, Maury's father intervened. "I was just about to set a trap when a terrible squawking disrupted me. A raven flew at me several times in a great state of agitation. I couldn't understand it and then it dawned on me that the bird was Blackie. I called its name and it landed on my shoulder. Several times it flew off towards the cabin screeching loudly. Only then did I realise that something was wrong. The bird wanted me to follow it and it flew directly to the creek where my woman was lying in great pain."

"That bird saved my life because if my husband had continued along his trap line he would have been gone for a long time," said Maury's mother. "Sadly the raven is no longer with us. It just disappeared one day, shortly after that incident. I think its purpose had been served."

"Ravens are as old as time," added Maury. "They are hardy birds that can withstand the meanest temperatures and they are as cunning as foxes."

"In our culture, the raven is a brother-in-law to the wolf, who is our guide and protector," stated Maury's mother as she offered Eric another mug of tea.

In Maury's presence, Eric felt uneasy about what had transpired between himself and Meira. When Maury proceeded to tell his parents about his woman being confined indefinitely to hospital, he experienced a sense of guilt. Maury's mother replied that she hoped Meira would soon recover and she was looking forward to the day when Meira would join the family on a permanent basis. That statement spoiled the remainder of the week-end for Eric because he felt like a traitor amidst people who were extremely generous and kind. Eric felt relieved when he set foot on Fort Smith airport.

The following Friday evening found him walking along the hospital corridor with an enormous bouquet of flowers. When he entered the ward he was pleased to note that Meira's facial bruises had changed to a lighter shade. Her eyes were brighter and she was obviously pleased to see him. She held her hand out to Eric who took it between his own warm hands and retained it there, as he boldly stooped and planted a kiss on her forehead.

"Such beautiful flowers Eric. Thank you."

"I thought they would bring a touch of colour into your life, Meira."

"I am so glad to see you. It is a long day without visitors."

"I'm sure it is, but it is great to see that you are on the road to recovery."

"Being confined here means I won't be able to graduate this year, Eric."

"Don't worry about it. Concentrate on regaining your strength Meira. You can graduate next year."

I still have some course work left and I thought I might be able to work on it there but the Doctors don't want me to do that."

"Take their advice. You have your whole life ahead of you. I just want you to get well because I'm sure you know I have deep feelings for you".

Meira's flush tinged her cheeks and she lowered her eyes.

When Eric tenderly stroked the top of her hand she looked directly at him and replied.

"I have been aware of your feelings for a long time Eric and fought to avoid acknowledging them as well as my own feelings for you."

"How do you feel about the situation now, Meira?

"I have given up fighting. Whatever will be, will be."

"Exactly my sentiments. Your statement makes me very happy. I think my luck is changing."

Meira asked Eric to pour her some juice and as he did so Rachelle and Magnus appeared, followed by Maury, who held a bunch of roses in one hand and a small parcel of salted meat in the other. He looked hard at Eric.

"I didn't expect to see you here Eric. You never mentioned last week that you were visiting Meira again so soon. Maury turned towards Meira and informed her that Eric had spent last week-end at his parents' place.

"Oh! He didn't mention it. Did you enjoy the trip, Eric?"

"I had a marvellous time and heard some interesting stories from wonderful people."

Rachelle passed remarks on the flowers which the nurse had already placed in a vase. Suspecting that Eric had brought them she didn't enquire as to the donor.

Eric thought it best to leave the visitors with Meira and felt disappointed as he exited the hospital. It was obviously going to be a week-end where prime time with Meira would be at a premium. There were so many things he wanted to talk about but they would have to remain in abeyance until they could speak together privately. He arrived at the hospital the following day, earlier than usual, but his effort was to no avail. The visitors had arrived before him so there was no opportunity to express his desires to Meira. She detected his disappointment and before he left promised to write to him diplomatically avoiding making any reference to a visit two weeks hence.

Maury didn't fail to notice how Eric and Meira reacted towards each other and he was instantly consumed with jealousy. The woman he loved was slipping through his hands and he would have to do something about it. In his mind, Meira was more vulnerable than ever. She had lost her husband and now her only child had been taken from her. In her present state of mind it was only natural that she should respond to Eric's overwhelming generosity and attention. Maury had already made his interest in Meira known to Eric, Mimi, and Derek and he was feeling upset that Eric had chosen to ignore his claim. Although Eric's card beside the flowers wished Meira a speedy recovery, nevertheless, he was convinced that the words conveyed a deeper meaning known only to Meira. He allowed his angry feelings to simmer, fully aware that jealousy is an unsatisfactory and frustrating element of human nature which continuously feeds on the mind's imaginary foibles. When allowed to run amok it has the power to destroy.

He suddenly recovered from the negativity which had seized him unmercifully as soon as Meira remarked that visitors were supposed to be cheerful and his countenance was not a happy one. Maury apologised, using the excuse that he was concerned about his final exams. He then proceeded to ask Meira about her future plans since she would not be among the graduates. It was now Meira's turn to look gloomy. She replied that the Principal of the program was coming to Edmonton on College business and would be visiting her to discuss the situation.

"There might be some allowance made for your absenteeism Meira since you are one of the top students in the program."

"Who told you that, Maury?"

"Word gets around. I just wish I had your brains and determination. I must say, though, most of my courses haven't been too hard to handle. One or two did give me a headache but I sought Eric's help on a couple of occasions. He is quite learned in his field."

Meira ignored the reference to Eric and replied that her intent was to make a complete recovery, then proceed as originally planned in the field of education.

Rachelle had been sitting quietly absorbing the conversation. Maury then proceeded to question her regarding the Academic Upgrading program in which she was enrolled. The reply, that another year in the same program would enable her to obtain a Grade 12 diploma and allow her to pursue a nursing career seemed to satisfy his curiosity. He stated they would all soon be products of an institution that had served them well. He agreed with Meira that education was the road to enlightenment. Mind expansion was the forerunner of a well organized society. If the fruit of knowledge was still continued and applied as aggressively as it had been in the past, then the Northwest Territories would hold its own in line with the other Canadian provinces when autonomy was achieved.

Maury then advised Magnus to take the opportunity of an education. His retort, that he would wait until Rachelle finished because two parents with their noses in books would cause neglect of the children, caused Meira to smile and comment.

"I never expected to hear such a statement Magnus. I am so glad that both of you are now taking parenting seriously."

"We realised the error of our ways Meira after we lost Maya. It is just a pity we had not done it sooner," he replied sadly.

"It's all in the past Magnus and we must move forward. Life takes many twists and turns before we reach a straight road which leads to better things," said Meira as she patted his arm.

Maury pondered on these words uttered by Meira. Was she already on the straight road and was Eric at the end of it with open arms? He suddenly decided that he needed a drink and left Rachelle and Magnus at Meira's bedside with the excuse that he had to meet some friends. He imbibed in alcohol for a couple of hours which made him ill tempered. In this frame of mind he decided to confront Eric in his hotel and settle matters regarding Meira once and for all time.

After hastily downing another drink he carried out his intention and arrived by cab in an ugly mood. Maury's vile language did not endear him to the occupants of the room on whose door he was violently pounding, nor the occupants of some of the other rooms who were gathering in the hallway. He was on the wrong floor and was quickly removed by the house detective and a burly porter who threatened to call the police if he didn't remove himself from the premises forthwith.

Eric, completely unaware of the fracas on the floor beneath his, was quietly enjoying a television documentary and sipping a scotch.

Next morning, Rachelle, Magnus and Maury met Eric at the airport. He observed that Maury looked slightly rough and made the remark "You look a bit under the weather Maury. Were you partying last night?"

"No," replied Maury rather sheepishly. "I just got into bad company."

"You have been too heavy handed on the bottle Maury" laughed Magnus as he slapped him playfully on the back. "You should have stayed at the hospital with us."

This statement saddened Eric. Instead of being closeted alone in his room he could have been enjoying the company of Meira, Rachelle and Magnus but Maury hadn't given any indication that he was leaving early.

Although Maury still had a chip on his shoulder he was still able to converse with Eric without displaying any resentment. During the journey Maury lay back and closed his eyes in an attempt to ease his thumping headache while Eric ate heartily the breakfast provided and made plans for Meira's recuperation.

CHAPTER 23

Meira had a setback. Unforeseen circumstances, relative to her internal injuries, detained her in hospital longer than anticipated as she underwent further surgery. This shattered the arrangements made with the Principal of the Teacher Education program and the graduation ceremonies proceeded without Meira's inclusion. The Surgeon's prognosis had not been one that lightened her depressed state of mind. It necessitated a once-a-month trip to Edmonton for the purpose of attending the Outpatients department. Meira was already in residence at the College having refused Eric's invitation to move into his home. Despite the fact that their relationship had developed into a full-bodied love affair, she was adamant about remaining on campus until she had completed the program.

Meira buried herself in her course work in a brave attempt to overcome her anguished thoughts. She was still mourning Nuniye. Eric was very patient and made a tangible effort to conform to Meira's whims. The only time he couldn't comply with the caring routine was when she travelled to Edmonton for her monthly check-up.

Maury also showed great concern for Meira's relapse. Although he was aware that she spent a considerable amount of time at Eric's house, the fact that she was still in College residence gave him a degree of comfort. It meant that he could visit her, when he so wished, without any conversational restraints being imposed. Several times, he had attempted to make his deepest feelings known but on each occasion Meira cleverly circumvented the remarks. This tactic, instead of crushing his ardour, made him all the more keen. Meira had become an obsession. Every waking hour he thought about her. Several times he had witnessed Eric and Meira shopping in the Bay and Drug stores. This caused him to become incensed, but he always managed to compose himself enough to converse with them, in his estimation, pleasantly. Eric, however, sensed Maury's underlying antagonism but decided against discussing it with Meira until she was discharged from the Hospital's Outpatient department with a clean bill of health. He was of the opinion that she should not have to deal with the intense situation. Meira didn't need any more complications in her life by having to cope with the unwanted emotions of another man, who apparently idolised her as much as he did.

After graduation, Maury, helped by his excellent summer work experience record, obtained a position as a Park Warden. Although he spent a considerable amount of time outdoors he still needed to consult with Eric occasionally. During these conversations he was quite affable. It was only when Meira was present did the carefully hidden resentment of Eric's relationship with her surface.

Meira still intended pursuing a Degree. The Principal was negotiating with the University of British Columbia for her admission to the Faculty of Education, even though the University of Saskatchewan had a fixed agreement with the college to grant credits for all courses taken, including the internship towards a B.Ed Degree. Meira had requested this change of location because Eric would be returning to British Columbia on termination of his contract. Both of them had arrived at the conclusion that neither wished a prolonged separation so marriage was the obvious solution. It would take place after the next College graduation but meantime, at Meira's request, the decision would be kept secret. Eric was inclined to agree with her because he had no idea how Maury would react to the news. He had a feeling that Meira was possibly of the same mind because she hadn't divulged her reasons for the secrecy.

When Meira announced her intention of attending summer school at University Maury was delighted. She would be separated from Eric and he could rest more comfortably in his bed at night, without erotic images of Meira and Eric together assaulting his mind. She had just returned from Edmonton and the news was good. Her attendance at the Hospital had been reduced by half. Maury was sitting on the other side of the table in Meira's residence when she circled on the calendar the date of her next appointment. He looked at the red circle and stated with a chuckle, "What a coincidence. I happen to be going out on the same day to a workshop Meira, so you will have me as your travelling companion. Maybe we can get together in the evening and live it up."

Meira was not enthralled. Her reply was that after enduring the boredom of hospital waiting areas and being subjected to pokes and prods she just wanted to be left alone.

Recently she had noticed a darker side to Maury, one which she didn't like. He had strange mood swings and she had caught him several times again looking through various windows before he approached the door. In the beginning, it was Maury's strong resemblance to Trolin, and his excessive generosity with gifts of food, and toys for Nuniye that had forged the friendship. When she became involved with Eric she noticed a new meaner side emerging. He appeared to have developed a Jekyll and Hyde personality It saddened Meira but it also frightened her.

The next day when she mentioned Maury's workshop date to Eric his reply was that he would take time off and escort her. Only then, did she confide in Eric her concerns regarding Maury's constant visits and his continuous references to both of them making a life together after her graduation. Even though she had tried to disillusion him by using realistic scenarios that would prevent such a relationship, he remained impervious and continued the barrage. Eric was aware that Meira's charitable attitude made her easy prey for those wishing to impose on her generosity of spirit. He cautioned Meira to exercise caution around Maury. He too was glad that she was going to summer school but for reasons different to Maury's. Her indisposition had caused a break in her studies. In order to enter the University of British Columbia the extra courses were required. Secondly, the constant pressure of study would help relieve the suffering in her mind, and thirdly, for two months she wouldn't have to suffer Maury's blatant disruptions in her life. Eric intended visiting her as often as possible and would be in constant contact by telephone.

A week after Maury had revealed to Meira that he was going to Edmonton Eric was approached and told verbally that his attendance at the same workshop would also be necessary. It was confirmed in writing and the memo happened to be lying face up on his desk when Maury perched himself on the edge. While Eric was engaged in a telephone conversation Maury casually read the contents. He was livid and hastily scrambled off the desk scattering papers on to the floor as he exited the room. Eric followed his movements in amazement. It was only when he had finished his conversation and was about to replace the receiver did he notice the cause of Maury's rash retreat.

Maury's big plans had once again been dashed by Eric's invitation to the workshop. For a week he had been conjuring in his mind an evening with Meira that she would never forget. He had planned to surprise her by ordering dinner for two in her room, and entering behind the waiter with a bouquet of flowers. He wasn't into treating women in this fashion but it seemed to work for Eric so why not him. It looked as if Meira was a woman who preferred the white man's fripperies and if that were so he would show her that he could compete just as competently in the same field. He even intended expanding on the surprise by purchasing a bracelet with her name inscribed. He sat and fumed at his desk for a short time before deciding to leave his chair and go out into the park.

When Eric had gathered his papers off the floor, he went directly to Maury's office but when he saw the disturbed countenance he returned to his own office. He was glad that he was accompanying Meira, and although accommodation had been provided for all participants of the workshop, he had no intention of occupying it. His first concern was Meira. She needed to be protected from whatever sinister thoughts were in Maury's mind.

During the journey to Edmonton, Maury was on amicable terms with both of them. The workshop grouping kept Eric apart from Maury and during lunch Maury ate with some of his friends. Eric overheard them making arrangements for an evening out. When one of the Wildlife officers asked Eric to join them he declined and it was then that he saw the pure malice in Maury's eyes. It was at that particular moment he realised just how unpleasant the situation could become. Once he arrived in Meira's room he encouraged her to have a quiet evening and they decided to forego eating in the dining room.

As Eric lay in the darkness, holding Meira in his arms, listening to her steady breathing, a whole gamut of emotions assailed his senses. Once again he had reached a step which was going to lead to matrimony with a woman he loved deeply. From the moment their minds and bodies had spiritually and physically come together as one, in an act as ageless as time itself upon which the seed of perpetuation constantly feeds, Eric knew it was his last conquest. Meira and he were destined to sail together, on the calm and turbulent seas of existence towards the horizon, where the eternal sun never sets. Then, why was he having such disturbing thoughts about the materialisation of the happy event? Could it be that the dregs of past misfortunes were still nestling, like weeds, among the beautiful flowers of love, or was it the malevolence emanating from Maury that was making him uneasy. Deep in his heart, he felt that some awesome volcanic element was about to erupt, maybe punishment for daring to grasp, once more, the rings of destiny which entwined both of them in an eternal hold. The idea that he should lose her, brought a lump to his throat. He drew her closer, into a tighter embrace, and capped the unruly thoughts of disaster as he recalled a poem entitled 'Softly' she had written for him after their first night of exquisite lovemaking.

Softly steal into my mind
Be warm tender and kind
Let your vision linger long
Fill my heart with song
Softly as the moon rides high
Let love take wings and fly,
To the pillow on my bed
Caress my face and head
Softly in the silent night
Bring me sheer untold delight,
Gently touch my hair
Tell me that you care

Next day Meira was safely on her way back to Fort Smith while Eric persevered with Maury's hot and cold moods for another day.

Charles had arrived to spend a long week-end with Eric and he was being entertained in the Canadian Legion. They were engrossed in deep conversation when Brian, the town Lawyer, arrived at the table proffering two drinks. He had been on Eric's Curling team and stated that he owed him a drink. Eric asked him to join them.

When he had fetched his glass from the Bar counter, he was introduced to Charles, and having a lot in common, besides Law, they were very soon chatting like old friends.

In a short space of time, the discussion eventually took on legal tones, when they commenced to compare Aboriginal justice with the Federal system of justice. Brian stressed that Community justice looks at an offence in a different light going to the root and cause of the trouble and dealing with it by prescribing a healing program; whereas Canadian justice deals with the offence by handing out punishment to fit the crime irrespective of the cause that brought about the action.

Aboriginal people have ambivalence towards Canadian justice. They have never felt comfortable with the white man's judgment and sentencing. To them jail sentences are cosmetic covering abrasively the action and ignoring treatment of the root. They are forever pointing out, that prisons are full of people who, when released, commit further crimes, so the period of incarceration fails to heal their inner conflicts with society.

The Aboriginal people have great faith in the healing circle. For them the circle has deep spiritual significance.

The conversation then switched to Circuit work in which Charles showed an avid interest. Some of the Circuit Court Judges have to travel vast distances from Yellowknife, to where the Sitting is to take place, in order to dispense their mitigated brand of justice which has to be viewed from a different perspective.

Administering justice in Canada's icy outback can be difficult for a Judge. He requires a good sense of humour and an inordinate amount of empathy for the people who appear before him, and their problems, because justice, in Aboriginal terms, takes a more lenient approach towards the perpetrator. It seeks to, once and for all time, rid him of the criminal disease afflicting him.

Nearly all Aboriginal people in the communities have a hard time understanding legal jargon. The pretentious language means nothing to them. Even an interpreter, who has graduated from the College, with an extensive knowledge of legal and medical terminology, can sometimes fail to grasp the true meaning of a particular term. This makes it all the more difficult for the community to accept the justice administered.

The traditional healing circle is a more effective way of abolishing actions that lead to criminal activities and recidivism.

As the two Lawyers parried back and forth their own brand of justice, which they considered suitable for a land, where Aboriginal treaty rights were sometimes put under legal scrutiny, Eric excused himself.

He telephoned Meira and was happy to hear that Maury hadn't bothered her since he returned from Edmonton. Although he had seen Maury several times, he had ignored Eric and failed to respond to his greetings. Before he terminated the conversation, he asked Meira if she would like to join Charles and himself for lunch but she declined because she was working on an important assignment which had to be handed in on Monday.

Comfortably seated in his own house Eric introduced into the conversation his plans for the future with Meira. Charles was delighted for his friend. He raised his glass in a toast to long lasting life and happiness together. Having already enjoyed the pleasure of Meira's company he approved wholeheartedly of Eric's choice. Charles then posed the question of whether Eric would live in British Columbia or the North.

"Until Meira finishes her Degree we will be living in Vancouver."

"What happens then, Eric?"

"I have already discussed it with Meira. She hopes to return to the North to teach."

"Will you be able to find a position? I can't imagine you being a house husband."

"I think I might have difficulty but I will try to find something suitable."

"Love is a strong emotion, Eric. It can turn one's life upside down. Somehow, I can't see you, for the rest of your days, living in a small community, surrounded by snow and ice for nearly six months of the year. You are too gregarious."

"As long as we can spend four to six weeks in the year away from the North, it will always be something to look forward to. Meira has already agreed to this arrangement."

"What about children, Eric? Have you given any thought to that important side of the marriage? The gene pool will be a controlling factor in their lives."

"Meira and I have already discussed this issue and we hope our children will have a stable balance of both sides of their ancestry in their lives."

"After all you have been through you certainly need a change of pace. Let's hope the tables have been turned and everything goes your way."

Eric was silent for a moment before he replied to the last statement.

"Actually there is something niggling me. I can't help feeling that something dreadful is going to happen and we will never stand before a Justice of the Peace."

"I think it's a case of pre-wedding nerves, Eric. Every prospective bridegroom suffers this complaint. I wouldn't worry too much. Put it down to past experiences haunting you.

"I wish I could be sure of that, Charles. Anyway, I'll try to dismiss this portent from my mind."

"That's my boy. Think positive. Where is the wedding going to be held?"

"Meira wants to be married here but no one except Mimi and Derek is aware as yet, of our intentions. It will be a very quiet affair with only four people present. We will be travelling to Vancouver the same day. Anyway, it's still a long way off.

"Keep me informed of the date, Eric. We can't let your wedding day slip past without a proper function to mark such an auspicious occasion."

"As soon as a date is set, you will be the first to know, Charles."

The remainder of the evening was spent going over old times together and catching up on recent events in the picturesque city on the shores of Burrard Inlet and the Pacific Ocean.

During breakfast, Charles remarked on the good work the College was doing bringing such a medley of skills to the people of the North. He thought the Interpreter program was one which would have far reaching effects in government, law, and medicine, allowing the Dene and Inuit to evaluate in their own languages these three complex disciplines. The College also had many far flung campuses able to cater to the needs of its students. He was totally impressed by the overall structure of the institution.

Fort Smith fascinated Charles and he began to elicit some more information about its history. Eric did his best to facilitate him.

"The town was established in 1874 on a high bank of land overlooking the Slave River. The only way the western freight and supplies were carried was by water transportation.

There were four sets of Rapids. This meant the goods had to be portaged around them. Fort Fitzgerald, in earlier times known as Smith's Landing, in Alberta, was the beginning of the twenty-six kilometre portage route and the trail ended in Fort Smith. Warehouses, established by the Hudson's Bay Company, at both ends of this trail brought employment to both communities.

In 1942 the occupation by the United States Army brought vast changes to the town. They improved upon the portage trail by building the first winter road between Fort Smith and Fort Fitzgerald and they also built an airport and a U.S. Government Supply Depot. However, in the 1950s a railway was built to connect Hay River to the south, and from there a new centre of transportation left Fort Smith literally 'out in the cold.' To make up for this loss it became the educational capital of the Northwest Territories. It also became the regional administrative headquarters for a large area of outlying communities.

Government is still the biggest industry. Fort Smith. Is a town in a picturesque, wilderness setting on the edge of Wood

Buffalo National Park, a UNESCO World Heritage site, larger than Switzerland, where many species of wildlife, some of them on the brink of extinction, can be found. Its aboriginal name is Thebacha which means 'at the foot of the Rapids.'"

"It appears to be a town that from its infancy has undergone many face lifts, before it emerged, in its own right, into a sophisticated centre. I understand it also has a Ballet Society."

"Yes. Rachelle's child is a member and just a week ago the children gave a delightful performance. Besides dancing, she is also learning piano, so there are many cultural activities. Children can also ice skate and play ice hockey. It is a very self-contained community where there is really no social deprivation.

"I rather like this little town. That's why I came back."

"I thought the fire scare would have put you off ever visiting again."

"No. It did not. While conversing with Brian, I was mesmerised by life on the Court Circuit. As a matter of fact, I wouldn't mind being on that Circuit myself for a year."

"Don't tell me Charles that the North has bewitched you."

Charles gave a hearty laugh as he replied, "It may very well have done so, because once I commenced looking at the slides I took on my last trip, I just felt compelled to return. I took your advice, of course, and avoided the mosquito season."

"Another thing, Charles, the cost of living is very low here compared to other communities farther north."

"No doubt because of high transportation charges."

"I have been told Fort Smith is the Garden Capital of the North."

"Because of the warm summers and not too harsh winters. Last year, Mimi had quite a garden full of vegetables. I had fresh lettuce, carrots, potatoes, peas, beans, beetroot, all summer. We take these ordinary common vegetables for granted here but in the High Arctic they would be more precious than gold. There is no doubt that it is a community worth living in.

Eric then took Charles to Fort Fitzgerald.

"You are now in the Province of Alberta, Charles. This was once a thriving little community but there are only a couple of families living here now. Most of the residents moved to Fort Smith, and elsewhere, after the collapse of the transportation system.

"It's quite a scenic little place. It would be nice to have a week-end cabin here like the one we occupied in Pine Lake."

"Actually, Meira and I discussed living here if a position became available for her in Fort Smith. It might also give me a chance of finding something permanent with government."

"What about the Affirmative Action policy. Would that not affect your chance of employment?"

"It would depend on the job description."

After returning from Hay River, Eric and Charles spent an evening entertaining Meira, Derek and Mimi. The conversation centered around the pioneers, like the bush pilot, Wop May, and others who flew planes over the uncharted icy wilderness.

"On a wing and a prayer," exclaimed Derek, "without proper navigation equipment, captive to the elements. Men like Wop May have to be admired for their dauntless courage, flying blindly through snow storms, relying on their inner compass and Omnipotent guidance. Eric interrupted Derek's conversation by telling the group that flying blindly through a snow storm reminded him of an incident, in which he nearly perished. He had been caught in a whiteout as he made his way to Valerie's house.

"What would a whiteout entail, Eric?" asked Charles all agog.

"It is blowing snow, so thick, that you feel as if you are enveloped in a white blanket. It obliterates everything. You wouldn't be able to see a finger in front of you. You have to feel your way and eventually become so disorientated that you have absolutely no idea where you are. In this particular instance, I felt as if I had been walking for miles, losing all track of time. I became so exhausted that I was about to throw in the towel and sit down. Then I staggered against a door of a house which wasn't Valerie's where I had to spend the night. Valerie, of course, was frantic when I failed to reply to her numerous phone calls. She was very relieved when I eventually phoned to let her know I was still alive. That taught me a lesson. Never venture forth in a whiteout. If you happen to get caught in one it will be the most frightening experience you will ever encounter."

The conversation then switched to another pioneer, an Ophthalmologist, who had lived and practiced in Fort Smith. In the early years the Doctor had braved the elements, covering many kilometres by dog team, in the high Arctic, to examine and treat patients with eye disease. Her research led her to the International podium where her findings and papers were widely accepted. Her fortitude earned her the Order of Canada.

Not all pioneers succeeded in their quest. Some failed with dire consequences. In 1845, the ill fated Franklin expedition, comprising one hundred and five officers and men left their ships, which were trapped in the ice, to try and make it to Hudson Bay on foot. Their goal was to discover the Northwest Passage but not one of them survived. If they had paid close attention to how the skilful and tenacious Inuit survived in the inhospitable land, they probably would have reached their destination. The Inuit have never let go of their hunting skills.

Eric then told the group about a journey he had made to Axel Herberg 1sland, in the High Arctic, where the remains of a fossilized forest had been discovered. The forest, resembling the Florida Everglades, housed the remains of giant sequoia trees, found only in China. They flourished forty million years ago and would survive where there is plenty of light and water. There were seeds and pods scattered everywhere, which the Scientists harvested, so that they could unlock the mysteries of the tropical Arctic's past. The forest is still in its organic state. Petrifaction should have turned the wood into stone, but it remains wooded because it is waterlogged.

The information, which had been distributed during the evening, made Charles all the more keen to venture farther north on his next visit.

At the end of the evening, it was unanimously agreed that the true pioneers of the incredible North were the first Aboriginal people who inhabited it.

CHAPTER 24

Maury had been seething inwardly for weeks. His intense obsession was beginning to make him very morose. Some of his co-workers had remarked on his complete change of temperament and went out of their way to avoid him. He had also begun to drink heavily. On the first occasion he had failed to turn up for work he had been reprimanded verbally. The second time, a letter had been placed on his file. He was aware that a third warning would have to be avoided because he had no desire to leave Fort Smith while Meira was still at the College.

The cause of his ill temper was the scene he had witnessed of Meira and Eric in a passionate embrace. He went to visit Meira one evening, and as was his usual habit, he looked through one or other of the windows before approaching the door. There was no one in the living room, so he went to the bedroom window where a chink of light was pouring through the partly closed drapes. It enraged him when he witnessed the lithe brown body of the woman he loved, being violated by a white man. It was a struggle to force himself away from the window and return to his residence, without resorting to the blinding violence that assaulted every nerve in his body. On the next occasion, when he went to the window, he turned away in disgust vowing to make Eric pay for his folly.

Every time the mental picture of Meira and Eric, as lovers, flashed before him he went into an outrageous mood. In his opinion she had no right to flaunt her charms and indulge so shamelessly in acts of passion of which he should be the recipient.

Meira deserved to be punished for her licentious behaviour but he would deal with her after he had dealt with Eric. He decided not to make any more visits to Meira for a while.

Maury then formulated a plan and decided to ignore Eric, but what he had in mind for Meira meant he would need to remain on friendly terms with her. It would be foolish, at this stage, to cut ties. He needed her trust and confidence.

Maury arrived at Meira's residence as she was about to insert the key into the lock

"Hi, Meira. How are you? I meant to call earlier in the week but I have been so busy. The Park is a big place."

"Hi, Maury. I have just finished my last assignment and went to have a word with the College Dean. She has really been taking a great interest in my progress, and has scaled many obstacles to have me admitted to the University of British Columbia."

"So that's where you are going. Why there? The Teacher Education graduates don't use that University to further their education."

At this question, Meira was flummoxed but she smiled and answered, "I decided to be different. I might end up teaching in that Province."

"You mean to say you are going to be leaving the North. That's not what you indicated when we first discussed our respective dreams Meira. I have partly realised mine."

"People's views change. I lost a husband and a child so I have decided to leave the North for a while. I will probably return sometime in the future."

Maury then laid the large bag of food, he had been clutching, on the table. "Here Meira, this is for you. It will save you going to the store this week."

"Please take it back, Maury. Thanks all the same but I have more than enough food to last me until term ends."

"No. I won't take it back. I brought it especially for you. If you don't want it, you can share it with some of your classmates. He waited expectantly for Meira to ask him to be seated but she stood, with coat in hand, staring at him. Without any further ado, he seated himself at the table.

Meira hung her coat on the peg and moved towards the sink, where she filled the kettle and prepared to serve tea.

As they sat facing each other, consuming cookies and drinking tea, Maury decided to have a bit of fun at Meira's expense.

"Meira, over a week ago, I came one evening to pay a visit. There was no one in the living room and seeing a little bit of light between the drapes, I peeped into the bedroom."

Meira's face went crimson but she managed to compose herself.

"You shouldn't be looking through anyone's windows. The door is the proper entrance and if your knock remains unanswered there is obviously no one at home."

He was about to say, I did knock Meira and you were at home but very much occupied, then decided against it. "I thought you must be at the College. The living room and bedroom were both empty so I didn't bother knocking."

"It still isn't right, Maury. I could have been in a state of undress in the bedroom."

Again Maury was tempted to say, so you were Meira and giving the most debauched performance of your life, but again he refrained from mentioning the erotic scenes in his mind. Instead he replied, "I'm sure nothing could be lovelier, Meira."

He regretted mentioning the crack in the drapes because Meira was clearly becoming upset. She lifted her mug and rinsed it giving a clear indication to Maury that it was time to leave. He knew instantly Meira was aware that her lovemaking with Eric had been observed by him.

Nothing must foil his well laid plans. He would have to tread more carefully in the future. He must not incur Meira's wrath because he would not succeed if the situation between them could not be maintained on a friendly basis.

Maury lay in bed, going over his plans. When he closed his eyes he could still see the beautiful face reddened by the drape remark. He had already observed the glorious body of Meira in the nude and it only increased his desire to possess it. When conversing with her his mind had been aflame with fervent passion. He would have liked nothing better than to have led her to the bedroom and got her to re-enact the last scene he had witnessed, which had sent his pulse out of control and his heart thumping in his chest. It must have been evident, in his eyes and on his face, because Meira had immediately dismissed him. While walking towards his residence his mind had been preoccupied by thoughts of Meira relishing his passionate embraces which, without doubt, would subjugate what he had already witnessed. All thoughts of controlling his obsession, instead of dissipating, had now reached the pinnacle. It was time for action.

He poured himself a beer and decided to keep it at one only. He needed clarity of mind. He mulled over several scenarios before he produced some sheets of paper and commenced to jot them down, one after the other, in alphabetical order. Then he sat back and carefully perused them. He had four options but he would wait awhile before settling for the one he considered would best suit his purpose.

Meira felt extremely embarrassed, as well as annoyed, by Maury's remarks. She knew that their passion had been observed by Maury's prying eyes and he obviously found it offensive. She was flushed with anger because of his 'Peeping Tom' actions.

While she waited for Eric, she busied herself preparing his favourite meal.

"Hi, sweetheart. Sorry I'm late." Eric drew Meira close and kissed her.

When she related what had transpired between her and Maury, he was aghast as well as being very surprised that Maury would stoop to such an indelicate act. They went together to the bedroom and inspected the drapes.

"There is a slight space when they are drawn Meira but not enough to cause any anxiety. I'm surprised neither of us noticed it."

Meira fetched safety pins and fastened the drapes tightly together.

Eric smiled. "Is that an invitation Meira?" She turned, draped her arms around his neck and replied "Why not!" Then she slowly began to undress.

As they lay satiated in each other's arms Meira told Eric she had received wonderful news during the afternoon.

"And what would that be my darling?"

"Our child has been conceived Eric."

Eric drew her towards him and covered her face with kisses. "How exciting, Meira, I am so thrilled. How do you feel about it?"

"Deliriously happy," she replied, as she made her way to the bathroom to shower.

They were both ecstatic as they sat down to enjoy their meal and clinked glasses as they made a toast to love, happiness and new beginnings.

As Eric drove home he again experienced a feeling of dread. He knew he would heave a great sigh of relief when Meira graduated, his contract ended, and they were on their way to British Columbia as husband and wife. The situation was even more precarious now that Meira was an expectant mother.

Maury, who had been a good friend, was now his enemy. Maybe he should have a heart-to-heart talk with him in an effort to put things right. Instead of going directly home he detoured in the direction of Maury's apartment. He knocked several times before Maury opened the door and admitted him.

"This is a surprise, Eric. You haven't visited me for ages."

"I have come for a specific purpose, Maury. We used to be the best of friends but recently you have been ignoring me, even refusing to acknowledge my greetings."

"Sorry about that, man. Sometimes my mind is focussed on other things that I fail to notice someone trying to attract my attention. Some of the boys were saying the exact same thing today. So it's not only you, my friend, who is being ignored."

"I think it goes deeper than that. Ever since I commenced keeping company with Meira you have definitely chosen to ignore me. Isn't that so?"

"No way. Meira has always been a friend to both of us and nothing has changed."

"But it has, Maury. Meira and I are more than friends. I think you are aware of that and it has caused your change of attitude towards me."

Maury was very calm. This wasn't the time to display anger which was slowly beginning to build. How dare this white man come here to let him know that he and Meira were lovers. He needed to maintain an unruffled appearance, if his plan was going to work. He held out his hand "Sorry Eric. No hard feelings."

Eric grasped it, surprised that Maury was quite docile about the situation. Maury then offered Eric a beer which he accepted.

"Meira was telling me today that she is going to the University of British Columbia."

"That's her plan."

"Well, I suppose it's only natural to want to be near the man she fancies."

"Meira will be very busy when she enrols in the University. There will be a lot more work to do."

"I'm sure it won't faze Meira. She's a clever one. Do you have any long term plans together?"

Eric hesitated before replying and Maury noticed it. "No Maury. We just take every day as it comes."

"That's the best way to live. Too many plans can go awry in the blink of an eye. Isn't that poetic?"

Eric smiled, finished his beer and left, still feeling uneasy but more comfortable because the isolation factor had been removed. He was back in Maury's good books.

Maury had another beer and sat sullenly dwelling on the conversation he had just had with Eric. The hesitation when he had enquired about long term plans bothered him. Maybe they were planning marriage. If that was on the cards his plan for Eric would have to be moved forward. The following evening he went to visit Mimi and Derek.

"Hi, Mimi. Long time, no see. Here is some caribou meat."

"Thanks, Maury. Where have you been? Eric says he hasn't been in your company for ages."

"I have been very busy but now I have time for my friends. I went to visit Meira yesterday and she told me she and Eric are getting hitched."

"Oh! Did she tell you? I thought it was going to remain a secret. It won't happen until next summer."

Maury was immensely pleased with himself. His ruse had worked. The information he had just elicited had accounted for

Eric's hesitancy. He replied with a smile, "Well, it isn't a secret anymore."

"It isn't going to be a big affair so that's the reason for the secrecy. Did Meira extend an invitation, Maury?"

No. Not yet, but I expect as the time draws near, I will receive an invite. Is Derek flying tonight?"

"He is and he will not be home until the wee small hours. I'll get you some coffee."

"No, don't bother. I have to make another call."

"Thanks again for the caribou, Maury. When I cook it I'll have you round to share it."

"It's a pleasure. See you, Mimi. Say hello to Derek for me."

"Will do. Bye."

Maury went away whistling. He had cleverly trapped Mimi into divulging what he had already suspected. He decided to take the long way home, past Meira's residence. Eric's truck was outside. There was no one in the living room and because of his 'big mouth' the drapes were tightly closed. Not a chink of light escaped but his imagination served him well. He didn't need to find out what was happening behind the drapes. He already knew.

He decided to have a glass of milk so that his decision making would not be clouded. He again perused each one carefully. He could not afford to make any serious mistakes. Place and timing were two important factors as well as maintaining a very pleasant countenance and friendly attitude.

Maury entered Eric's office with a cheerful smile and greeting. "It's time we went out on that moose hunt we promised ourselves, Eric. Are you still interested?"

Eric looked up and met Maury's intense gaze. "I will let you know tomorrow, Maury. Is that O.K?

Maury knew that Meira would be consulted and she would be the decision maker. No problem. Tomorrow will be fine. See you then Eric."

Eric ruminated on what had just transpired. Maury appeared to be back to his usual self. He was obviously making an effort to put the friendship back on a level footing so he would take up his offer provided Meira didn't need him. Even though Meira had her friends she still desired his company. She had an incessant appetite for affection brought about by the loss of her child. He was not complaining but a few days moose hunting would be a nice change.

When Eric mentioned Maury's proposal to Meira she again showed a reluctance to be deprived of his company. When he lifted the phone to ask Maury to postpone the trip to a later date she then relented and encouraged him to go.

CHAPTER 25

George Kardoz, a Penal Institute escapee had furtively managed to cross America's border eluding his searchers. No stone had been left unturned in an effort to trace and reincarcerate him but the trail had gone cold.

He knew that posters had been widely distributed but with the four hundred dollars he had been lucky to snatch in the hospital, he had been able to support himself in cheap lodgings and alter his appearance with several aids. Now the money was running out he would have to do something drastic in order to retain his freedom.

A complete new identity would be required to enable him to move more swiftly into an area where he would be accepted without question. Vancouver was a large city, where a wanted criminal, if he was alert, could evade detection by being lost in a crowd. It had also forced him to be constantly looking over his shoulder. He had his sights set on a small community, where a new identity might present a much better opportunity for melding into the landscape and societal framework.

As he was about to pass a car park containing only six vehicles, he observed a woman, her features partially obscured by an umbrella, striding hurriedly towards her car. Kardoz lengthened his stride and as the motorist inserted her key into the ignition, he whipped open the door. With a startled, frightened look on her face, the terrified woman, like a zombie, obeyed his instructions without a whimper. He was elated. On the seat beside her was a money bag for night safe deposit and her shoulder strap purse.

He instructed her to place both items on the back seat. Here was the cash to enable him to eat, sleep, change his appearance, purchase suitable clothing, and most importantly travel by bus or plane to the destination he had in mind.

During his stay in the Penal Institute, he spent innumerable hours planning his escape. He had been a model prisoner who obeyed the rules, but made few friends. His obsequious attitude had earned him brownie points from the staff, but black marks from some of the other inmates. Kardoz spent many hours in the library studying geography.

He had, in his mind, planned a precise route to a little town close to the Province of Alberta border, where there were numerous acres of park land, and a small number of Royal Canadian Mounted Police. The name 'Smith" appealed to him. It had been his grandmother's name and even though he had brought great misery upon her, she had never turned her back on him. Possibly, a place with the same name might have the same effect.

Before he could reach his destination, he would also require a social security card and that might entail a re-enactment of the crime which had put him behind bars in the first place—attempted murder. To achieve this goal there would be no mistakes. This time, the person who was unlucky enough to be chosen would not live to tell the tale. He had made a fatal mistake by ignoring his sixth sense and not checking that the grisly job had been carried out properly. The badly scarred victim had lived long enough to put him into his rightful place, but had succumbed to the fatal horrific injuries shortly thereafter.

He was still treading the perimeter of his lucky escape and would need to move cautiously. The woman would have to be disposed of in a way that ensured she would not be in a position to describe her attacker. Quickly grabbing the silk scarf which hung loosely knotted around her neck, he pulled both ends into a tight knot. The woman, who had initially been plunged into motionless shock failed to react in the first instance. She now struggled frantically but her gasps and kicks ended feebly as life left her limp body. The sound of footsteps, approaching in the direction of the adjacent car, caused Kardoz to take the dead woman in his arms and drape one of her lifeless arms around his neck. The reversing car's headlights momentarily depicted two lovers in a passionate embrace, as Kardoz lowered his head and fastened his lips to the still warm skin of his victim.

The danger past, he took note of the interior. On the back seat he found a carrier bag containing groceries, as well as a man's overcoat, which had obviously been collected from the cleaners. He couldn't believe his luck as he donned the coat which fitted the lean body of his six foot two inch frame. The sleeves were slightly short but that was a minor detail. He would dispose of it as soon as he purchased another one. Kardoz was a charismatic, handsome man, who had kept himself in excellent physical shape despite his confinement. He had been living meagrely for one month and lost a lot of weight. The goatee he thought was unsightly, but that would soon be disposed of, and his thick straight hair which had grown would be cut and curled.

Under the groceries, he found a brief case into which he stuffed the bank lodgement of eleven hundred dollars and a further seventy five dollars and some loose change from her purse after disposing of some papers. He was very satisfied with the rewards.

Kardoz found a small motel. After purchasing hair dye, perming lotion, a pair of rimless glasses, comb, razors, scissors, jacket, several shirts, sweaters, jeans, underwear and strong boots, he turned himself into a respectable upright citizen, who from all appearances could have passed himself off as a professional gentleman. He was pleased with his reflection in the mirror and decided to wait until the reception shift changed before checking out. He would have liked to have rented the room for a few days longer, to enable him to enjoy the company of some of the curvaceous women he had seen walking the streets and loitering on corners, but that would have to wait. The sooner he put a greater distance from his point of entry into Canada the better.

Kardoz felt more at ease as the bus swept smoothly towards Edmonton. The carelessly opened newspaper, which lay across his knees, had not made any reference in the headlines to an unknown murderer. Now that his appearance had been satisfactorily rearranged there was still the question of identification cards. He would need a driver's licence as well as a social security card.

His fellow passengers were unimpressive, but across the aisle a very attractive woman kept glancing surreptitiously in his direction. Although he wanted to return the enquiring glances, he decided against such an action as he had not as yet acquired a suitable alias. As he looked out of the window at the passing landscape, a light tap on the arm startled him. It made him jump.

"Sorry for disturbing you, but would you mind if I borrowed your newspaper?"

The woman's soft tones were pleasant and her even white teeth complemented the soft luscious lips that smiled at him.

He hesitated before replying. "Not at all. You may keep it. I have finished reading it."

Kardoz's reply seemed to be an invitation for further communication. "May I introduce myself? I am Gina Whitley. She held out her hand. "And you are?"

Kardoz was so taken by surprise that he was momentarily stumped for an answer. He managed to stutter, "Just call me "Gordo." He immediately realised that he had made a foolish mistake because this had been his nickname in the Institute.

"Pleased to meet you, Gordo. Do you mind if I sit here?" She pointed to the vacant seat beside him. He felt like telling her rudely to piss off because her intrusion had caused him to make a stupid mistake regarding his name. He also knew he could not afford to be ignorant and make a scene therefore he acquiesced to her request. As the journey proceeded, it was obvious that Gina was not interested in reading the newspaper. Her total interest was Kardoz. He felt uncomfortable as question after question assailed him. His replies were curt and he decided to redirect the same questions towards Gina.

"Enough about me. Let me hear something about your background. Do you live in Edmonton? I observe you are wearing a wedding ring."

"Still wearing it, although my husband died six months ago as a result of a road accident. I live in Edmonton."

"How sad for you. Do you have any children?"

"Luckily I don't have any. I don't think I could cope being a single mother. I have been visiting my sister in Vancouver, still trying to recuperate from my terrible loss.

"How about you? What is your destination?"

"I am heading east to Toronto. I have a brother there."

"Nice city. I used to work there before I was transferred to Edmonton. In which part of the city does your brother live?"

Kardoz hesitated for a moment, giving himself time to recall his geography, before he replied. "He used to live in the north of the City but by the time I reach Toronto he will have completed his move to Montreal. "Oh! Look at that. A truck upended in the ditch." He was glad of the disruption in the conversation as he pointed at the mishap which had slowed the traffic. This guided the conversation in another direction and allowed him to breathe more evenly. He decided to feign sleep, laid his head back and closed his eyes before saying, "I hope you don't mind. I'm going to have forty winks."

Kardoz opened his eyes to the subtle fragrance of perfume and a head on his shoulder. He had fallen asleep and Gina had followed suit but her head had obviously slipped sideways. Not wanting to disturb her, he remained motionless as the perfume numbed his senses and sent arousing thoughts through his mind. It had been a long time since he had held a woman in his arms. Gina was obviously attracted to him. If he could keep his mind alert, and bluff his way, a few nights of lovemaking would add variety to this freedom he was now experiencing.

Kardoz became aware of Gina's intense gaze. As he looked down at her he couldn't resist brushing her lips lightly with his own. She smiled, her head still on his shoulder, and her eyes revealed an invitation for further romantic exploration. He complied and both of them became completely engrossed in a kiss that spoke volumes.

The scene was set. When they arrived in Edmonton, Gina proffered an invitation to Kardoz to stay for the night at her home before continuing on his journey. To her delight he accepted.

Kardoz lay inhaling deeply the aroma of the delightful woman by his side, which had satisfied some of his deep desires. Gina rolled over and made eye contact.

"Do you know why I couldn't keep my eyes off you, Gordo?"

With a deep laugh Kardoz replied "It must be my good looks."

"The looks certainly, but you bear such a close resemblance to my dear dead husband. You could be his twin."

Gina lifted the photograph off the bedside table and held it towards Kardoz. He studied it closely and agreed that the resemblance was uncanny. Immediately a thought occurred to him. There might be personal documents belonging to Gina's husband somewhere in the house, possibly a driving licence and social security card. Kardoz gave the framed photograph back to Gina with the remark that there was a strong likeness. He then drew Gina into his arms. Again he indulged in a steamy session of lovemaking which he hoped would leave Gina anxious to adhere to his request. Before she had time to recover from his ardent advances, he whispered in her ear that he couldn't bear to leave her just yet. He would stay a couple more days before proceeding to Toronto. Gina, her husband's image looming above her, was positively responsive to his suggestion as she willingly gave herself up to his overpowering caresses.

Kardoz awoke to find Gina fully dressed, standing at the bedside with a steaming mug of coffee. He took the mug and laid it on the bedside table. As she bent to kiss him, he pulled her down on the bed with the intention of satisfying his demanding urge. Gina rebuffed his overtures, with the remark that she would love to accommodate his desire but she was already late for work. "It will keep," stated Kardoz as he slapped her playfully on the bottom. He assured Gina that he would be able to occupy himself, until she returned, by replying to some outstanding correspondence.

"I will make you a special meal this evening, Gordo. Meantime have a nice day," remarked Gina cheerily as she left the bedroom.

Kardoz leisurely sipped his coffee and smoked a cigarette. He felt like a cat with a bowl of cream but also realised that he must not become too complacent. He reminisced on his break-out and congratulated himself on its success. It amused him to think that the warden and screws could have been so dumb as to fall for his bogus epileptic fit routine. He laughed heartily when he thought of the foam spewing from his mouth. He had no idea what the small packet of powder which had been smuggled in at an enormous price contained He remembered the acute pain, frothing at the mouth and thrashing around it caused but he adhered strictly to the instruction that he had to get himself out of hospital before the following morning when tests would be done to confirm the diagnosis. Consultants would have already left the hospital before he was admitted.

When he was transported to the hospital, because of suspected severe epilepsy, restraints were not imposed. The night nurse assigned to his room was a male, the same height and build as himself. The nurse's uniform fitted Kardos perfectly. The mask across his mouth and nose had been an effective disguise, leaving the unconscious nurse covered up in the bed as he went past the warder sitting outside his door engrossed in the evening newspaper . . .

He had to resort to intense violence against an unsuspecting victim relieving himself at a urinal. This enabled him to dispose of his white uniform trousers and add to the cash for his bus ticket to Seattle and other necessities.

He had not encountered any difficulty leaving the hospital, wrapped in a light jacket, which had been temporarily abandoned on a chair in the casualty department.

Now he was in Edmonton, in a luxurious apartment, having spent the night making love to a very attractive woman. The only faux pas, so far, had been the use of the name Gordo.

He flicked on the radio in time to hear the news but there was no mention of the unfortunate woman, who had lost her life in a car park in Vancouver.

He decided to luxuriate in a hot bath before commencing the task of rifling through drawers. He poured a liberal amount of Gina's bath essence and the foam it created caused another gale of loud laughter. If those fools could only see me now, he thought, as he vigorously scrubbed what he thought to be a sweet smelling shampoo into his hair then he lay back to relax. When he commenced to dry it with the towel he was horrified to see a head covered with multicoloured hair, ginger, brown, and subtle streaks of black. He looked like a clown.

He examined the bottle and found it was a special substance for blondes to bring out the highlights. The whole effect was absolutely bizarre.

"Hells bells" he shouted aloud. He had not intended leaving the apartment but now this recent catastrophe would necessitate a trip to a hairdresser. While he dressed, another thought struck him. Gina hadn't given him a key so how was he going to re-enter the building. The only solution to the problem was to commence the search and leave with or without identification documents. After having rummaged through each drawer carefully, he went through the closet but to no avail. It was some time before the second bedroom yielded the required documents. The closet contained some of Gina's late husband's suits and in one of the inner pockets he found a wallet. He studied the photograph on the driving licence and had to agree with Gina, the likeness was amazing but the hair would have to be attended to. Finding some writing paper and envelopes, he wrote a few lines thanking Gina for her lavish hospitality. He also stated that he decided to leave earlier than anticipated but would definitely keep in touch.

Wearing one of Gina's husband's caps on his head, Kardoz checked into a motel. He found a hairdresser and after several hours of sitting with towels wrapped around his head, pints of water enveloping his scalp and eventually another black dye ended an afternoon of torture at a tremendous cost and a bumping headache. However, he was pleased with the final result and began packing.

With an elaborate story in mind, he felt confident that he would be able to pass himself off as an unemployed carpenter, seeking work in the North. His carpentry skills in the prison wood shop had earned him praise from inmates and staff alike, so he had no qualms about seeking employment in that field.

As he sat in the airport, waiting to board the flight, his thoughts centred on Gina. He regretted the rash action of having washed his hair, because he had been looking forward to the meal she had promised and a few more nights of passion. He knew she would be disappointed when she read his note, as her response to his romantic advances had been overwhelming. As he reminisced on what pleasures he had forfeited, he became aware of a woman studying him. The petite blonde lowered her eyes as he returned her focussed gaze. He wondered where her deplaning point was since the flight would be making two stops before reaching Yellowknife. He felt her eyes on him again as he casually leafed through a magazine. He looked directly at her and smiled. He hoped that she was going to Fort Smith. It would be good to have a contact. The smile was returned and boldly he walked across to the empty seat beside her. Using a familiar cliché he introduced himself.

"Hi. I'm Terence and I have a feeling we have met before."

"Your face is also familiar but I just can't place it at the moment. I'm Donetta. Are you travelling farther than Fort Smith?"

"No. That's where I am alighting."

"So am I. Are you visiting someone there?"

"Not really. I am searching for work and have been advised to try the North."

"What is your occupation?"

"By trade I'm a carpenter but I can turn my hand to many things."

Before the flight was called, Donetta and Kardoz were chatting like old friends. As the plane was not very full, Kardoz moved from his numbered seat to one beside Donetta. The camaraderie continued until they were forced to part at the motel which Donetta had recommended. However, he received an invitation to supper the following evening.

Next day, Kardoz took a short walk around the town. He was particularly interested as to the location of the Royal Canadian Mounted Police compound, and wondered whether or not notification of his escape had reached the outpost. As he walked past the building, he shivered. Now that he had experienced true freedom, he had no desire to return to a prison cell. It was a small town, and he stood out like a sore thumb but the people he encountered were extremely friendly.

Donetta provided a very appetising repast along with ample beer and spirits to quench a traveller's thirst. Kardoz didn't even imbibe cautiously. He couldn't afford a loose tongue. Donetta was impressed by his sobriety and remarked on how unusual it was to have a male guest refuse a beer.

"Perhaps you would prefer a soft drink, Terence. I have oodles of orange and grapefruit juice in the fridge?"

"Orange would be acceptable. I have managed to suppress my desire for alcohol."

This statement led Donetta to believe that her guest was probably a recovering alcoholic.

Kardoz elicited as much information as he could concerning the town and surrounding area. He learned that there might be a possibility of procuring a carpentry job with a local builder, which would be preferable, since Fort Smith was mostly Government controlled. A few weeks work would enable him, financially, to move on. He needed some place more heavily populated, and from all accounts Yellowknife might prove more suitable.

As the evening progressed, it became blatantly obvious that Donetta was romantically attracted towards him. He decided he was not going to let the opportunity of seducing her pass. Before midnight, he was comfortably ensconced in her bedroom, indulging in all the hedonistic fantasies he had, for so long, been deprived of, and which had seared his mind, as he had lain incarcerated in a bare prison cell. He found Donetta a more flexible and co-operative partner than Gina. This liaison would satisfy his needs until he decided to travel farther north. Donetta appeared to be a kind, caring person, whose sensual appetite matched his own and her invitation to check out of the motel and move in with her was accepted without any hesitation.

CHAPTER 26

Mimi arranged with Meira to throw a surprise birthday party for Derek.

"Anything for an opportunity to liven things up before the barometer plummets to the low thirties, Meira. Not that Derek wants to be reminded he is another year older."

"I'm sure he will be delighted Mimi. Derek is definitely a social animal. He loves parties."

"I have included Donetta and friend on the guest list. She is definitely keeping him under wraps. Even though I have extended a dinner invitation to Donetta and partner on several occasions, she has always politely declined with a suitable excuse."

"I think Donetta must be in love, Mimi. She doesn't want to share the tall dark handsome stranger's company with anyone, until she is confident that she has snared him."

"I think there could be some truth in that statement. Anyway, I am not excluding her even though I expect a refusal."

When Meira mentioned the conversation between herself and Mimi to Eric, he replied that Donetta seemed to be besotted with the new man in her life. Since he had moved in with Donetta, she had cut herself off completely from all her friends. Even the curling team and ice skating club in which she had played prominent roles were being deprived of her expertise.

"Well, I think I understand how she feels, Eric. "Love is a wonderful emotion to be shared with a partner," answered Meira as she wound her slender brown arms around his neck and nuzzled his face.

"When is the party, Meira? Don't forget Maury and I are going out on a moose hunt."

"I don't think there will be a problem. If Maury hadn't postponed the hunt you wouldn't even have to think about the suitability of the invitation. When is he expected back in town?"

"I think it is sometime next week. I'm not sure. Is he on the guest list?"

"Mimi wants to include him. That's why I am enquiring as to his return.

In Donetta's household, Kardoz was assisting Donetta in the preparation of omelettes for breakfast. He had already been in residence with Donetta for three weeks and was thoroughly enjoying being pampered. Several times, he had found himself in a position where he had to exercise control over Donetta's enthusiasm to accept invitations to various functions. By applying large doses of his ardour, it always rendered her incapable of acting on her own initiative. He was always consciously aware of his precarious situation which could be blown apart at any moment. He felt very safe behind closed doors with only Donetta for company. On numerous occasions there had been short intrusions, but he had always made himself scarce by retreating either to the bedroom or bathroom. Donetta began to take notice of this behaviour. While she felt flattered that this man seemed to be enraptured with her nevertheless she could see it leading to a severe obsession As she vigorously whisked the eggs, she made a firm decision that the invitation on her dressing table would not be ignored and discarded. She and Terence would be attending Derek's birthday party.

"I'll have to purchase a birthday present, Terence. What would you recommend as being most suitable for a man?"

"In this climate, I think a warm sweater would be a useful gift. Whose birthday are you honouring, Donetta?"

"We are going to Derek's birthday party on Friday evening."

As Donetta emptied the eggs into the pan, Kardoz rinsed and dried his hands, before he carried the plate of chopped tomatoes and onions to where she stood. He laid the plate on the counter top adjacent to the stove, then standing behind her, he commenced caressing her.

213

"Do we have to attend a noisy party, when we could be enjoying each other's company, Donetta, in the solitude of this house? It is sure to be a raucous gathering fuelled by alcohol."

Donetta felt she could easily succumb to his arousing advances but she extricated herself from his embrace and soundly declared, "Mimi and Derek are long standing friends and I would consider it a rather shoddy act to ignore the invitation, Terence. I will be attending this party with or without you."

Kardoz knew from Donetta's stance, and tone of voice, that her decision was final. He had no option but to accede to her request, otherwise, it would only attract unwanted attention from the partygoers if she attended unescorted. It did not, however, detract from his amorous feelings.

"O.K. Donetta," he said with as much enthusiasm as he could muster, before he once again resumed the pleasurable activity which had met an untimely disruption.

Donetta's influence had procured temporary employment for Kardoz. He was putting his carpentry skills to good use, in a new building being erected to house Government employees. His boss, a long time northerner, was not too inquisitive regarding Kardoz's background. Once employed, his expertise had been enough to convince the employer that he had hired a competent man.

Kardoz, while trying to build a good rapport with his workmates, still maintained an aloofness when asked to join them on a Friday evening in the hotel bar. He was running out of excuses and eventually decided to use religious beliefs as a reason for not accompanying them. He was quite comfortable within the confines of his small work circle and the seclusion of Donetta's home. He had no desire to increase the limitations he imposed upon himself. As long as he kept a low profile, responded to Donetta's carnal needs and displayed an interest in household affairs his accommodation was secure.

A cursory glance in the mirror reflected a problem. Excessive showering was having an effect on his hair colouring. It was beginning to fade. He wondered why Donetta had failed to remark upon it. Being sequestered with a woman didn't give him much privacy. He had another box of the dye hidden amongst his belongings and he would have to make an attempt to use it before Friday.

Kardoz had left the job an hour earlier. He was just in the last stages of attending to his coiffure, when he heard Donetta entering the house. Quickly, he gathered together the bottle, cotton wool and empty box, wrapped them in the towel and deposited it in the laundry basket. When Donetta arrived at the open bathroom door, he was running his comb through the dark curls.

"You are home early, love," said Donetta as she stood on tiptoe to kiss him.

"Yeah. We ran out of materials and knocked off early."

"Well, it's parent/teacher interview time again this evening, so we will have an early meal. Would you mind preparing the carrots and potatoes while I have a quick shower."

Donetta began to disrobe in the bathroom and Kardoz had no alternative but to adhere to her request. He was concerned about the towel in the laundry basket, but he would wait until Donetta was safely enclosed behind the shower curtain before removing it. He had just lifted the vegetables from the rack when the phone rang. It was Mimi asking to speak to Donetta. As soon as Kardoz entered the bathroom he noticed discarded underclothing had already been carelessly pushed into the basket, as part of it protruded. When Donetta went into the bedroom to take the call, he quickly removed the towel and hid it. He noticed it was badly stained, the dregs of the bottle having leaked. Kardoz then returned to the kitchen.

Donetta finished her toilette. She lifted the lid off the basket, with the intention of removing the stained towel she had observed, before adding further garments. She was surprised when she found it had already been removed.

As she applied her make-up, her mind focussed on the towel. She was sure it was hair dye, and now that the soiled item had been removed, it was apparent that Terence didn't want her to become aware of this quirk. She had observed that his eyebrows were a shade lighter, but not enough to make an outstanding contrast. He didn't strike her as being too fastidious regarding his looks, but men were becoming more daring in the cosmetic field. If he didn't want to share his secret she would ignore it, but deep down she felt that something wasn't quite right. He had given her a good account of himself, from early childhood to the present time, but it could very well be a fabrication. The incident, although in her mind a perfectly innocent one, still made her feel uneasy. As they ate their food, Kardoz remarked on her quietness. He had a feeling that the stained towel had not escaped her notice. His position was perilous and he needed to act quickly.

"You are very quiet Donetta. Anything wrong?"

"I have a lot of things on my mind, Terence. Just school stuff," she replied with a wan smile. Her reply disarmed him.

"I hope I haven't made a mess of your towel, Donetta. I was touching up my curly locks. Have been doing it for years, ever since my ex-girlfriend said she preferred tall dark handsome men, so I have just kept that image. It appeals to you, I hope."

His frankness and flashing smile dispelled all doubts from her mind. "It certainly does, Terence. You are the most handsome man in Fort Smith."

Kardoz, with a broad grin on his face, walked around to her side of the table. His hands on her body banished the gloom, and sent her pulse racing as they became immersed in a river of passion.

Eric began to wonder if Maury would arrive home in time for the party.

Maury popped his head around Eric's office door, a cheery grin on his face.

"How's it going, big fellow?"

"Glad to see you back, Maury, safe and sound. How were things in Whitehorse?"

"Great. I love the Yukon with its ice-capped mountains and sweeping valleys. The Gold Rush put it on the map in 1898 and it hasn't looked back since then. Whitehorse is still a lively place. Although the meetings kept us busy during the day, we found plenty of entertainment in the evening. Now that's over we can seriously plan our hunting trip. How about this week-end, as tentatively arranged? We could leave Friday afternoon."

"We could, Maury, but I understand you are being invited to Derek's big birthday bash. Meira and I have already accepted."

There was a silence before Maury replied.

"That's unfortunate. I had my sights set on leaving Friday afternoon. I suppose we could leave early Saturday morning but we might not be in a fit state to pursue a moose." As Maury uttered these words, the thought struck him that a hunter with a severe hangover could very well have an accident. Let's leave early Saturday then, Eric. I'll see you and Meira at the party. Till then take it easy, friend."

Gina sat down on the settee with a glass of white wine in her hand. It had been a long tiring week and she was glad of the opportunity of putting her feet up and relaxing. As she idly cruised through the various television programs, a face on America's Most Wanted caused her to hesitate. "George Kardoz, nickname Gordo, one of America's most wanted criminals, believed to be in Canada and responsible for the murder of a Vancouver woman." Gina gasped loudly. She sat for a few moments immobilised, her eyes glued to the screen, digesting the details of the wanted man. She had no doubt in her mind that the man she had made mad passionate love with was Kardoz. They had travelled on the same bus from Vancouver and she had been foolish enough to invite him into her home and share her bed. She trembled when she thought that she could very well have been another statistic in the coroner's files. She still had the note he had written. Gina lifted the telephone.

In Fort Smith, Donetta also relaxed on a settee with a glass of wine and the head of her lover on her lap. The party the previous evening had been an enjoyable one with lots of food, wine, spirits and camaraderie. Everyone had a good time. Kurdoz had insisted on their arriving very late by keeping Donetta occupied in the bedroom. He knew almost all of the guests would be intoxicated and his appearance would not be as noticeable. Only the hostess was sober as she welcomed him by saying to Donetta "Why have you been keeping this luscious man all to yourself?"

As Kardoz had expected, his introductions made little impact, except for Derek's wife, and a tall fair haired man, whose glances at first made him feel uncomfortable. As time wore on into the early hours, the fair haired man became another alcoholic dropout. Donetta had insisted on staying until the end and it was 5:00 a.m. when they crawled into bed. It was 1:00 p.m. before they surfaced, Donetta the worse for wear, complaining of a pounding headache. After a few mugs of strong coffee and another rest she was back to her usual form. They had just finished a late supper and were reclining on the settee before retiring for the night.

"Donetta, who was that tall fair haired man you spent some time speaking to in Mimi's kitchen? Mimi forgot to introduce me."

"Oh. That was Denis. He's R.C.M.P."

Kardoz froze at the words he had just heard, and then he casually said, "He's very young. How long has he been here?"

"He just arrived, a couple of months ago, from some little settlement in the Arctic. He is not as young as he looks. Boyish looks can belie age."

Kardoz said nothing more and lay with his eyes closed.

Donetta became aware of the silence and as she ran her fingers through his hair she said softly, "Do you feel like going to bed?"

Kardoz would not have hesitated to accept the invitation if the word R.C.M.P. hadn't been mentioned, but he had other things on his mind now. He hadn't liked the way in which the officer had been scrutinizing him.

"Not at the moment, Donetta. What were you discussing with baby face in the kitchen?"

"Oh ho!" A little touch of jealousy, Terence. I assure you it was business. He is attending my classroom next week to discuss drugs with the children. He was also discussing his daughter's progress. Anyway, he is married to an attractive wife. You saw her. The woman with the flaming red hair. They have two beautiful children,"

Her reply did not satisfy him. "Was he asking about your new boyfriend?"

"As a matter of fact he was. He just enquired, in a jocular manner, how long I had known you and it ended there."

This was enough to spur Kardoz into thinking about making a move. He was angry with Donetta for making him accompany her to the party. Warning bells rang in his head. He felt as if invisible forces were at work. Inwardly, he knew that his luck couldn't hold out for ever. He should have paid heed to the shiver he experienced, the first day he walked past the R.C.M.P. compound.

"I think I will go and wash my hair."

Do that, Donetta. I'll just relax here and have another coffee."

Donetta, aware of his change of mood attributed it to jealousy because she had spent a considerable time with Denis. She didn't like it and her mother's words "Never get involved with a jealous, possessive man" came to mind. She had just entered the bedroom when the phone rang. Kardoz lifted the phone beside him, at the same time as Donetta lifted the bedside phone. He listened intently to what was being said.

"Donetta, turn on the television quickly, America's Most Wanted program," said Mimi breathlessly.

Donetta complied and was astounded to see a man resembling Terence before her eyes. Despite the rimless glasses and jet black hair, she realised Kardoz, a wanted murderer, could well be the man downstairs in her living room.

She was stunned as she studied the features on the screen.

"Donetta, get out of there pronto. Come to my place. We will phone the R.C.M.P."

"There is a slight resemblance, Mimi, but he might not be the wanted person." She so desperately wanted to believe that the man, who had wormed his way into her affections, was not the same person, whose features she was still carefully scrutinizing.

The hair dye incident then came to mind, as did his reluctance to accompany her on extended invitations, and his sudden disappearances when visitors arrived. Only a few moments ago, he was also questioning her regarding her conversation with Denis. She realised it was too much of a coincidence. Kardoz and Terence was one and the same person. She began to feel threatened.

"Is he there, Donetta? Can you speak?" "He is downstairs. I am so confused, Mimi. This is very unsettling. I don't want to raise any suspicions, by suddenly leaving the house, after indicating I was going to shampoo my hair. I will begin to make some of those little cakes you like. I'll tell him you phoned to remind me that they are required for tomorrow's coffee morning with the skating club committee."

"I don't think you should spend another minute in the house with that man, Donetta. Your life could be in danger. Leave now."

"No, Mimi. Let's do it my way. I should be with you in an hour, or shortly thereafter. I'll be O.K. Don't worry."

As Mimi rang off Kardoz quietly replaced the receiver. He knew the game was up. He had to get away using Donetta's car and there was no way Donetta was going to Mimi's house. Donetta entered the living room smiling. "That was Mimi on the phone. She was reminding me about the cakes I promised for tomorrow morning's meeting. I completely forgot all about it, so I will just make them now and take them to her."

Kardoz returned her smile. "What a good friend Mimi has. I hope she appreciates you as much as I do, Donetta."

Donetta walked into the kitchen and Kardoz went upstairs with one thought in mind, preservation of his freedom. He searched through his bag for the Swiss knife.

Donetta's hands were shaking as she weighed the flour. She then became aware of Kardoz, standing close behind her. She was so cold, that the heat from his body, still made her shiver as he put and an arm around her waist and nuzzled the nape of her neck and right ear.

"Not now Terence, I must get this task finished. Let me, at least, get the cakes into the oven then we can go to the bedroom or into the living room".

The tension in Donetta's strangulated voice and her trembling body excited him. "But this is one of your favourite places, Donetta," he whispered, as he drew the knife, with deft precision, across her throat the baking bowl and contents cascading to the floor.

CHAPTER 27

Eric removed his boots and placed them inside, at the bottom of his sleeping bag, before he zipped himself in. He then leaned on one elbow, sipped his second cup of coffee and thought of Meira. The temperature was in the low twenties. He would have preferred snuggling against Meira instead of being cloistered in a small tent with Maury.

They had trudged quite a few kilometres following moose tracks, but luck hadn't smiled on them. Maury's statement, that the animal had probably doubled back and was a long way behind them, made him feel despondent.

Eric's thoughts then centred on Donetta. He was pleased that she had found someone to love, although he wasn't impressed with her choice of partner. There was something about Terence, which didn't ring true, and it disturbed him. He couldn't pinpoint it. When introduced, he noticed the lack of direct eye contact, and the rapidly shifting gaze around the room. The man had appeared to be on pins and needles, and more so, as he watched Donetta conversing with Denis. He decided to speak to Denis about his concern, when he returned.

Maury lay inside his sleeping bag with his eyes closed; giving the impression that he was about to lapse into a well earned sleep. He was still very alert. In a few hours time, he intended carrying out the plan that had been fermenting in his mind for months. His violent jealousy had been refuelled, when he observed Meira draping herself around Eric in Mimi's kitchen the previous evening and Eric's loving response, so he had no qualms regarding his deadly intention. While Eric was alive and well, he knew he had no chance of winning her affection. He was sure his plan was foolproof. It meant, of course, some suffering on his part. A deep slash on the leg by a supposed stranger would be painful, but he would gladly suffer the agony in order to win the only woman who could make him happy. He had brought along an extra pair of boots, a size bigger, which would account for the third set of footprints leading to the tent. Maury was pleased with his proposed plan. Eric wouldn't feel a thing. A quick bullet to the brain and it would be all over. He would have to go out wearing the boots and carefully dispose of them as he made his way from the camp, before reporting the crime and seeking medical aid. He had a high pain threshold and knew he would be able to cope with his self inflicted wound.

He listened to Eric's even breathing and bided his time.

Quite a while had elapsed and Maury began to rationalise his intended behaviour. What gave him the right to take another man's life, especially a friend? The more he thought about it, the very idea of such an unforgiving, atrocious action appalled him. He began to realise that his jealousy, a mortal sin, had gained control of his life. If he allowed it to continue the woman he was supposed to love was the person who would really suffer as well as Eric's family in England and Canada.

The consequences of such an action would also be horrendous if traced to him. His parents and family would be horrified and have to suffer the disgrace of losing a son behind bars, but he would be the biggest loser. His reputation would be in tatters and he would end up as a criminal, so he intended heeding his conscience and abandoning such wilful and evil thoughts.

After all, Eric was Meira's choice not him and he needed to accept that. There were lots of other woman to choose from who could make him just as happy. He would relax now with a clear mind and dispose of the larger size boots before Eric wakened.

Maury awoke with a start. He sat up straight expecting to see his parents. His dream, or was it a nightmare, was so realistic? His mother was weeping as she held her arms towards him. His father was trying to comfort her and both appeared to be deeply distressed. He considered it weird and took a long time to compose himself.

As Meira drove past Donetta's house, she observed a shadowy figure at the rear of the car in the drive way. She slowed down and when she looked again, she saw Kardoz lift a bag and throw it into the front seat, on the passenger side. Meira glanced at the clock which registered 9:00 p.m. She travelled slowly along the road and saw the headlights of Donetta's car, which was directly behind her, disappear as it turned off into the avenue leading towards the highway.

Meira made a three-point turn and went in the direction of Donetta's vehicle. It wasn't long before she saw it being refuelled at the gas station. When the car emerged on to the main street, the flashing right hand indicator led Meira to believe the driver was going on a long journey, as the vehicle sped down the highway. It was usual for people going to Edmonton to travel the sixteen hour journey during the night.

She suddenly became aware of her intense interest in the movements of Donetta's friend. It was so unlike her to concern herself with other people's affairs and she couldn't find an excuse for her irrational behaviour.

As Meira drove towards her residence, she pondered on the tall, black-haired, man who had accompanied Donetta to Mimi's get-together the previous evening. It was obvious that his looks complemented his charm but she had perceived an uneasiness about him. He had given the impression that he was constantly waiting for something significant to happen as he glanced furtively around the room, on more than one occasion. On the way home from the party, Meira had drawn Eric's attention to Donetta's escort. His reply was positively in alignment with her thoughts. Eric mentioned that one of Maury's friends, who worked with Donetta's beau, on the building site, had indicated that their new colleague was a religious character, who abhorred alcohol. He carried out his duties conscientiously, by always being back on the job, before the coffee breaks ended. On hearing this, Meira replied that Terence had probably felt as uncomfortable as she did; being in the midst of a group, imbibing in beer and spirits, because she noticed that he had drained Mimi's coffee pot dry and refused all offers of liquor.

Meira parked outside her residence, still ruminating on Kardoz's departure. She attempted to put it out of her mind by thinking about Eric, somewhere out on the ice covered land, dreaming of a moose. Recently, the unfriendly situation which had existed between Maury and Eric had become more ameliorative, for which she was thankful. Also, Maury had not been forcing his unwanted attentions on her, since she spent more time in Eric's home than her own. She had noticed, though, while at Mimi's house party, a look of great displeasure on Maury's face when Eric had put his arm around her and pulled her close.

She wished Maury could find a woman to love. It would take the pressure of her, because she felt she had, in a way, contributed to his all consuming interest in her, by accepting the food and gifts forced on her and Nuniye, even though she had tried to discourage his generosity.

Meira drank tea as she leafed through a text book. No matter how hard she tried, she couldn't concentrate. She felt strongly that there was something amiss. She wondered if she should phone Mimi. She lifted the receiver, but quickly replaced it, as the thought entered her mind, that she might be making a fool of herself by discussing the car episode. It was really a matter between Donetta and her boyfriend, and there was probably a simple explanation for the journey. Meira emitted a deep sigh and returned to the textbook.

Mimi paced the floor. She looked occasionally at the clock before going to peer through the window. It was already fifteen minutes past the hour for Donetta's appearance. She wished Derek hadn't been targeted to pilot some government officials to Inuvik. He always seemed to be chosen at the most inopportune moment. When something explosive was about to erupt, Derek seemed to be assigned duties, which took him out of town for more than twenty four hours.

The sound of a car again drew her quickly to the window, but it was her next door neighbour's son. She observed the night was frosty, and a lot of dark cloud was obscuring the moon, which radiated its bright light at sporadic intervals.

Mimi sat down, lifted her knitting, and tried to control her churning emotions. After a short while, she found she couldn't contain her anxiety any longer and lifted the phone. Donetta's line was busy. She quickly replaced the receiver, as she thought Donetta might be trying to contact her. She waited sometime before redialling, only to hear the same tone. She stood beside the phone idly drumming her fingers on the work top. The third redial, after another seemingly long wait, produced the same result. Enough, thought Mimi, I'm going to Donetta's house. As she donned her parka, the shrill bell of the phone made her jump. She dashed across the room and answered it.

"Hi Mimi, Meira here. Sorry for phoning at this late hour, but I feel I need to talk to someone about my concern."

"Yes, Meira. I was just on my way out, but I can spare a few moments. What's the problem?"

Well, it may not be a problem. My concern may be unfounded. I saw Terence, Donetta's friend, taking off in her car tonight, shortly after 9:00 p.m. It looked as if he was making his way towards Hay River. I have a strong feeling that something is wrong. I followed him as far as the garage, where he filled the gas tank and departed."

"Oh no, Meira. Don't give me this awful news. I'll pick you up immediately and we will go to Donetta's house."

As they proceeded in the direction of Donetta's residence, Mimi relayed the story to a shocked Meira. Both women were in a state of heightened anxiety when they arrived there. The house was in complete darkness. After knocking loudly and repeatedly on the back and front doors and receiving no response, Mimi drove rapidly to the Royal Canadian Mounted Police compound.

When the officers forced their way into the house, Meira's concern and Mimi's fears were realised. It was too late to help their friend. One of America's Most Wanted criminals was now also fleeing from Canadian justice.

Kardoz drove erratically along the icy road. Before he left Donetta's home, he had taken the phone off the hook. He hoped it would give him extra time. He had no idea how long it would be before the engaged tone aroused suspicion and someone went to the house. He suspected that after an hour had elapsed, Mimi

225

would be worried and decide to investigate. She would probably seek the aid of her friend Denis. He wondered how far he would travel, before his crime was discovered. He was aware the road led to a place named Hay River and it would take a couple of hours to reach there. Kardoz intended abandoning the car near the town and stealing another one. A truck would be preferable as there would be better traction. The road from Hay River led to Edmonton. If he was lucky enough to reach that city, he could hibernate for a while, until the trail ran cold. It would give him time to plan his next move. He would have to avoid Inns and Motels. He thought about Gina, but realised that to approach her could be risky, because she also may have seen the television program. Acutely aware of the desperate circumstances, in which he was now placed, he decided to wait outside Gina's apartment block until he caught sight of her, provided he reached Edmonton. When he confronted her, any sign of fear in her eyes would alert him, and govern his behaviour.

He was loathe to admit that his plan to seek a small town had been flawed. He would have been better staying in a large city and taking his chances. All these thoughts ran wildly through his brain, they diverted attention from his driving skills. His foot suddenly pressed too hard on the accelerator. The car slewed violently before catapulting across the icy road. He fought to right it, but it careered across a deep ditch and veered around some trees, before making contact with one which brought it to an abrupt halt. Kardoz was shaken. His only injury was a bruise on his forehead, where it had come into contact with the steering wheel.

A few vulgar expletives poured forth from his mouth. It helped to relieve the tension he felt, at being stranded in a desolate snow covered wilderness without transport, very soon to be pursued by the Mounties.

The door on the driver's side refused to budge but he managed to squeeze through the door on the opposite side of the vehicle. He donned his heavy parka, wound a scarf around his face, pulled down his ear flaps and grabbed his backpack. He wanted to get away from the main road as quickly as possible. He followed a narrow path until he saw a tent. By the side of it were two snowmobiles. Just what I need, he thought, as he stealthily approached.

Kardoz, clutching his Swiss knife, was about to put his hand on one of the machines, when a man emerged from the tent. He had a rifle in his hand, and boots hanging around his neck. On being confronted by the startling appearance of Kardoz he momentarily froze. Kardoz immediately lunged knocking him to the ground and plunged the knife into his neck. He lifted the fallen rifle just as another man emerged through the flap of the tent. Eric stood as if in a trance. Was his vision hallucinatory or was the tall dark man enshrouded in ice fog real. Momentarily he was paralysed with fear, unable to react to the spectral intrusion until the rifle was raised in his direction. Eric quickly twisted sideways to avoid the deadly discharge Suddenly an explosion of pain gripped him in a vice, as hard as the ice which tenaciously held the surrounding land in its freezing grasp. The force of the bullet had caused him to somersault sprawling face down on top of the tent which had collapsed. Eric lay on top of the demolished canvas which had sheltered him from the frigid elements. Now he was exposed to their unpredictable caprices. The scene was one of cold savagery. The man who had been fatally stabbed lay crumpled in a heap, a black splodge on the stark white landscape. The crimson rivulet, which had seeped from the mortal wound, made an obscene blot on the chaste terrain.

Despite the horrific pain, a gamut of emotions assailed Eric's still functional mind from the first day he had made the decision to set foot on the North's icebound perimeter to his present incapacitated state. A multitude of photo frames flashed successively before his tightly closed eyes. He was held captive to their succinct imagery, impervious to the hypothermic danger which threatened him. until he lost consciousness.

From behind a dark cloud an orb of brilliance appeared and cast its crowning glory over the detritus of man's 'inhumanity to man.' It was ironic that the man who planned to murder his friend, then decided to heed his conscience, had now become the victim of a deranged murderer.

CHAPTER 28

Sergeant Davidson had gathered together a posse comprising Hay River and Fort Smith officers. The skid marks on the road led them to the smashed car crumpled against a tree and the footprints to the sad scene outside the tent. They discovered that Eric, with a very weak pulse, was still alive and immediately went into action to keep him in that state while waiting for the medevac team.

Meira was overwhelmed with anguish as Mimi did her best to comfort her on the way to Edmonton. She didn't know what to expect when she arrived at the hospital. Eric could already be another victim of the man who had murdered Maury. Even though Maury had considered himself as the only man who could ever fulfil all her dreams and bring her perfect happiness as a married couple, she was very distressed and mourned, as she would for a brother, at his brutal passing. He had always been very kind and helpful to her and Nuniye. He certainly didn't deserve to die at the hands of a maniac nor did her friend Donetta.

A shiver ran through Meira, as the image of Donetta lying in her own blood on the kitchen floor, amid a smashed bowl of cooking ingredients, hit her forcibly. It was a sight she would never forget. Donetta was a loving, kind, gentle woman with a big heart who unwittingly had offered accommodation and hospitality to a psychopath.

As Meira's thoughts meandered haphazardly, she recalled the evening she and Eric had raised a toast to their future happiness with the unborn child In mind. This caused copious tears to spill down her cheeks as abysmal thoughts of living without Eric assailed her.

Meanwhile examination of Eric revealed a badly torn shoulder muscle and from the elbow to the tip of the clavicle acute grazing of the bone. His injuries were quite serious. Had Eric not had the presence of mind to twist hastily aside the bullet would have entered his brain, the intended target. The wadding in his padded jacket had also helped to absorb the force of the bullet. He was still In the intensive care unit.

As he was regaining consciousness he had to be strapped down as he struggled to free himself from an imaginary attacker. Two more male nurses had to be called to take control of his legs and feet before he finally succumbed to his supposed capturer.

Eric opened his eyes and stared vacuously into space for a second before uttering the word 'Meria'. The doctor, a syringe in his hand, about to inject him asked one of the nurses to fetch Meira. When Meira entered she knelt at his bedside glad to see him still alive. He gripped her hand and held it tightly refusing to release it until he was sedated.

The prognosis for Eric was a long road to recovery. Meira moved to Edmonton to be near him and give much needed support and encouragement. He was totally devastated when he heard that Maury never survived the vicious attack. He clearly remembered Maury's last words before they settled down for the night. "Don't be disappointed Eric, tomorrow is a new day and I have a feeling that a lonely moose will be mourning her mate. Sleep well my friend.".

Meira was in agreement with Eric that before they left the North they would visit and pay their respects to Maury's parents who had been deeply shattered by the way their devoted son had lost his life.

Eric persevered with the physiotherapy and made good progress. It was a joyous day when the consultant informed him that his treatment and medical appointments were at an end. He congratulated him for his perseverance which had resulted in his quick recovery but mentioned that he could be afflicted later in life with arthritis. Eric replied that it couldn't be any worse than what he had already suffered and he hoped to enjoy pain free freedom until the children, he intended having, were adults and able to take care of themselves.

The RCMP exercised their usual expert capabilities in tracking and apprehending Kardos. Still in control of the rifle, when commanded to put it down. he did so willingly, surrendering his freedom to whatever fate awaited his sordid grisly existence.

Eric held Meira's left hand on which a plain gold band encircled the third finger. As the plane flew over the extensive swathe of green forest, he felt a sadness at leaving Canada's north. His life in the Northwest Territories had been a mosaic of adventure, love, sorrow, pain and happiness. Now it was time to pursue a new path beside the woman whose roots were deeply embedded in the land they were leaving and whose strength was as indomitable as the unique and beautiful land in which she was born.

> But what of life whose bitter angry sea
> Flows at our heels, and gloom of sunless night
> Covers the days which never more return?
> Ambition, love and all the thoughts that burn
> We lose too soon, and only
> Find delight in withered husks of some dead memory.

Desespoir—Oscar Wilde

Lightning Source UK Ltd.
Milton Keynes UK
UKOW052344260112

186126UK00001B/56/P